Ally McBeal

HarperCollins books may be purchased for educational, business,
or sales promotional use. For information please write:
Special Markets Department, HarperCollins*Publishers* Inc.,
10 East 53rd Street, New York, NY 10022–5299.

First Edition

Videograbs provided by Omni Graphic Solutions.

Interior and cover design by
Tanya Ross-Hughes and David Hughes, HOTFOOT Studio

Library of Congress Cataloging-in-Publication Data is available

ISBN 0-06-098813-4
99 00 01 02 03 10 9 8 7 6 5 4 3 2 1

THANKS TO
Caitlin Blasdell, Lois Draegin, Mindy Farabee, Virginia King,
Katherine Koberg, Jeffrey Kramer, Michele Macklis, Steve Reddicliffe,
Shannon Smith, Neely Swanson, and Pam Wisne.

Ally McBeal

the official guide

Tim Appelo

A HarperEntertainment Book
from HarperPerennial

CONTENTS

○ ▶ ◀ ▶ ▶ ■

INTRODUCTION

In 1997, a tightly wound bundle of contradictions in a miniskirt lit up TV, but few expected *Ally McBeal* to be a monster hit. Her creator, David E. Kelley, was more of a cult show rebel than a ratings behemoth. His series such as *Picket Fences* won passionate fans but dodged a mass audience, quirkily jumping the fences separating comedy and drama, TV's strict standard categories.

But when 18 million viewers got a look at Ally (played by Broadway actress Calista Flockhart), the show hit fans' hearts like a crossbow with home truths about love, and cracked funnybones with some of the strangest ensemble comedy ever seen. Sex, religion, and politics, but this was not business as usual, politically incorrect and loving it—it was an equal-opportunity offender.

Something was clearly missing from TV. It turned out to be *Ally*. Maybe what people needed was a good laugh and a brisk argument. For audiences awash in gloppily obvious social issues, dramas, and comedies with under one calorie of social commentary, *Ally* was the antidote. The jokes and melodramas broke beaucoup rules, colored outside prescribed political lines, and made people actually talk about issues—hostile work environments, what constitutes adultery, discrimination legislation, the moral implications of the one-night stand, the stubborn persistence of first love, the ethics of prostitution, whether size matters.

Conversation heated up at office watercoolers nationwide. There were raucous ad hoc *Ally McBeal* debating societies and *Ally McBeal* bar nights. "That show is one big watercooler," said a psychiatrist writing for the *Journal of Popular Culture*.

"It's all pretty out there and pretty intense, and I guess it is daring," says Jonathan Pontell, a longtime David E. Kelley producer and sometime director of the show. "But David has certainly proved that it works."

So what makes it work? For one thing, it's interactive entertainment. The story, written death-defyingly close to airtime, responds to rumors and critiques with scripts packed with jokes, using sight gags and newspaper headlines as springboards for speculative fancies and dizzying triple-flips of satire. And did anyone make more meaningful and original use of the themes raised by the president's woes than *Ally McBeal*?

The perverse mixture won folks over: sensitive emotions and slapstick fantasy, sharp courtroom drama and madcap song-and-dance routines, flopping tongues and inflating breasts and flashes of Ally catapulted into Dumpsters. Incidentally, Ms. Flockhart's beloved dog Webster was rescued from a Dumpster.

At first, it was the simple things in Ally's life that got America's tongues wagging. Her biological clock caught the nation's imagination when it was personified by the computer-generated Dancing Baby. "That really hit, man, that dancing baby really put us on the map. I mean, we were doing actually rather well right from the beginning. But that one got people perked," says Pontell.

Topic A on the national agenda, however, was the Unisex, a restroom where both men and women meet and utter things most indiscreet. "Well, he certainly stirred the pot with that one," said Peter MacNicol, who plays Ally's boss Cage, to a reporter. "That has been the single most talked-about thing in the whole show."

Swiftly, the constellation of the *Ally McBeal* repertory company, a group of some of the most talented actors and actresses from stage and screen, swung into place, and the warmly bizarre machinations of the story became the show's chief fascination. Again, Kelley was a responsive writer, not only giving the big cast (and hordes of guest actors) ample spotlight time but painstakingly crafting the roles to fit their myriad gifts, and tinkering with the rich mixture of personalities. Many members of this talented ensemble have enthusiastic followings of their own. This focus on the group also freed up Flockhart somewhat, but her long workday still demands plenty of grueling physical pratfall feats. "She's a better athlete than people give her credit for," says visual effects man Mike Most, who has put her through countless ordeals. She's also an unusually subtle actor, as unconventional as her part.

The odd combo of iron will and willowy fragility is what got Flockhart the job, and it's central to what made her a star. "I think people are drawn to Calista as an archetype of the Little Match Girl," Michael Hoffman, her director in *A Midsummer Night's Dream*, has said. "This very sensitive waif who at the same time houses a remarkable strength."

Both come in handy in creating the character of Ally. Her nerve endings seem to throw sparks, and the most audacious things come out of her mouth—things some people would secretly like to say but don't dare. Things nobody could possibly think of saying unless they were as spontaneous as Ally, and in such an eccentric orbit. Ally's friends also say the darnedest things—the dialogue is like a Ping-Pong game at a table with more than two sides.

Ally is just a character in an alternately funny and touching story. She comes from an important pop culture lineage, a long line of strong heroines. Ally is descended from Lucille Ball and Mary Tyler Moore.

The change from them to Ally does say something about what we want in a heroine these days. Ally is all about love, but she's not enslaved by it. She has moments of the deepest sweetness imaginable, but nobody could imagine calling her America's Sweetheart, as people have been calling popular actresses since Mary Pickford's day.

By the '50s, America liked Ike, but it was significant that it was Lucy they loved. Love had to be stressed, and Lucy's power toned way down. She was imprisoned by that big heart that formed the show's logo. It was a great role, but a woman's role. Mary Tyler Moore was a giant, graceful dancer's leap from Lucy's restrictive world: She lived alone and supported herself. Her theme song was "Love Is All Around." Mary could "turn the world on with her smile."

Ally has a heart as big as Lucy's logo, and can turn the world on with her smile, if she feels like it. Or she can turn on the world and kick its ass—assault friends and strangers and get sent to jail. Her smile is private, and half the time what she's smiling at (or yelling at, or throwing things at) exists strictly in her inner world.

Ally is living fictional proof that, in our day, a female character can wear a miniskirt and still play on the boys' field. When she was lambasted for skirt brevity, her skirts got briefer. She is a woman who defies certain orthodoxies and demands the right to speak her mind and articulate her heart's most politically inopportune promptings.

Ally is all about living in the moment. *Ally McBeal* is a show about low laughs, flying tree frogs erupting from toilets, love and longing, reconciling irreconcilable drives and desires, colliding in close quarters with people you adore and abhor by turns.

And who's to say that Ally's demand for romance, for the triumph of hope over experience, is as fanciful as her hallucinations? Part of why the show resonates with viewers is that we can identify with these characters. There is always the truth at the heart and soul of each situation.

It's also true that at least three people on the show—David E. Kelley, Peter MacNicol, and Courtney Thorne-Smith—met their life's mates on blind dates. Ally may just find hers yet.

These people, their workplaces, and their situations seem to live in all of us. For every three steps forward, we may take two steps back. But we are gaining, we are moving forward, and we will remember Ally and her crew for holding a mirror up to us all.

an
INTERVIEW
with
David E. Kelley

Tim Appelo: *Ally* fans will be delighted to discover that besides the new hour-long episodes in the 1999–2000 season, there will be half-hour shows blending previous episodes with never-before-seen scenes. What's in those "lost" episodes?

David E. Kelley: There really aren't lost episodes. The genesis of it was sort of a financial one— one of those rare occasions that has a creative upside. When it was going out for syndication, half hours syndicate better than hours. And I always felt this show played better as a half hour than an hour. Because usually when people are watching reruns, they aren't too inclined to invest in the emotional parts of the story. So I started cutting shows in half on my own just to see how they played as comedies. And in doing so, discovered that they played pretty well, and when I talked to Fox about it, they got excited and started talking about actually programming it. There are scenes that never have been seen before in some episodes because they were just too long. We had to cut some scenes out of various episodes.

TA: Can you tell me one?

DEK: There's probably about fifty. The one that's the most memorable for me is a very touching scene between Renee and Ally. It took place in the episode where Ally had just kissed Billy and then was going into therapy over it. Ally was really having a bit of a crisis over it, and there was a lovely scene, about a minute and a half to two minutes, between Renee and Ally. But the episode itself was about nine minutes too long, and sometimes you just have to lose scenes altogether. That's one that killed us to lose because it was a nice—it was a wonderful, wonderful scene. But we just—something had to go. So there are scenes like that that this would give me an opportunity to bring back, which I'm excited about. There will be some episodes, however, that have no new scenes, the episode will be re-cut from an hour to a half hour and will probably look a lot different, and the transitions will be different. But probably some of the episodes will consist of footage that has aired in its entirety. There are some half hours that are very emotional and stay on the emotional pulse from beginning to end, and others just play more like comedies. More times than not, I'm discovering as I go through them that it's the court cases that will either be taken out or truncated.

TA: In both the court cases and the emotional sagas, there is a certain logic that obtains. However wacky the case is, it's never simply whimsical.

DEK: No. There's always an idea behind it.

TA: The ideas on the show provoked a lot of debate, but most of the commentary seemed to center on Ally's wardrobe and Calista

Flockhart's lunch plans. What aside from her Broadway credentials in *The Glass Menagerie* and *The Three Sisters* made you cast her as Ally?

DEK: Yeah, well, she's an amazing actress. And I think one of all of the greatest crimes of all the publicity this past year is how people haven't really acknowledged that or focused on it. I don't think I've ever worked with anybody with the range of Calista Flockhart. Whether it's comedy or drama, she's able to access it with such a facility it's amazing. It's a hard quality to find in any actor, the ability to be strong and vulnerable at the same time. And Calista can do it. And if people have a complaint or don't like the character, trust me, it's the character or the way it's written, or the way we're doing it, it's not her. Because she's playing the character as we write it.

TA: So she's not an Ally, she just plays one on television.

DEK: Right, exactly.

TA: What inspired you to focus so much on Peter MacNicol's Cage character?

DEK: Peter kind of just—he always makes me laugh. And again, it's such a complex interpretation of character. I found that on *Chicago Hope* with this lawyer character we wrote named Birch. And you know, most of my scenes try to find conflict, and if I have a character where there's always conflict churning within, it probably fuels me as a writer. Fuels ideas and stories. And Peter's always got that going on in Cage. You know, even in his body language. Even if things appear to be going right, you can tell with Cage that he's still churning. For something more. And if you watch dailies of Peter, he is constantly making choices, making it one way or another, like with his hand movement. Nothing is arbitrary with Peter. Peter and Calista are really very interesting actors who can be sort of funny and emotionally accessible at the same time.

TA: Flockhart told one reporter that she likes the way the show can "turn on a dime." The show is constantly doing that, and it's a quote from a song sung on the show by Vonda Shepard, "The Wildest Times of the World." Did you respond to that lyric?

DEK: It's funny that you mention that. It was that song—I was at, I think it was called the Billboard Club, listening to Vonda Shepard, and it was while she was singing that song that it hit me that Vonda really was the voice of this character. And then I took it a step further and actually went out and hired Vonda to sing and be the voice of the character.

TA: And what was there about the song that relates to Ally?

DEK: I think it was the fragile nature of the song combined with the hope of it. And that there was a loneliness to the song and yet a hope for the future even though there was no clarity or clear path to how you arrive at that hope. So there was a sort of both loneliness and optimism in that song, and in Vonda's voice, that sort of spoke to the core of Ally.

TA: Have the actors influenced your creation of their characters?

DEK: Well, certainly Greg Germann's ability, the way that things roll off his tongue with such simplicity, allow me to put sometimes the most ridiculous yet complicated thoughts—or not necessarily complicated, but provocative thoughts—in his mouth. And it allows me to say things that I don't think I could say through any other character. You might be inclined to take them too seriously. Or be offended even.

TA: He says the most outrageous things.

DEK: He does, and he says it in such an unapologetic way that the audience's response is: Well, it's no big deal. Because Greg has this no-big-deal intonation in his delivery. And you can be seduced by that delivery and you go, yeah, it's simple, it's simple. And then you stop for a second and replay what he just said. And you think, how could he get away with saying that? Well, in a way, you sort of expect it from him. That's just Fish. I can't tell you how many people say, I think that, or I say that, but when I do I get my head taken off. How does he get away with it?

TA: Lucy Liu (Ling Woo) says what attracted her about the show was that it says things that people are afraid to say.

DEK: Well, those two characters definitely do. And Ally also says quite a few things that people are either able to dismiss or lay off on her character and not perceive it as being an endorsement of the program.

TA: The views expressed by the characters are not necessarily those of—anyone but the characters. But part of the show's notoriety owes to the anger it incites, among feminists and others. Do you ever respond within the show to headlines about issues?

DEK: Not too much, most of the stuff that we do emanates from characters. If it's organic to the characters of our people, then I'm certainly willing to take on an issue and have fun with it, but I don't usually find an issue and then try to jury-rig it into the show. That's why most of our cases are a version of a man-woman issue or sexual harassment. It's really women and men struggling, striving to work together. The other issue that is thematically very common is one of just loneliness. I think the show demonstrates that that one crosses the gender line. But there aren't many social issues that we take on just because it would be a good issue to explore. If it doesn't really coincide with these characters and what they would find important, then I don't usually stray there.

TA: It's remarkable how many shows end up with somebody walking off home alone.

DEK: Well, it's a big underlying theme of the show that a lot of people are lonely at the end of the day. Some people are better at covering up than others. But there's more of it out there than one would think.

TA: When you want to express an idea, do you think about which character will best illustrate it? Are they each daubs on your painter's palette?

DEK: It's certainly true that when I'm hatching a story idea, you think which character it will resonate the most through. I do the same on *The Practice* as well. Usually you're hoping that in addition to just some straight storytelling, there'll be a texture to the story that's coming through your character. So the character's own history or personality is always a factor that you put into the equation.

TA: How do they affect each other's equations?

DEK: These people are all in each other's lives. That doesn't mean they all love each other. Nelle and Ally don't have any great affection for each other, for example, but they're all in

TA: But you write best under pressure? Does it enhance your work?

DEK: I'm not sure that deadlines work as well for others as they work for me. I'm sure for actors it can be a bit oppressive when you're asked to learn a lot of lines at the last minute.

TA: In one of the scripts there was a long, kind of a cool monologue for Ally, and you wrote in parentheses, "Sorry, Calista."

DEK: Yeah, I think it was like a page long. I don't write that anymore because she can—she just does it [nonverbally]. I don't know how, but I mean, I don't know how any of them do it, to tell you the truth. By the time I've finished writing a script, I could probably recite almost the whole thing because I just remember how the lines flow. But to do it with a sense of pace that they're required to do, I don't know how they do it.

each other's lives. So accordingly, each of their lives is, if not a reflection, at least a consequence of all these other people that are around them.

TA: They're like billiards bouncing off of each other in unpredictable ways. Ally's world is chronically shifting.

DEK: Right, which this show will always do and will always have to do. And I feel we're just getting started, too. There are nine, I think, characters in the show, but exponentially I don't know how many, maybe sixty different relationships depending on who's in the room—whether it's Ally and Georgia, or Ally and Billy, or Ally, Billy, and Georgia, all in the same room. And the dynamics shift depending on the recipe of characters.

TA: Flockhart said that you probably don't know what's going to happen next season. Is that true?

DEK: I'm just actually getting to the point where I'm actually starting to figure out next season. That's what hiatuses are for.

TA: I've found many allusions to *The Music Man* in the show. How deliberate is that?

DEK: *The Music Man* was the first musical, the first play, that I ever saw in my life. And of course I loved it. I was only six or seven, but I loved it. I tried to use *The Music Man* as the opening for *Picket Fences*, but we couldn't get the rights. Tom Skerritt's character was in the barbershop quartet, and in the original script, they were singing "Lida Rose." But Meredith Willson's widow was untrusting that we would be faithful or that it would be the kind of material that her late husband would be proud to be associated with. And she denied the rights. Then I think *Picket* won two Emmys or something, and she may have softened on her stance. And we continued to request the usage because I'm such a fan, and finally she became convinced that I was genuine—sincerely a fan of both her late husband and the musical—so she blessed us with the rights to the material.

TA: The degree varies of course but there are aspects of the actors that seem to appear in their characters. There's a cleverness in the way Germann talks that feeds the character, for example.

DEK: I'm sure that that's true. And you know, after five or six episodes, when I'm sitting down writing and conceiving stories, in my ear I'm hearing their voices and their rhythms, so there is definitely a collaboration. Even if it's an unconscious or unwitting one sometimes, it's still a collaboration.

TA: When you set out to do the show, there was a sense of adventure about it. Ally doesn't know where she's going. How has the show changed?

DEK: Probably the most obvious one is that it's become much more of an ensemble show. And that's probably just a function of these other characters emerging as successfully as they have. In terms of storytelling style, if you look at the first few episodes, two or three or four episodes, you'll see a lot of voice-over that now would probably strike you as being strange, because I don't think we used voice-over last year at all. If we did it was maybe once or twice. We just didn't need it. At the outset I really wanted to get inside Ally's mind, and we've been able to do that with visual fantasies or other fantasies, and on the occasion where we haven't used fantasies, just she's so expressive as an actress that the voice-over I found was quickly redundant. And it almost reduced the moment, with us telling the audience what she was thinking instead of allowing the audience to read her.

TA: The smile therapy thing, wasn't that supposed to be just a one-hit gag?

DEK: I never, when I write something, say that I'm going to use this once and never again. The same thing with the Barry White. I mean, you just see how effective it is. And once we did the smile therapy, I knew it was something

that would actually get funnier as it would reoccur. So I never know at the time of the first usage whether it will be the only usage or not. Usually I just wait and see if it works.

TA: Was there anything that particularly surprised you during the first two seasons? A development in a character?

DEK: Let me see. Well, I think one of the pleasant surprises was the dramatic subtext that Jane has. I mean, when casting Elaine we weren't looking for that. It was just kind of not a multidimensional character on the page at all. And a lot of Elaine's development I credit to Jane because that story [about how Elaine as a child saved up for a bell for a bike she would never get to own], that's certainly not something I had in my mind with the creation of the character. That kind of thing was inspired by Jane's interpretation of it. There was something fun and yet slightly desperate about the way Jane was playing Elaine. And add her musical abilities on top of that—when casting I wasn't looking for someone who could sing and dance—that was a real pleasant surprise, that she turned out to be as versatile.

TA: Do we wind up with more musical routines because you've got this remarkable wealth of song-and-dance talent?

DEK: Certainly hers, yeah. Again, it fits right in with her character that all you have to do is ask her to sing and you know, in come the backup singers and she's ready to do a number.

TA: The evolution of Billy and Georgia is interesting, too. At the beginning it seemed to me that they were kind of the viewer's stand-in, the normal people. But now it's changed.

DEK: Yes, and people haven't really noticed yet, but it's only a matter of time before they will. That Billy is emerging as probably the most indefensible chauvinist of the entire bunch. Despite all the things that come out of Fish's mouth, he's not dangerous because they are seemingly . . . you're not afraid of Fish corrupting the guy next door as he talks. But Billy, it's much more subtle and entrenched and much more persuasive.

TA: He could run for office.

DEK: It's almost the difference between Swaggart and Falwell. Swaggart, you know you're not afraid of someone listening to him and being persuaded. Falwell, what makes him dangerous is he sounds so plausible sometimes. And Billy's chauvinism is very subtle, but it's very much there. And that will continue to emerge next year.

character
PROFILES

CHARACTER	PLAYED BY
ALLY McBEAL	CALISTA FLOCKHART
BILLY THOMAS	GIL BELLOWS
JOHN CAGE	PETER MacNICOL
RENEE RADICK	LISA NICOLE CARSON
GEORGIA THOMAS	COURTNEY THORNE-SMITH
RICHARD FISH	GREG GERMANN
ELAINE VASSAL	JANE KRAKOWSKI
NELLE PORTER	PORTIA de ROSSI
LING WOO	LUCY LIU
"WHIPPER" CONE	DYAN CANNON
DR. TRACY CLARK	TRACEY ULLMAN
VONDA SHEPARD	HERSELF

ALLY
mcbeal

Ally McBeal (played by Calista Flockhart) is a serious lawyer and a serial kisser, single-minded about what she wants yet subject to multitudinous moods that mutiny against the reign of her Harvard-trained brain. She is bent on marriage and motherhood (but on her own terms) and in the meantime is swept up in the familylike whirl of the weird yet warm Boston law firm where she works.

She says what she thinks and especially what she feels, and though she passionately defends the passionate life, she often instantly regrets the words that fly out of her mouth like mischievous spirits. Just as often, she stands by the outrageous things she says. Busted by a judge for wearing short skirts, Ally demands the right to wear them on principle: No judge presumes to dictate men's attire,

and besides, she's got an inalienable right to make guys talk about her legs. Asked for comment, she calls the judge a "pig."

She is emotionally exoskeletal, but mostly, she likes it that way. She can be an excellent lawyer in court—not quite as outrageous as her boss Cage, infinitely superior to her boss Fish—but her legal arguments almost invariably serve as a lens on her private life or on romance, her personal cause even when the romance in question doesn't concern her. As she exasperatedly tells Yorkin, a prison warden who is trying to block an inmate with a life sentence from wedding Ally's client: "Why are you insisting that it all make sense? If you want to be practical, would any marriage make sense? They love each other . . . that's not just enough, it's everything."

We don't know everything about Ally's past, but we share the nuances of every instant of her present life, both inside and outside her teeming mind. Her dad is a lawyer, and after majoring in art history, she followed his career footsteps (and those of her childhood sweetheart and Harvard Law classmate Billy Thomas). In high school, she was thought a bit of a prude, if not a Julie Andrews in the making. She had a heartrending affair with a married professor at Harvard, and Billy sort of stepped on her aorta by transferring to Michigan and leaving her for another woman (his future wife, Georgia).

Billy was always too practical-minded to believe that he and Ally could've met their life partners in childhood (something he never confessed to her), until their unexpected reunion years later at their Boston law firm. Ally's hard-to-shake devotion to Billy (and her affair with her professor) could be related to her own parents' shaky liaison. When Ally was three, she caught her mother in bed with another man while Ally's dad was away. Ally's parents' marriage endured for life, though empty of love. That's why she's so picky, determined to find the real thing and make it stick.

Most people see things as they are and say, "That's the way it goes." Ally sees hallucinations and holds out for dreams to come true. Her visions put her in touch with the deep emotional undercurrents that run through everybody's lives. Her hallucination of the unicorn signifies hope and love to the pure and lonely, and that's Ally all over.

Not that she's alone. Ally's life is rich with erotic collisions (see "Ally's Passionometer"). She could write dissertations on the various kinds of dancing and what they mean, the theory and practice of the kiss, and the importance of wearing your lucky underwear on a first date with a hot prospect.

On the playing field of romance and in the close, quarrelsome company of her friends, Ally proves she's got a big heart. She's not all heart, however. She can be selfish. She had a purely physical one-night stand with a snowboard dude and intimated to her friends that his prodigious private parts were all everyone thought they would be. When she throws a party, Billy lets her have it for being more concerned about her own reputation as a hostess than about how her pals are enjoying the party. Cage marvels at her gift for turning a conversation about someone else's problems into one about hers in six seconds flat. Georgia acidly asks the endlessly kvetching Ally what makes her problems

so much more important than anyone else's. "Because they're mine," Ally defiantly replies. Ally's temper has provoked her to yell at perfect strangers, and she's even tripped and tackled a couple of people who irked her, but it all made perfect sense in her emotional context, and besides, the targets of her ire started the arguments, more or less. And when, in a rare instance, she spent the night in jail on a misdemeanor charge, it was mostly just bad luck.

Although Ally isn't the chief meddler at the office—that would be Elaine—she does her share of getting into other people's business. When Fish cheats on Whipper by fingering Attorney General Janet Reno's wattle, Ally orders him to stop it. When Georgia has a false pregnancy and sobs alone in a Unisex

stall, Ally is so curious that she peers over and falls on top of her. Later, Ally tongue-lashes Georgia for hanging around an old boyfriend (Ray Brown) because Ally senses Georgia still has feelings for him.

Even when Ally tries to do the right thing, she often does it in the wrong way. When she's been courted by guys she doesn't want, instead of just rebuffing them gently and directly, she has attempted to turn them off with an elaborate act: She has impersonated a brainless makeup-obsessed narcissist and a lesbian (twice). When Ally decides to play Good Samaritan to help a girl on the street, the girl's ingratitude provokes Ally to attack her, attracting the police.

In short, Ally can turn the world on with her smile—but only when she damn well feels like it. In fact, she thinks smiling has its perils: When her twenty-eighth birthday is looming, Ally tells her roommate, Renee, that one's face starts to "crack" by age thirty: "It loses moisture. The only reason I look as young as I do is because I had the good sense not to smile growing up."

Ally can nail an opponent with legal logic, but her true mission in life is to make the case for love. Bravely, she sails unruly seas of emotion, and in her world, emotions are matters of practical consequence. If Ally is with a guy who makes her feel like she's walking on air, her feet physically appear to rise above the floor. If she feels dumped, we feel for her as she's flung from a truck to a Dumpster. For every strange vision that confronts her, there is a perfectly reasonable explanation, even if Ally is the only one who can see it. She makes us see things her way, by the passion of her arguments, the purity of her visions, and the infectious melodies that fill her head.

Ally is her own woman—and she hopes this won't mean she winds up on her own forever. Not likely. Her charm and beauty will certainly win out.

She embodies the hopes and dreams most folks hold inside, and not just womenfolk. She's a walking, dancing, air-swimming, pratfalling example of what life might be like if the irrational, inspirational internal world each of us lives in could get loose and take over the world around us. She's a dream girl who won't settle for a drab reality, and her dreams are widely shared.

Calista Flockhart

Calista Flockhart grew up in Illinois, Iowa, Minnesota, New York, and New Jersey, the cheerleader daughter of a teacher and a Kraft Foods executive—both her mom and dad were responsible for quality control.

A drama student at Rutgers University, Flockhart was a pro of note from the start, holding her own onstage with Christopher Reeve, William Hurt, Lois Smith, Amy Irving, Lili Taylor, and Julie Harris and making a splash at Massachusetts' Williamstown Theater Festival and in New York and Chicago. The *New York Times* found her performance as Juliet "luminous." The powerful critic, Frank Rich, deemed Flockhart "excellent," and the most cruel, erudite, and hard-to-please critic, John Simon, raved her as "one of our best young actresses." Her biggest hit was a tough role to make fresh—Laura in *The Glass Menagerie*—which won her the 1995 Theater World and Clarence Derwent Awards. *Time* magazine called Flockhart's Laura "beautifully poised and tender...winning your heart and breaking it, too." Often, critics praised Flockhart's sensitivity to the moment and ability to balance tricky, tense, contradictory emotions in a role.

Success led to small movie parts and then to Ally, the most innovative role for a woman in recent TV history.

Fame for Flockhart has been a bit of a bear. When she walked out of a restaurant with a reporter interviewing her for *In Style* magazine, Australian tabloids instantly came out with photos and a headline about "Calista's New Love." She chose to be amused and focused on her ongoing stage career, her promising film career, and the round-the-clock job of bringing Ally to life.

It's not easy squeezing a significant performance in between TV seasons, but Flockhart has done fine work for two playwrights while taking a break from *Ally McBeal*: William Shakespeare and Neil LaBute. Flockhart's Helena in a film of Shakespeare's frothy early comedy *A Midsummer Night's Dream* got thumbs-ups from critics and audiences, and she demonstrated her range in LaBute's dark, scary stage piece *Bash*. "Flockhart is riveting

and harrowing as a young woman confessing a monstrous crime," raved *Newsweek*'s Jack Kroll.

Flockhart the actor is versatile and well-known, but is there any scene in which Ally expresses Calista's emotions? Her mother saw one aspect of her daughter come out in a scene where Ally walks out of court after one of Cage/Fish's many victories and thinks, "I won. I don't need men. I don't need anything." Flockhart told a *Cosmopolitan* reporter that her mother said, "That was so you—did you write that?" For the record, David E. Kelley wrote it; but it was brought to you by Calista Flockhart.

BILLY
thomas

In the first episodes, Billy Thomas (played by Gil Bellows) appears pretty much as a nostalgic reflection in Ally's eyes: the perfect guy, the childhood sweetheart who got away. His transfer to the University of Michigan, allegedly for Law Review (Ally made Law Review at Harvard and Billy didn't), was in reality to pursue Georgia, a woman he felt fated to marry ten minutes after they met.

But for a perfect guy, Billy has just a wee flaw or two. When Ally discovers he once shared a bachelor-party hooker with "Happy" Boyle, she busts him big-time; when he says, "Old girlfriends don't have rights," she snaps, "This one does." It's a turning point: Being mad at Billy is more intimate than longing for him from afar. Because he has known her for so long (age eight onward), Billy can bust Ally when no one else can—as he does after she undermines his defense of her defiant miniskirts in court by calling the judge a pig.

The better we get to know Billy, the more cracks we see in his perfect facade. ("It's a long-fuse role," Bellows observes.) He's hardly on his best behavior in the case of Ling's sister's implants—does he need to inspect those naked breasts at such close range? He claims he's checking "for scars" and really has a professional obligation to try some hands-on fact-finding.

His marriage with Georgia develops cracks, too, giving us a deeper glimpse into each character. Yet Billy has an integrity that remains intact through it all. In the second show, Ally has to save him in the nick of time from wrecking his marriage (and Georgia's ego) by confessing his party indiscretion. Usually, Billy is far more orderly in court than Ally is, but his emotions often take him by surprise. Part of what attracts Ally to him is a certain boyish earnestness, a groping toward doing the right thing, his extreme kindness along with an instinct for self-preservation. He defends Nelle from her critics, but warns Nelle not to trifle with his friend Cage's affections. He feels responsible and thinks Cage should be told about Stefan the frog getting flushed—but he finds reasons for Fish to be the one stuck with breaking the truth to Cage.

Until the arrival of Nelle and Ling in the second season, Billy (and Georgia, too) served partly to mirror the world of the firm, often playing straight man to Ally and the other characters with weird behavior. He and Georgia unleash their unruly inner selves more often as the show progresses, perhaps most memorably by having—or trying to have—passionate sex in a unisex stall.

One thing Billy never wants to put a leash on is Ally's idealistic faith in romance, or in the Maxwell case, or anyone's hope for higher love. Billy defends the guy who believes in unicorns not only because he's a great, straight-ahead lawyer who can pull off legal miracles but also because he respects unicorns and what they stand for, even though he's usually too sensible to see unicorns himself.

To those who are hard on Billy for yielding to the urge to kiss Ally—try looking at it this way: Billy married Georgia because they're a better match, but he feels the tug of Ally because sometimes she helps him see shimmering possibilities of what might have been.

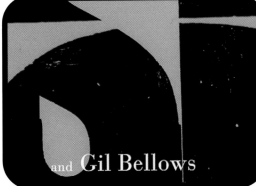

and Gil Bellows

CREDITS

Film and Television Roles

Dinner at Fred's (1999), Richard

Judas Kiss (1998), Lizard

The Assistant (1997)

Snow White: A Tale of Terror (1997), Will

Witch Way Love (1997), Michael

Looking for Richard (1996)

Radiant City (1996) (TV), Bert Kramer

The Substance of Fire (1996), Val Chenard

Black Day, Blue Night (1995), Hitchhiker Dodge

Miami Rhapsody (1995), Matt

Silver Strand (1995) (TV), Brian Del Piso

Love and a .45 (1994), Watty Watts

The Shawshank Redemption (1994), Tommy Williams

Law and Order (1991) (TV series), Howard Metzler in "The Violence of Summer"

Books on Tape Narrated by Gil Bellows

Exit to Eden, by Anne Rice

Gil Bellows left Vancouver, B.C., to attend the American Academy of Dramatic Arts in Southern California. Then came a promising stage career in the Northeast, and a still more promising film career. Bellows has costarred with Tim Robbins in *The Shawshank Redemption*, with Joan Plowright in Bernard Malamud's *The Assistant*, with Parker Posey in *Dinner at Fred's*, in *Witch Way Love* with Jeanne Moreau, and in *Judas Kiss* with Emma Thompson.

He and his wife had a daughter in April 1999.

Q: When your character reveals some new fact or personal quirk and the story takes a new turn, does it just show up in the script or does Kelley sit down and talk to you about it?

Bellows: If there's ever something within a script where we explore something more in depth, that's when the discussion happens. It's usually very brief—he's very good at articulating your point of view when you have questions about your character or the scene. I think that's an aspect of David that probably separates him from a lot of people: He has a very economical yet acute sense of what you're thinking, and he will consider it and respond and usually in a way that's very collaborative.

Q: Can you give us an example of that collaboration in action?

Bellows: Well, I think . . . um, I think that . . . I guess . . . I remember at the beginning I had concerns because, uh, the second episode I guess I was supposed to have slept with, uh, a hooker at my bachelor party.

Q: Your hesitant way of bringing up this delicate matter reminds one of Billy's abashedness about his embarrassing bachelor-party lapse. You clearly feel protective of Billy and his reputation.

Bellows: Here I am, this character, and I have a very large burden to carry for the audience. I'm Ally's first love, and I have a lot of social and plot-driven barriers that separate me and Ally, but I'm going to be seeing her in every episode, so I don't know if I want to be somebody who is doing things like that. I wanted this person to have a chance to almost be perfect and then slowly see the cracks—and I think that's kind of what's been happening. And as an actor, I always feel like my desire of pace is different from his—but I do say that

David has this wonderful internal rhythm overview of the entire show that's pretty amazing.

Q: In retrospect, some of that early rectitude that Billy projected in the first episodes seems kind of a front. Billy has all kinds of cracks inside, behind that perfect suit he wears like a knight's shining armor.

Bellows: That's essentially what the character's got to be. Because there's a lot of flamboyance around him, and at the same time, he has an opportunity to be a sort of a legitimate point of view in the show.

Q: You're the sane person witnessing often nutty events.

Bellows: I don't know if it's sane, necessarily.

Q: You're the closest thing to sane we're going to get at Cage/Fish, anyway.

Bellows: On a certain level, I would say yes, absolutely. Or at least, I think Billy would be in the position of being put forth as *seemingly* more sane.

Q: Billy is the one most mortified by his wacky colleagues in the crossover episode with *The Practice*, when more normal lawyers confronted Ally's world, because Billy is the closest to that real world.

Bellows: Yeah. It's a very interesting dynamic to play.

Q: Kelley observes his actors and puts bits of them into the characters they play: Peter MacNicol's bagpipe playing, Greg Germann's cigars, the flutter Ally's hands sometimes acquire as she talks. Are there aspects of you somewhere in there in Billy?

Bellows: I'm hoping as my character goes on to filter more of those in. I just feel like—

Q: Sometimes, do you feel like Clark Kent waiting to be Superman? Get the wind in your hair?

Bellows: [Chuckling.] That's kind of funny. Yeah, every once in a while you get to muss up the hair a little bit, and that's fun. The Clark Kent/Superman image—I don't want to own it, but I think it's a good one. But Billy is a long-fuse kind of role, you know. Thirty-eight

episodes in, I got to express my [Billy's] own frustrations. The one right before the "Trouble in River City" one, right before I confess to Georgia, I get to tell Ally how I feel, and it was a lot of fun to do. Extremely enjoyable to play and very powerful.

Q: Billy seems to have this compulsion to confess. He seems like this pillar of rationality that Ally can lean against, but emotions can unhinge him. Ally had to stop him from telling Georgia about the bachelor party, and when he sees Ally finally getting serious with her on-and-off boyfriend Dr. Greg Butters, he just can't keep from blurting out his love for her.

Bellows: Right, right. Which is an interesting lesson.

Q: What does Billy see in Ally and Georgia, respectively? What sides of him are being pulled at?

Bellows: The head and the heart. And I think that the thing is that they're both very sexy in very different ways. So if you can embrace the head or the heart, you've got a full package in front of you to lose yourself in.

Q: Until that moment when he blurts in Episode Thirty-eight, Billy is too intellectually pragmatic to accept the notion that he may have met his life's love at age eight. To believe that, he'd have to be as romantic by nature as Ally—or see the romantic in himself. Whereas Georgia and Billy get together as a pair of feet-on-the-ground practical types—when they get a positive pregnancy test, they shake hands. You're on unfamiliar emotional turf, you don't know how else to express it.

Bellows: Yeah. You know, there are certain intrinsic forms of communication and upbringing that are slightly different between Billy and myself.

Q: What do you share, and how do you differ?

Bellows: Let's see, the one thing that I share is this profound affection for women. I think that Billy definitely does have a strong affection for the feminine persuasion. I think, as well, I'd have to say there's something about wanting to discuss a point of view. He's a lawyer, I'm an actor; you have an opportunity to debate, I think.

Q: There's a similarity in the slightly syncopated rhythm of your speech and that of Billy's, except that your inflections are a little looser—kind of jaunty and jazzy. What's different between you and Billy?

Bellows: I wouldn't get up to wear a suit every day. I'm kind of a jeans and T-shirt kind of guy.

Q: You can take the boy out of Vancouver, B.C., but—

Bellows: Exactly, you still wear the jeans and the shirts.

Q: Grunge was always in in the Northwest. You were grungy when grungy wasn't cool.

Bellows: That's true. I had a little leather jacket with a band on the back. When I was twelve, I had Boston on for a couple of years. And then I had the Stones, of course.

Q: This isn't the first time you had a chance to play opposite Calista Flockhart. You started out at the same time in New York theater, and you did a reading of a play together.

Bellows: It was like nine years ago. It was a lot of fun, but it was never done. It was about a snake charmer and the woman he loved.

Q: At first, it was you and Georgia who were a kind of straight mirror on the strange goings-on at Cage/Fish, and then with the two new characters, Nelle and Ling, they formed another point of view on it.

Bellows: Yeah, I agree.

Q: You never know who's going to bump into whom on that show or what's going to happen next. Each character reacts subtly or violently to the others, and that can't happen unless the actors are perfectly in synch. Would you say you run with the best pack of actors on TV?

Bellows: I think everyone in the cast would say that it was a really wonderful moment to receive that award for best ensemble because there are some great ensembles out there—we're not saying we're the best. But we're not children, you know, we've been doing this, all of us, for a while, and we're good, and we're enjoying it, and we're given a wonderful opportunity. You can put any two people in a scene, and it would be interesting.

john CAGE

John Cage (played by Peter MacNicol) is the most miraculously effective attorney in the firm, by far the strangest of a strange crew. He shares a name with the composer John Cage, who is most famous for a composition consisting of several long minutes of silence. In court, Cage orchestrates manipulative silences—those "moments" he takes—but he has many, many other sounds at his disposal: nose whistles, stomach rumbles he can throw ventriloquist-fashion, squeaky shoes, clickers, whooshing blowtorches, tapes of noises making fun of opponents' cases, the clangorous bells from *Rocky*, show tunes, pop songs, and the theme from *Mr. Ed.* He tends to call opponents "wily" or "tricksters," but nobody is as wily a trickster as Cage. On the other hand, some sounds exert a power over him that he can't control—"Gimme Dat Thing" makes Cage a dancing fool, the first seven notes of "Can't Hurry Love" make him urgently want to do just that, and anything by Barry White catapults him into the seduction zone.

Although his longest relationship was with a frog named Stefan (a liaison lasting twice as long as his longest relationship with a woman), women from Renee to Nelle have been strongly drawn to him from time to time. For a guy nicknamed "The Biscuit," he's not really soft—in fact, he can be hard-nosed. And he's the only member of the firm whose inner world is as weird as Ally's. Or more so.

The key to Cage is that even in his weirdest moments, he is unapologetic. He plays it straight when he tells a court considering the case of a nun that as a kid he himself wanted to be a nun, because he thought that then he could fly, and that he asked for feminine napkins for Christmas so he could bike and swim and ride a horse (as ads claimed a napkin-wearer could). He knows that others don't share his obsession with a fresh bowl and that Ally won't feel his pain when it's necessary to break his favorite toilet to free her butt from its clammy grip.

He is an enigma, but as Renee observes, a cute enigma with no intention of surrendering his mystery.

with Peter MacNicol

CREDITS

Film and Television Roles

The Pooch and the Pauper (to air on ABC, 1999)

Baby Geniuses (1999), Dan Bobbins

Silencing Mary (1998), Lawrence Dixon

Bean (1997), David Langley

Abducted: A Father's Love (1996) (TV), Roy Dowd

Mojave Moon (1996), Tire Repairman

Toto Lost in New York (1996), voice of Ork

Dracula: Dead and Loving It (1995), Renfield

Chicago Hope (1994–1995) (TV series), Alan Birch

Radioland Murders (1994), Son Writer

Roswell (1994) (TV), Lewis Rickett

Addams Family Values (1993), Gary Granger

Cheers (1993) (TV series), Mario, motel manager in "Look Before You Sleep"

Housesitter (1992), Marty

The Powers That Be (1992) (TV series), Bradley Grist

Hard Promises (1991), Stuart

By Dawn's Early Light (1990) (TV), Sedgewicke

American Blue Note (1989), Jack Solow

Ghostbusters II (1989), Janosz Poha

Days and Nights of Molly Dodd (1987) (TV series), Steve Cooper

Heat (1987), Cyrus Kinnick

Johnny Bull (1986) (TV), Joe Kovacs

Faerie Tale Theatre—The Boy Who Left Home to Find Out About the Shivers (1983)

Sophie's Choice (1982), Stingo

Dragonslayer (1981), Galen

Selected Theater Roles

Black Comedy/White Liars (1993) (off-Broadway)

The Dream Theme (1991) (off-Broadway)

The 52nd Street Project (1990) (off-Broadway), Human Nature

Romeo and Juliet (1988) (off-Broadway), Romeo

Twelfth Night (1986) (off-Broadway), Sir Andrew Aguecheek

Rum and Coke (1986) (off-Broadway), Jake Steward

Found a Peanut (1984) (off-Broadway), Little Earl 5

Crimes of the Heart (1981) (Broadway), Barnette Lloyd

Crimes of the Heart (1980) (off-Broadway), Barnette Lloyd

Books on Tape Narrated by Peter MacNicol

Beach Music, by Pat Conroy

Imajica, by Clive Barker

Shiloh, Saving Shiloh, Shiloh Season, by Phyllis Reynolds Naylor

Peter MacNicol grew up in Texas and Minneapolis and hit the stage at age nine, taking a long moment as a statue of St. Peter that eventually came to life. An early role as Louis Pasteur healing a dog helped hone his gift for improvisation when the dog jumped up and chased him around the stage. MacNicol came of age at the Guthrie Theater in Minneapolis, one of the launchpads of the American regional-theater

renaissance. Instead of work emerging from Broadway and being exported to the provinces, the provinces began feeding Broadway with plays and actors. MacNicol was launched nationally alongside Holly Hunter in Beth Henley's 1981 Pulitzer and New York Drama Critics Circle Award–winning import to Broadway, *Crimes of the Heart*. Legendary caricaturist Al Hirschfeld scribbled him. The *New Yorker* said MacNicol "couldn't be better" as the star of the twenty-one-character play *Rum and Coke*.

MacNicol's most historically important movie is probably the part of the narrator/hero (based on author William Styron) in *Sophie's Choice*, the Oscar-winning movie with Meryl Streep, but his funniest may be *Ghostbusters II*. He wound up in the film by accident: His manager proposed another actor for the part, but the tape accidentally included MacNicol's performance as a young man courting TV's Molly Dodd.

MacNicol's *Ghostbusters II* turn as the mad Carpathian Janosz Poha, a character largely concocted by MacNicol, stole the film from Bill Murray and Dan Aykroyd, in the opinion of most viewers, including the *New York Times*. Even Pauline Kael cracked up over MacNicol's unearthly comic style: "The pure silliness of it—all the childish playacting it recalls—can make you surprisingly happy." MacNicol persevered, juggling distinguished stage and screen roles, the lawyer Alan Birch on David E. Kelley's *Chicago Hope* perhaps being the most conspicuous.

Of course, it is as the inimitable John Cage that MacNicol will probably forever be most renowned.

RENEE
radick

Renee Radick (played by Lisa Nicole Carson) is Ally's roommate, confidante, fellow aficionado of ice cream and "Good Night, My Someone," occasional courtroom nemesis as assistant district attorney, attender of weddings and burner of bridesmaids' dresses, and giver and receiver of lots of mostly sound love advice.

Renee has been steamrolled in court by Cage and refused to plea bargain on one of Ally's cases, but she never takes their legal roles personally. Renee is almost always down with the Cage/Fish crew dancing at the Bar, at parties, running into Ally on the street at emotionally significant moments. Renee is a de facto part of the whole firm's life, not just Ally's.

Renee is a great singer—and this gets her into trouble with Ally when she impulsively cuts in on a solo love song Greg is crooning to Ally at the Bar, turning it into a steamy duet and taking the spotlight from the

jealous, serenaded Ally. In terms of their relationship, Renee usually sings a pragmatic, mildly sarcastic counterpoint to Ally's arias of neurotic romantic lament. "Here's a flash," she'll tell Ally, when Ally is bewailing a man's lack of response, "men are shy." She also tends to take a more nuanced position on love than Ally does. When Ally identifies with the outrage of clients whose lovers get stolen, Renee is the one who astutely notes that nobody gets stolen: "People find each other, and sometimes, there's a bump involved."

Not that Renee doesn't need Ally's advice, too. When Renee's outrageously provocative overtures encouraged one guy to try to compose a sexual finale beyond what Renee had in mind, she broke his neck, being the kick-boxing champ of greater Boston. And Ally busted Renee's chops afterward. Renee's fun's-a-poppin' approach to sexuality, her way of defusing it by playing the hot mama, was wrong, and only Ally is entitled to order Renee to "get it" about what she's doing wrong.

Renee does get it when Ally talks the tough truth to her, but she's still capable of teasing Ally even then. "Look at what my life has come to," she mourns. "I'm taking advice from you." Renee and Ally are each other's greatest defenders and most well-informed accusers. Maybe that's because Ally sees the private side of Renee more than others do. After all, the fatal attraction of Matt Griffin for Renee is the fact that he knew her before she acquired her tough persona, and she feels he can help her to get in touch with her weak inner self again. Ally has that access, too, in a way, and Renee has an all-access pass to Ally's heart in a way nobody else does.

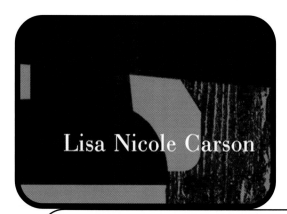

CREDITS

Film and Television Roles

Life (1999), Sylvia

Eve's Bayou (1997), Matty Mereaux

Love Jones (1997), Josie Nichols

ER (1996–1998) (TV series), Carla Reese

Devil in a Blue Dress (1995), Coretta James

Divas (1995) (TV), Jewel

Jason's Lyric (1994), Marti

The Apollo Comedy Hour (1992–1993) (TV series), Regular Performer

Law and Order (1991) (TV series), Jasmine in "Aria"

Lisa Nicole Carson was born in Brooklyn's Clinton Hill and moved at age twelve to Gainesville, Florida. Her theater debut was in second grade, and her first professional job was in *Little Shop of Horrors* at age fifteen. Her parents split up, and Lisa moved to New York, where her mom taught in the South Bronx. Her dad teaches journalism at the University of Florida. Carson, a determined person, made it on stage (and in big roles in small movies), and after initially scorning TV, scored stellar roles as the mother of Dr. Benton's kid on *ER* and Ally's best friend. She doesn't like to drive, her nickname is "Gypsy," and she confesses to having skinny-dipped on a first date.

Q: In the wonderful movie *Devil in a Blue Dress*, weren't you the woman whose "spot" was found by Denzel Washington?

Carson: Yeah, he found the spot.

Q: It's not easy to steal a scene from Denzel.

Carson: Well, it's not easy to find my spot.

Q: And it wasn't easy to break into showbiz, especially starting out in a white community in Florida. How did you make it in New York?

Carson: Definitely on-the-job training. I've never had an acting lesson or a singing lesson. I just kind of jumped in and started doing it, and made a lot of mistakes, and met a lot of interesting, wonderful, talented people, pounding the pavement with *Backstage* magazine as my Bible.

Q: Renee is completely unfazable. Who else could drag Ally by the ear and not wind up dead?

Carson: I think that Ally and Renee are beyond roommates. They're sort of like sisters. And you can call your sister on anything, and she has called me on some of my things, too. Like last season when I kicked that guy's ass accidentally. Well . . . it wasn't accidentally.

Q: You fronted the all-woman rock band Mascara. How do you like doing the singing scenes on *Ally*?

Carson: Anytime, anyplace, I'm there 100 percent. I am a total music junkie. So as soon as we're in the Bar and there's Vonda singing, or Barry White, or whatever they're playing, those are really great times for me. A release.

Q: What are your own musical faves?

Carson: I'm primarily a rhythm-and-blues girl.

Carson: I thought that was cool, too. Definitely, Ally is sensitive to Renee. I mean, I think Calista is pretty sensitive in real life, too. The two things about Calista that I think of the most—that I will carry with me after this is all said and done—is she has amazing endurance, she works excruciating hours every day. And she is on it. All the time. And that's impressive. And also she has an amazing emotional range and the ability to manipulate it at the drop of a dime. She's really good.

Q: What is Renee's chief virtue and frailty?

Carson: She's smart and probably she does like to keep a front going, a real tough exterior. And you know it's just real hard to get to the goo. And it's all the richer then.

Q: Tell us about the Renee-Cage relationship.

Carson: Cage is crazy. That is just it.

Q: My theory is that he's David E. Kelley's fantasy of what he'd have liked to get away with when he was a lawyer.

Carson: He's so much fun. He just came in and rocked it. I love that the most. He was just supposed to come in and do his thing and leave, but he just rocked it so hard. I have to say. I mean, who else could have taken a glass of water and wound up with that character? He adds so much flavor to the show. I mean so much of his character defines *Ally McBeal* the show to me. It's wonderful.

Barry White, Teddy Pendergrass, Peabo Bryson, Stephanie Mills, and you know, Diana Ross and all of those guys, Stevie Wonder, but I also listen to jazz, Ella Fitzgerald and Sarah Vaughan, and then I'm also into rock and roll, you know, real heavy-duty, Guns 'n' Roses, Aerosmith, just everybody. I love voices and Rickie Lee Jones, and I think I'm a voice person. If the voice moves me, the music will follow.

Q: How does Renee relate to Ally's work pals?

Carson: They're more of an ensemble and my contribution to the show is really with Ally. Mostly. I do have some interaction with them and we have established a rather catty and aloof relationship between me and some of the female characters on the show and then I have an interesting relationship going on with Cage.

Q: I've always wondered about that.

Carson: Yeah, me too.

Q: It was touching how concerned Ally was for Renee when Renee's Billy equivalent—her long-lost love—came back and discombobulated her life.

GEORGIA
thomas

Georgia Thomas (played by Courtney Thorne-Smith) walks into Ally's life as a problem and swiftly develops into a close friend. Like Ally, Georgia was better than Billy in school: Not only did she make the University of Michigan's Law Review but she was Billy's editor. Billy had known Ally since age eight, but that's exactly why he doubted that she could possibly be his sweetheart for life. The first time he laid eyes on Georgia—on a trip to check out Michigan's law school—he knew she was the one for him.

Unfortunately for Georgia, when Ally walks back into Billy's life at Cage/Fish and Associates, Billy becomes less sure about his urges. And when Georgia winds up working there alongside both of them, libidos erupt and tempers flare. Georgia is quick to pick up on the ancient intimacy that reignites between her husband and Ally, and she's the one who's smart enough to sum up the ironies of their triangle when the three of them see a therapist. Georgia is peeved to find that Ally's presence seems to improve her relationship with Billy, resents her own growing friendship with Ally, and is understandably enraged that there are areas of her husband's heart that only Ally can access.

With Dr. Tracy's loud cheerleader-like encouragement, Ally consents to kick-box with Georgia, to get their rivalry right out in the open. Georgia lands the first blow, but it winds up a mutual K.O. This scarcely settles the contest. Georgia maintains a vicariously pleasurable interest in Ally's affairs, voicing enthusiasm (and even occasionally letting her tongue flop to the floor) over such Ally amours as Glenn the model and Bobby Donnell. Meanwhile Ally gets more and more wrapped up in Billy, culminating in the kiss heard 'round the world. Georgia's got grit as well as great looks. She challenges Ally to bed Billy to get it out of their systems once and for all. Ally is a live wire, confrontational by nature, but Georgia (somewhat like Billy) has a slower fuse. When Ally absent-mindedly sits on Georgia's lap in the toilet, Georgia is more patient than most women would be. And she doesn't erupt the way most people would upon learning that her spouse is kissing his ex again, but she does do a slow burn, and even when the threat subsides, she doesn't instantly forgive Billy or Ally.

Georgia has other vulnerabilities besides the Ally dilemma. She's stunned by a pregnancy scare, then moved to tears in the Unisex when the positive

pregnancy test turns out to have been false. When Nelle joins the firm, Georgia confesses to the Unisex mirror what it feels like to be the fairest of all no longer.

Georgia is also the worst singer in the world: Her renditions of Dusty Springfield classics are so abominable that everyone in the room bursts into song to drown her out. She mistakes this for encouragement and warbles on horribly. Later, Billy helps her face the fact that she is among the singing impaired. Just as Georgia's quasi-musical outburst made her a rounder character by revealing her impulsiveness—prior to this she's been pretty much the model of self-restraint—her reaction when Billy breaks the bad news about her talent-free singing shows a new, winning vulnerability. She sure deals with a bad performance better than Ally, who earns comparable shame onstage when she proves to be "the world's most incompetent teller of dirty jokes."

In the final analysis, Georgia's marriage troubles aren't Ally's fault. She and Billy are more alike than Ally and Billy: They're a pair of reasonable minds, and Ally is in an orbit all her own. When Georgia's marriage slips into a rut, she slips into something slinky. She walks in on Billy naked in red high heels and lies down on his desk, has such athletic sex with him in a Unisex stall that he winds up with a black eye, and scandalizes him by day by donning thigh-high slit-skirt attire to make tongues wag, or worse.

Caroline Poop calls Georgia a Barbie doll, but when it comes to Georgia, Poop doesn't know squat. This is one Barbie doll with a brain and a lot of brass.

Courtney Thorne-Smith

CREDITS

Film and Television Roles

Venus Conspiracy (1999)

Chairman of the Board (1998), Natalie

Duckman (1997) (TV series),
voice-over in "Bonfire of the Panties"

The Lovemaster (1997), Deb

Spin City (1997–1998) (TV series), Danielle Brinkman in
"Starting Over" and "It Happened One Night"

Melrose Place (1992–1997) (TV series),
Alison Parker Armstrong Hanson

Beauty's Revenge (1995) (TV), Cheryl

Breach of Conduct (1994) (TV), Helen Lutz

Grapevine (1992) (TV series),
Lisa in "The Lisa and Billy Story"

Anything But Love (1990)

L.A. Law (1990) (TV series),
Kimberly Dugan in several episodes

Side Out (1990), Samantha

Day by Day (1988) (TV series), Kristin Carlson

Infidelity (1987) (TV), Eileen

Revenge of the Nerds II: Nerds in Paradise (1987), Sunny

Summer School (1987), Pam

Fast Times (1986) (TV series), Stacy Hamilton

Lucas (1986), Alise

The Thanksgiving Promise (1986) (TV), Sheryl

Welcome to 18 (1986), Lindsey

Courtney Thorne-Smith grew up in the Bay Area, a national theatrical capital. Her professional training began in her last year of high school at Mill Valley's Ensemble Theater Company. Originally, she was named Courtney Thorne Smith, but since her middle name was her mother's maiden name, she decided to honor both families by hyphenating it. Being tight with her family paid off in her acting career: When she got her first huge break playing the tormented Alison on *Melrose Place*, one suspects Thorne-Smith got insightful input from her mom, a therapist. And since Alison was an ad woman by profession, it must have come in handy that Thorne-Smith's sister was an advertising executive.

Q: Tell me about how Georgia has evolved as a character.

Thorne-Smith: Well, she talks now. She didn't in the first couple of episodes. That was an issue.

Q: Georgia was like the straight man, along with Billy.

Thorne-Smith: We were the eyes of the world. We were the observers. Which we continue to be, but we're also allowed to have some humanity and our own problems. We've gotten to lose it completely a couple of times, which is fun for us.

Q: What was your favorite losing-it moment?

Thorne-Smith: When Georgia gets up and sings Dusty Springfield and then completely loses perspective on what's OK and what's not OK. It was so much fun, and it's the first time that I've really gotten to do one of those David Kelley things where you're doing something completely ridiculous but it makes absolute sense for the character. Vonda was helping to produce the number, and I sang it once, and she goes, "Whoa, we've got it; it really can't get any worse, can it?"

Q: Only Georgia has been normal enough up to now to pull off that scene—nobody else has as much room to be embarrassed.

Thorne-Smith: Right. Unfortunately, it's also because the others can really sing. You can't put Lisa Nicole or Jane up there [to sing off-key]. They're too talented.

Q: What's the key to Georgia's character?

Thorne-Smith: She's very earnest. I admire how committed she is to her marriage. And yet Georgia seems to be able to stay committed to her marriage and herself. She doesn't seem to abandon herself. Though she stays in a situation that makes most of us go, "I would leave, I would leave!" she seems to be able to stay and keep her pride and find ways to do it.

Q: It must be an acting challenge, to maintain her pride.

Thorne-Smith: I rely a lot on denial. It helps me through. And I believe that long-term relationships can do with a little bit of denial. You can't pick at every little thing that someone does wrong. Even though I know that a lot of the things that Billy and Georgia go through are big things, the reality is, if I'm annoyed with a friend, or my fiancé, if I could just sit on it, if you can just sit on it for two weeks, you'll be amazed at how much of it fixes itself. This is something my sister taught me. Words to live by.

Q: Did you get any other good advice early in life?

Thorne-Smith: I did have an incredible high-school drama teacher who told me when I went to my first movie, "Remember you're there to do a job. Everybody's there to do a job. They'll treat you differently because you're an actor, but remember you can be one of a few hundred or you can be all alone." And that has served me so well. As an actor, I could sit there in my chair and say, "Get me this, get me that," and they'll do it, but then you're separate and alone. Or you can get up and get your own coffee and offer some to somebody else, and you're one of a huge team. And that's why Ally works, because we're all a member of the team. The cast gives the crew a Christmas gift every year, and this year we gave them a bowling party. Just us, the cast and the crew. And it was so much fun. It was a statement of "We are in this together." You know, all of us.

Q: In the rehearsal for the scene where Billy confesses he's smooched Ally and Georgia is aghast, I'm told you make a joke like, "Well, I kissed her first, why shouldn't you do it, too?" [Georgia and Ally had faked a kiss in an earlier show to discourage an unwanted Ally suitor.] That was a joke take. But have any improvisations really worked for the scene?

Thorne-Smith: In one scene, Peter says something, and I do the "Georgia look"—the double take. So Greg says, "Why don't we try and do it all together?" So Greg and Gil and I all did it together, the "Georgia look." Which made it so much richer. And the crew laughed, so we go, OK, we got it. There's a lot of stuff like that. You're constantly being challenged, and I think David has a lot of faith in his cast. I think he has more faith in us often, or certainly more faith in me, than I do.

Q: You're marrying a scientist. He's probably in one of the few professions where your hours seem normal.

Thorne-Smith: Yeah, except for he's the boss and he gets to make his own hours. It's easier to work a twelve-hour day when you decide when it starts and when it ends.

Q: What does it say about Billy that the most prominent women in his life are the two of you?

Thorne-Smith: That he's very lucky. They're both smart, career-oriented, they're both feminists. I know that people argue that Ally isn't a feminist when she's looking for love, but I disagree. I think she's a strong woman trying to be an individual. I mean, for me feminism is about women being whatever they want to be, need to be. Freely. And I think that she's truly an individual and so's Georgia. They both want to be happy. And they both make sure they're heard. It depends on what your idea of feminism is. If you think feminism is about presenting perfect women, that's one thing. If you think feminism is about creating realistic women and allowing there to be different kinds of women, different sizes of women, different personalities of women, different colors of women—that's what feminism is about.

Q: I liked Georgia's speech about not being "the fairest one of all" once Nelle arrived.

Thorne-Smith: I didn't even know about that until I had that speech. I didn't even know about this pressure I had going on! And then Portia came in and started letting her hair down. It was sort of a release. I didn't realize it that that was part of my role and I didn't have to do it anymore. Great!

Q: Somebody claimed your nude scene was the first in the history of the network. Does this make you feel historic?

Thorne-Smith: It wasn't my butt. So I don't care. The body double made history.

Q: Also, it wasn't just "objectifying"—it invited us into the experience with you and him, there on the desk, working on your marriage. It was very sweet.

Thorne-Smith: Very sweet!

richard
FISH

Richard Fish (played by Greg Germann) was Ally's most avaricious classmate at Harvard Law before she joined his firm, and he loves to say he's only in it for the money— "piles and piles of money . . . Heaps. *Big* piles." Still, Fish's very exuberance in saying so betrays a deeper motive: He really started his firm for the sheer morally malleable fun of it. Not that money isn't important to him—he's been known to get aroused by perusing his stock portfolio—but the crucial thing to him is to make sure everybody knows he's wealthy and winning the game. "Let me tell you something," he says in the debut episode. "I didn't become a lawyer because I like the law. The law sucks. It's boring. But it can also be used as a weapon. You want to bankrupt somebody? Cost him everything he's worked for, make his wife leave him, even cause his kids to cry? We can do that." He likes lucre—the filthier, the better. "It's not just winning, it's winning ugly that matters."

In practice, Fish's colleagues generally prevent him from executing his worst impulses, but if he couldn't appall people by what he blithely advocates, he'd be a sadder man. "Verbal spankings titillate," he tells Ally and Georgia. Fish can't resist telling a judge to reverse a Supreme Court decision because they're just dumb old men and then asking, "Do I win?" He calls a "continuance" "one of those continue doohickeys." But Fish knows he's got great lawyers at his disposal, and he seldom loses an opportunity to up the fun quotient of any conversation, in or out of court. And not only did he install the gender-neutral Unisex restroom but he was the first to eavesdrop on his colleagues there by putting his feet up on the stall door. (He claimed it was because of "an L-5 disk" problem.)

While we must never underestimate Fish's shallowness, he also contains deep concealed emotions. After many episodes of cracking us up with his eccentric devotion to wattles in general and to Judge Whipper's in particular and his dodging of Whipper's wish for a ring with comic denunciations of marriage itself, Fish reveals the grimace behind the clown mask. His parents' bitter relationship traumatized him into picking inappropriately older women as partners, so as to keep marriage at bay. His passion for Whipper is as sincere as his weakness for wattles—anybody's wattles (he even muses about Happy Boyle's).

Control is the key to his character. He likes a domineering woman—as a kid he yearned to be puppeteer Shari Lewis's little Lambchop—and when he collides with Ling Woo, the most intimidating woman in his world with emotional armor to match his own, she masters his heart.

The man who constantly reduces love to sex is reduced to loving Ling without any sex at all for the longest time.

Even in the throes of bedroom woes, though, Fish clings to bedrock principles. When Ling asks whether he's taking her cases just to court her, he replies, "I'm nice to you because I want to sleep with you. I kissed you because I want to sleep with you. But taking your cases? I do that only because you're a potential cash cow for the firm to milk in perpetuity."

Greg Germann

CREDITS

Film and Television Roles

Jesus' Son (1999), Dr. Shanis

Remember WENN (1996) (TV series),
Arden Sage in "Work Shift"

Ned and Stacey (1995) (TV series), Eric Moyer

Ellen (1994–1996) (TV series), Rick in several episodes

Assault at West Point (1994) (TV), Bailey

Clear and Present Danger (1994), Petey

I.Q. (1994), Reporter

Imaginary Crimes (1994), Mr. Drew

L.A. Law (1993) (TV series), in "Come Rain or Come Schein"

The Night We Never Met (1993), Eddie

So I Married an Axe Murderer (1993), Desk Clerk

Taking the Heat (1993) (TV), Assistant D.A. Kennedy

Big and Mean (1991)

Once Around (1991), Jim Redstone

Child's Play 2 (1990), Mattson

Equal Justice (1990) (TV)

Tour of Duty (1989–1990) (TV series),
Lieutenant Beller in several episodes

Miss Firecracker (1989), Ronnie Wayne

The Whoopee Boys (1986), Tipper

Streetwalkin' (1984), Creepy

Greg Germann was a theater brat looking for a break from Lookout Mountain, Colorado. His dad was a theater instructor at the University of Denver, and Greg, an usher at the Heritage Square Opera House, grew up to be a drama major at the

University of Northern Colorado and a rising star at New York's prestigious Circle Repertory Theater. For years, he cleaned apartments to support his stage habit. A role as John Hinckley in Stephen Sondheim's most perverse musical, *Assassins*, won raves for Germann. In Los Angeles, Germann played the hero Ned's nice-guy pal Eric in the sitcom *Ned and Stacey*. Then came Fish, wattles, extreme moral pragmatism, and global fame. Germann also wrote, directed, and starred in the film *Pete's Garden*, seen at the 1998 Sundance Film Festival and on the Sundance Channel.

Q: Fish describes himself as a "shark," but he's kind of a cuddly shark, a tub-toy shark, isn't he?

Germann: I think he's ruthless when he needs to be, but what's redeeming about him is he's guileless. He doesn't make any apologies for what he's doing. If I say something that may be off-color, you'll never see me backpedal about it. You always know where you stand with the guy.

Q: For a guy who runs a law firm, Fish isn't the world's greatest lawyer.

Germann: David told me right when I started, "You know, I don't know that you ever go to court." And the more I thought of [Fish], the more he became like my agent. I love to take meetings, go to dinner; I'm great about glad-handing clients. Can I litigate? If I have to. As ruthless as I may be, my intention really is to have a blast, and if everyone isn't having a blast with me, I'm kinda hurt by it.

Q: What's the essence of the Fishism?

Germann: Often, those Fishisms come out spontaneously. What serves me now becomes a Fishism.

Q: What percentage of David E. Kelley is in Richard Fish?

Germann: Beats me. You know, David is a cryptic guy. He's the kind of guy who, if you said, "David, you're cryptic," he'd say, "Am I?"

Q: Often, the writing is subversive. Most TV scenes touching on social issues come from an obvious point of view, but Kelley's are more provocative because you never know where he stands. The point of view keeps shifting.

Germann: I get the feeling that he likes to hold the mirror up a little bit and get a good laugh while he's doing it, and rabble-rouse if he can in a sort of intelligent, quiet way. Cage's whole defense of going out with that prostitute was, I thought, very bold. On the face of it, it doesn't really make any sense, but a lot of Kelley's writing is like that, where you look at it and you go, "Yeah. Yeah! I guess prostitution is OK! I gotta go make a call!"

Q: That's Fish's pragmatic switcheroo reaction to Cage's self-defense on the prostitution bust.

Germann: That was bizarre. I guess Kelley sees the show and decides we need a scene here, there we're short, so we do reshoots. And that was a reshoot. That was as much the character of Fish as anything we've done. "I've thought about it, and you know what? This is only going to make my partner a stronger, better person!" Which is another redeeming thing about Fish's character. He can take any situation, the worst situation, and turn it around and make it work for him. And I think that's something all of us want.

Q: Is Fish cynical?

Germann: I don't think he's cynical. He's actually very positive. Yeah, I want to make as much as I can and make things work for me, but underneath that is this motivation that, man, we're here to have a good time, and if we're not having a good time, then who cares?

Q: People often copy what they see on TV. Do you foresee Fish's wattle obsession sweeping the nation?

Germann: All across America! I'm waiting for that whole surge to happen. Suddenly, people will get plastic surgery. Wattle implants!

ELAINE
vassal

Elaine (played by Jane Krakowski) is the best secretary a law firm ever had, and also the worst. She's fast, she's organized, and she's willing to sue her own firm to the brink of bankruptcy when the mood strikes. Not that she minds a bit when her class-action lawsuit on behalf of the firm's women is crushed. Far from it—Elaine bounces right back to work on the magic carpet of her own inexhaustible good cheer. She expects to be welcomed back with open arms by the boss she'd almost taken to court, and she *is* welcomed back: Fish lets bygones be bygones.

The key to her character is that Elaine never met a spotlight she didn't like. The first time Ally meets her, Ally is new to the firm and feels nervous about jumping into a big case. Elaine makes such a point of how prepared and organized she is that Ally has a hostile fantasy of Elaine's head expanding to superhuman size.

Part of the reason Elaine acts so superior is that she *is* superior. If you want the relevant precedents on a capital case you've got to argue before the Supreme Court in five minutes, get Elaine on the case. She's a natural.

Mostly, Elaine was, is, and ever shall be clamoring, to be drawn into the family circle of the firm and to fulfill the limitless potential of her endlessly inventive nature. We're not talking strictly about the inventions she patents—the Face Bra, the Cool Cup, all the gizmos for which Ling will no doubt produce dazzling info-mercials that will quite possibly make both of them richer than Gates and Allen. The inventiveness of Elaine is the eruption of an indefatigable curiosity and ambition. Everybody at the firm eavesdrops; only Elaine does it with state-of-the-CIA-art equipment. In the love department, Elaine is a seasoned investigative reporter with an avid nose for news. She has a head for business and a body for monkey business, and practically any male of the species will do. She jokes about it—"It goes with who I am, 1–800-ELAINE"—and you can't hurt her by impugning her chastity. She's the one who reports that in high school, they called her "the human window of opportunity."

In a touching revelation that many on the set cite as the character's most affecting moment, Elaine opens up and tells how selling herself to the boys in

school to get nickels for a bicycle bell in her youth helped lead to her current nature. But the biggest mistake of all in understanding Elaine is to pity and underestimate her—a mistake that Ally makes big-time when she tells somebody in the Unisex that Elaine's obsession with a swing dance contest is "pathetic." How could Ally not know that Elaine would be in a stall with her feet up, listening? Ordinarily, such a mortifying overheard comment would occasion a smile, a sneer, or perhaps a Lingian growl of response from the insulted one. But Elaine sets Ally straight in no-nonsense terms. She simply tells Ally that she doesn't want what Ally and the other lawyers want out of life—she doesn't need status or even a husband, necessarily; what Elaine wants is life, in abundance, and she wants it all right now. Cue the lights, crank up the mike—this lady is going to make the world her stage.

Elaine is capable of snapping off that incandescent smile when she needs to. When she catches sight of Ally exchanging heart-to-heart glances with Elaine's boyfriend—a rare one (played by John Ritter) whom she wants as a keeper—Elaine matter-of-factly tells Ally, "You can have any man you want. Please don't take mine."

Of course, Elaine feels entitled to have a total-access pass to everyone else's private life: Embroidering gossip is her favorite hobby. If Ally gets flowers at the office and Elaine's there to sign for them, you can bet she'll read the enclosed card meant for Ally—"to find out if there were any special watering instructions." Elaine's spirit is a sturdy, extravagant growth watered with a few tears here and there, but forever in bloom. And in marked contrast to Ally, Elaine is essentially content with her life.

Jane Krakowski

CREDITS

Film and Television Roles

The Flintstones in Viva Rock Vegas (1999), Betty Rubble

Go (1999), Irene

The Rodgers and Hart Story: Thou Swell, Thou Witty (1999) (TV)

Dance with Me (1998), Patricia

Hudson River Blues (1997)

Due South (1996) (TV series), Katherine Burns in "An Invitation to Romance"

Mrs. Winterbourne (1996), Christine

Queen (1993) (TV miniseries), Jane

Stepping Out (1991), Lynne

Women & Men 2: In Love There Are No Rules (1991) (TV), Melba

When We Were Young (1989) (TV), Linda

Fatal Attraction (1987), Babysitter

Search for Tomorrow (1984–1986) (TV series), Rebecca T.R. Kendall

No Big Deal (1983)

National Lampoon's Vacation (1983), Cousin Vicki

Selected Theater Roles

Once Upon A Mattress (1996–97) (Broadway), Lady Larkin

Company (1995) (Broadway), April

Stepping Out (1991) (Broadway)

Grand Hotel (1990) (Broadway), Flaemchen

Starlight Express (1987–89) (Broadway), Dinah the Dining Car

Elaine Vassal is brought to life by Jane Krakowski, who was born Jane Krajkowski in Parsippany, New Jersey. (Try saying that, John Cage.) "Believe it or not, Krakowski is a stage name," says Krakowski. "How frightening is that? You would think if I was going to go to all the trouble to fill out the forms I would have come up with something else."

Jane's first great break was a job at the celebrated Williamstown Theater Festival in Massachusetts, probably the most star-studded summer theater in America outside New York. Future stars like Calista Flockhart and Jane acted alongside famous names who wanted to maintain their stagecraft.

Krakowski recalls Williamstown as a place rich in memories, though no place to get rich fiscally. "Gil [Bellows] and Calista and I worked a couple of summers in a row, making $200 a week for acting, and they were taking out $50 for housing. Gil met his wife that same summer. So I think because we knew each other then under those circumstances it made it much easier to have all this happen." Jane played Gwyneth Paltrow's sister in Paltrow's first performance in *Picnic* during Jane's first summer at Williamstown.

Broadway brought Jane nominations for the Tony and Drama Desk Awards, and she won the L.A. Drama Critics Award for Best Actress in *One Touch of Venus*. Although she remained a bigger presence onstage than onscreen, she has earned two Emmy nominations for playing Rebecca T.R. Kendall on *Search for Tomorrow*, and her film career, launched way back in 1983 with Cousin Vicki in *National Lampoon's Vacation*, now includes Irene in *Go*, and Betty Rubble in *Viva Rock Vegas* (currently in production).

Q: How did a nice kid from Parsippany wind up on Broadway?

Krakowski: One of my parents' main interests was going into New York City every weekend—I'd see every play and every show with them from age three. Instead of getting a babysitter, they would just take me with them.

So it was just always a very big influence in my life. And their hobby was this community theater in our neighborhood in New Jersey. Because I always saw my parents having fun, it all just sort of infiltrated that that's what I wanted to do. And be a part of. And I've been taking dance lessons since I was three. I would train in New Jersey during the week and went into the city into whatever the hot dance schools were at the time on the weekends. I didn't go to like any one formal drama school. I took classes all over the place.

Q: Comic secretaries are commonplace in sitcoms, but Elaine is no ordinary office vassal.

Krakowski: "Vassal"—there's definitely got to be a double entendre there. Elaine has been a gold mine from day one. Because I thought she had more freedom to get away with more things than many of the other characters.

Q: What's Elaine's secret?

Krakowski: I always wanted Elaine to be very smart, always very, very good at her job. I reasoned that she could get away and do all those things because she had already finished what she had to do as a secretary in the office. That's why she had free time to go and hang in the Unisex and get all the scoop. And go home at night and invent face bras.

Q: What's your favorite Elaine invention?

Krakowski: The Face Bra. I just think it could probably actually sell. I think the Ice Goggles could really make it on the market. The Husband CD was hilarious, and I think that there is a comedy album market that might be able to sell it. And this is a bit more Elaine than Jane, but because I've been playing the character for a long time, ideas seep in and I start thinking in a very Elaine way. If and when they ever market the Face Bra, they should get some sort of tie-in with Nike. You know the "swoosh" of Nike? You could put them on the cheeks, and they'd look like cheekbones to make it much more flattering.

Q: Even without experimental facewear, Elaine has changed dramatically on the show. On most shows, you get one simple concept per character, and if it hits, they milk it forever.

Krakowski: I wasn't sure in the beginning if Elaine would ever become one of them. I never knew if she'd become one of the group. And David has really done that for her. In the beginning, Elaine was sort of this gnat that you wanted to brush away. And then she evolved into a much more fleshed-out person. You've definitely seen her more vulnerable side. You understand more of who she is underneath all of her antics. What's odd is that when we first started, Ally was the normal one. She came into a crazy office full of crazy characters. And Ally has become one of the crazy characters with us. And Elaine has become a very full, understanding, almost wise person in the office. Which worries me. If Elaine is the sage in the office, then we've got trouble!

Q: Elaine is scarcely the only one who's changed—the whole ensemble is constantly evolving.

Krakowski: I think the whole tone of the show has changed. In the first six episodes, each is very, very different in its tone. And you could see that everybody was just trying to find their way with what it is. I thought it was a drama with comedic moments, and I think as we've figured out what the show is or what the audience wants, and just finding the tone, I think the show has turned into a comedy with dramatic moments.

Q: Vonda's musical grace notes to the show were part of it from the start, and then suddenly, you and other actors were up there on stage singing, too. How did that happen?

Krakowski: There is a company that makes a lot of compilation albums with Broadway performers, and I was very lucky to be asked to start doing these albums. David Kelley and the other producers didn't have any idea that many of the people on the show could sing or dance, and the story I've been told is that [executive producer] Jeffrey Kramer was listening to an all-musical radio station on his drive home, and a song I had recorded from one of those compilation albums came on. And he was, "Oh my

gosh, is that the Jane Krakowski who plays Elaine?" And they saw that Lisa Nicole could sing and that Greg Germann could sing. So within a couple of weeks, the Christmas episode was written. That first Christmas episode was such a highlight, because it was like show and tell. Everyone was just screaming and applauding from the crew, and it was just sort of like an unofficial Christmas party, even though we were filming it for national television. We always joke around that you have to be careful of letting them know what extracurricular activities you do because you could end up doing them in the office at some point. Greg and Lucy both happen to take accordion with the same teacher, so maybe that will sneak in one of these days. You never know.

Q: Even when she's not singing, Elaine is easier to like nowadays.

Krakowski: Who she is at her core is a fantastic person. She comes into work no matter what her baggage is and smiles. She loves being at work. And something I love about Elaine is that she doesn't apologize for her flaws.

Q: Why should she, when Fish and Ling are just as snoopy and tackily tact-free?

Krakowski: Yes. Elaine never apologized for being rude or snooping or saying the wrong thing. I just have better equipment for snooping. I always wonder where she keeps all that—she must have a hell of a storage space in the basement.

Q: Has there been a change in the response Elaine gets from fans?

Krakowski: When this show first started, fans would always say, "We have an Elaine in our office." But now people come running up to me and they're like, "I'm the Elaine in the office." With such pride and excitement! Something's going right if they want to be her.

NELLE

porter

Nelle Porter (played by Portia de Rossi) was originally conceived as a kind of a young, '90s version of the Rosalind Shays character David E. Kelley invented on *L.A. Law*—somebody who could cut through the warm world of the law firm like a well-aimed ice pick. Her nickname is "Sub-Zero Nelle," and Fish hires her because, like Cage, she is a famous "rainmaker" celebrated by *Boston Magazine.* A rainmaker is a lawyer who attracts cash downpours, but Ally's first impression is that Nelle looks like she makes sleet, not rain.

And at first, Nelle is on the icy side, sizing people up with a knifelike smile, "kidding" her new colleagues in a needling way. When she catches Ally in the Unisex doing a groin-grinding dance ("Do it and sue! Do it and sue!"), Nelle ridicules her. Ally has a point—that the firm takes way too many eccentric sex–related lawsuits—but Nelle acts as though she doesn't want to understand. She just wants to put Ally down with a cool, superior smile.

But Nelle, even in her colder moments, isn't simply frozen, she just becomes more complicated.

Granted, she toys with Billy and a jealous Georgia a little, shown by her reaction when he walks in on her dressing in the Unisex, by her telling him she likes to "give a cute guy a giggle," and by her teasingly asking Georgia if she can be Billy's date to Ally's party. But be fair: Georgia and Ally's first reaction to Nelle is "We hate her." Yet Nelle can't help it if her voluptuous cascading curls cause men's tongues to clunk the floor.

Nelle is a sex bomb—and a smart bomb, at that—but there's more to her than meets the eye. She has tact, even in an awkward spot. All three of the show's blond graces (Georgia, Whipper, and Nelle) have offered themselves naked to the man of their choice, and none handled the embarrassing consequences more graciously than Nelle. Georgia and Ally learn to like Nelle, because she's so soothing—Nelle buys Cage a new frog even though she loathes frogs, smooths over hard feelings between Ling and Elaine, and protects Ally from the true meaning of what the radio shock jock called her. (Nelle falsely claimed a "spinner" was a "perky" person, when in fact it's a sexual insult.) For the fairest one of all to see the prince lurking within that enchanted frog of a man, Cage, speaks well of Nelle's heart (if not of her eyesight). Or perhaps it was his mind that attracted her. Cage is a fine lawyer, too, and a fine soul. Why shouldn't she give him a chance to locate her "defrost" button?

Nelle's warm side may owe something to Rossi's real-life efforts to bond with the cast: Her colleagues say she's the one who organizes let's-get-acquainted events.

Most of all, Nelle bonds with Ling, the least warm person in the firm. She talks Ling out of suing her friends—and that's no mean feat.

Portia de Rossi

CREDITS

Film and Television Roles

Girl (1999), Carla

The Invisibles (1999), Joy

Stigmata (1999), Jennifer

American Intellectuals (1998)

Perfect Assassins (1998) (TV)

Scream 2 (1997), Sorority Sister Murphy

Nick Freno: Licensed Teacher (1996) (TV series), Miss Elana Lewis

Too Something (1995) (TV series), Maria Hunter

Sirens (1994), Giddy

Born Mandy Rogers in Melbourne, Australia, Portia de Rossi got her first TV commercial before she got her driver's license. At eighteen—partly inspired by Susan Dey speaking David E. Kelley's lines on *L.A. Law*, the only TV show she watched—she started a career in law by enrolling at the University of Melbourne. She supported herself by modeling part-time. But her life turned on a dime when she got cast in 1994 in *Sirens* as Elle Macpherson's bohemian colleague—they're artist Sam Neill's freethinking nude models, who cause Anglican priest Hugh Grant no end of stammering self-consciousness. Elle and not-yet-famous Hugh did well by the film. De Rossi got a new career in Los Angeles, with increasingly visible roles and a chance to be ravishing on camera while fully clothed.

De Rossi really arrived when she signed up with *Ally McBeal*'s company. She was daunted at first, she told TV reporter Dave Walker, when she stood "facing an enormous poster of the show's cast and thinking, 'How on earth am I ever going to get into this picture?'" Rossi got into the picture quite smoothly, in part by being very outgoing, in marked contrast with her originally frosty character, Nelle Porter. She organized get-togethers with the other actors, helping ensure the continuing smoothness of the already tight ensemble. Pretty soon, she was wearing a Cinderellaesque Valentino tulle gown and helping accept the 1999 Golden Globe Award.

LING

WOO

Ling Woo (played by Lucy Liu) is the latest addition to Cage/Fish and Associates, but she is in zero danger of getting overlooked in the crowd. If you thought Ally had impulse-control problems, check out Ling. Ling has no problem, because she sees no reason to control impulses. She says what she thinks and feels no guilt about her prodigious unreasonableness. Innocent of tact, dismissive of the little hypocrisies everyone else on earth uses to grease the wheels of social life, Ling speaks her version of truth to power, to weakness, to innocent passersby in wheelchairs, to glasses of liquid refreshment that displease her (and Ling is a stern judge of liquid refreshments). She sues, or encourages others to sue, whomever she pleases (up to and including God), quite ingeniously though perversely, for whatever whimsical reason occurs to her.

Ling is calmly confident in her awesome sexual power. She could kill a man simply by sleeping with him. She effortlessly accumulates wealth and is the mistress of many fields, including the fine points of the law, clothing design, and the retrieval of imperiled tree frogs from skyscraper ledges. At the steel factory she manages—one of her many enterprises, including her law career and women's mud-wrestling club—she intentionally dresses "trampy" to bend her dumb, horny male workers to her will.

Although she prefers shopping to sex (it's "messy"), Ling thinks sex can be good for women if they know how use it against men. Her wrestlers make almost six figures muddying up their figures, and Ling thinks their self-esteem is boosted: "They can go home and say, 'Even in mud, I look good.'" Here's Ling's philosophy: "We tease, we tantalize, we withhold it...we exploit men. They're pigs. Mankind is based on a kind of pigdom. In my club, the women basically control the dumb stick and take the men's money."

But Ling is not without compassion. Far from it. She feels sorry for beautiful women, like herself and her dear friend Nelle, because only good-looking guys have the courage to date them, and good-looking guys are idiots. Ling cares for her sister Leigh so much she bought her implants, so Leigh could feel "ample" like Georgia. When she cares most deeply, she keeps it to herself, the prime example being her love of the cancer-doomed child who inspires Ling to sue God.

Ling teases Fish because she cares about him, and she probably aspires to be more than his "little wattle of the month" (as Ally calls Ling). She keeps his interest (and dumb stick) up through sexy diversions (finger sucking, hair massage, hot oil drips), which helps Fish get over his feelings for Whipper ("the big-haired blond naked nude buttocks thing," as Ling sensitively puts it). Alas,

when at long last Ling literally yells "Action!" straddling Fish, she so intimidates him that he "turtles" and is unable to perform.

Not to worry. Viagra brought him out of his shell, and even Ling was impressed.

We know that despite the Wicked Witch of the West theme that accompanies her entrances and for all her guttural growls, somewhere *waaay* down deep, Ling really deserves to be pronounced with a soft "L."

The Big Bang Theory (1995), Hooker

ER (1995) (TV series), Mei-Sun Leow in "And Baby Makes Two," "What Life?" and "Do One, Teach One, Kill One"

Hercules: The Legendary Journeys (1995) (TV series), Oi-Lan in "The March to Freedom"

Coach (1994) (TV series), Nicole in "Out of Control"

L.A. Law (1993) (TV series), in "Foreign Co-respondent"

Beverly Hills, 90210 (1991) (TV series), Courtney, waitress at the Peach Pit in "Pass, Not Pass"

Home Improvement (1995), Woman No. 3 in "Bachelor of the Year"

Lucy Liu

CREDITS

Film and Television Roles

Shanghai Noon (2000)

Molly (1999)

Payback (1999), Pearl

True Crime (1999)

City of Industry (1997), Cathi Rose

Gridlock'd (1997), Cee-Cee

Flypaper (1997), Dot

Jonny Quest: The New Adventures (1997) (TV series), Melana in "The Bangalore Falcon"

NYPD Blue (1997) (TV series), Amy Chu, babysitter in "A Wrenching Experience"

Riot (1997) (TV), Boomer's Girlfriend

Guy (1996), Woman at newsstand

Jerry Maguire (1996), Former Girlfriend

Pearl (1996) (TV series), Amy

The X Files (1996) (TV series), Kim Hsin in "Hell Money"

Lucy Alexis Liu (rhymes with "woo") grew up in Queens, New York, went to Stuyvesant High, got a degree in Asian languages from the University of Michigan, and learned to dance, sing, act, and perform serious martial arts. In person she's approachable and chipper and down-to-earth. The biggest breaks in her career prior to 1998 were her guest roles on the titanic TV shows *ER*, *The X-Files*, and *NYPD Blue*. Playing the dominatrix Pearl opposite Mel Gibson in the movie *Payback* was a splashy success, too. She was only the runner-up for the role of Subzero Nelle on *Ally McBeal*, but after pondering it a bit, David E. Kelley called her back for a whole new role, Nelle's rich, litigious, comparably frosty client Ling. She clicked so well that she became a cast member and Ling a member of Cage/Fish and Associates.

Q: Why did Ling hit big with fans so fast?

Liu: Because she's challenging, and she adds conflict to the rest of the cast, which always makes it interesting. You know, to mix it up.

Q: Several women viewers have said they wished they could tap their inner Ling.

Liu: What it is, is that she's very forward and blunt and up front about her feelings, and she doesn't apologize for anything that she does or says. And I think that's very unusual, especially for women, who always feel like in some ways they have to . . . you know, be a certain way, do a certain thing. I think her character basically . . . demolishes all of those ideals and social foundations that have been around since the beginning of time.

Q: What's the secret of Ling's success with Fish?

Liu: The chemistry between them is extremely dynamic in the sense that it is *atomic*! [Laughs.] It establishes sort of a nuclear reaction between the two of them. They push and pull each other, and they're both very strong personalities. And they have a lot of the same ideas about life and money and—they might have different ideas about sex, but they definitely have strong career choices that I think definitely motivate them.

Q: Neither of them has ever met anybody as outrageous before.

Liu: Yeah, but oddly, they think of each other as quite normal, and everyone else as bizarre.

Q: On the set, I noticed an apparent rapport between you and Greg Germann.

Liu: He is a naturally funny person. I feel lucky to be working with him, because he brings really interesting creative ideas to the scene that will create such a charged moment, one that I never would've thought of.

Q: Such as?

Liu: We were doing this scene with this Rubik's cube, and I was playing with it, and he came up with the idea—wouldn't it be funny if by the end of the scene, Ling had completely finished the Rubik's cube and it was perfect.

Q: It makes perfect sense that Ling would solve the cube. Ling is perfect at everything. What's the difference between you and Ling?

Liu: Everything. And that's what's so refreshing about playing her. She's somebody I've hopefully humanized and made her somebody really tangible to people, but she should be fun. Not that I'm not fun.

Q: What appealed to you about the show?

Liu: My first impression was that it's really fresh and very politically incorrect, which I loved, and just broke a lot of the usual stereotypes. You know, not racially, so much, but the way it treated people as people on the show.

Q: Kelley's writing is sort of "race blind." It doesn't matter on the show, because it doesn't matter to him.

Liu: No, it doesn't. He doesn't mention it, because it's not an issue. It's not about—the relationship between Fish and Ling is about their sexual relationship, as opposed to their racial relationship. And the same goes for everything, like Jesse Martin's role with Calista is the same thing: It's not about anything but the relationship or that it is or isn't working out, but it's not because of race. I think that's wonderful and very true, and it's a very honest approach of looking at relationships. I hope that people out there also see that and realize to themselves that a relationship is simply that, if they see an interracial couple.

Q: Ling is blunt, as you say, but she's not completely up front. She hides her gentle side sometimes, as when she hires a blimp to lift a dying kid's spirits. She's like the Masked Man who will never let people say thank you.

Liu: She doesn't need anyone to know about it. I think the thing about Ling is she has a lot of emotions that go very deep and she doesn't really like to share them. I think that's the thing that hits people most: She's this and she's that, but when it comes to feelings, she doesn't feel like she can share them. That's what makes it so heartbreaking to see her when she's upset. It's her defense mechanism.

judge "WHIPPER" cone

Judge "Whipper" Cone (played by Dyan Cannon) is the only gavel-whacker who also plays a big part in the imprudent romantic jurisprudence that so preoccupies Ally and her colleagues. At first, Whipper ruled against the wooing of the decades-younger Richard Fish, but then she gave in, delighted to have a lover guaranteed not to stick around. Two miserable divorces soured her on love. Traumatized by his parents' querulous marriage, Fish was thrilled to have someone old enough to make marriage out of the question.

But Whipper finds that she wants to get wed after all. Fish tries to reassure her by serenading her with "I Love You More Today Than Yesterday." He's sincere, but he won't promise to love her tomorrow.

Whipper sneaks a kiss with Fish's client Cheanie, mostly for reassurance that she's still alluring. She catches Fish fondling Attorney General Janet Reno's wattle and knees him in the dumb stick. Whipper confronts Reno about "this administration's 'reach out and touch'" policy and dumps Fish.

But she still yearns for him, and he for her—until he's smitten by Ling. Ally, loathing Ling and liking Whipper, tells the judge to make one last bold move to win him back. Whipper still has Fish's apartment key, so she waits naked for him amid candles in his bedroom—and in walks Ling on the first night Fish takes her home with him. Dueling screams ensue.

Whipper endures, and she does good work, usually ruling in favor of long-term love. She rules against three-way marriage. On the question of a man's right to see unicorns, the embodiment of unreasonable romantic hope, Whipper's gavel gives hope a chance. (Ling thereafter refers to her as "that big-haired blond thing who believes in unicorns. She'll buy anything!")

Whipper won't buy a bad argument, however. She's been around, and she proves you can have a heart and a blond mane without impairing the brain beneath. Whipper stands for Ally's values, and she signifies beauty without youth, power without pants, and a woman without a man, for the moment. At any moment, that may change.

dr. TRACY clark

Dr. Tracy Clark (played by Tracey Ullman) first enters Ally's orbit as the "smile therapist" Cage urges her to see. Ally can't stop throwing shoes at people, so Cage convinces her Tracy is the key to a saner way of life. Dr. Tracy combines tact-free, cut-to-the-chase, horse-sense advice with a style that could get her committed herself. When Ally says something Tracy finds absurdly naïve, Tracy plays an extremely loud laugh-track tape, because her own guffaw just won't suffice. Tracy's not the "there, there," hand-holding type, but she is chipper. "Narcissism is a wonderful thing!" she tells Ally. "Nuts like you heat my pool!"

Besides, Tracy is sometimes on the money. When Ally frets that her lustful thoughts about an eighteen-year-old are abnormal, Tracy points out that if it were unnatural, there wouldn't have to be laws against it. "Did he have really amazing glutes?" Tracy asks. "Because that can do it."

Therapists are always more interested in talking about their patients' problems than their own. You'd expect Dr. Tracy to keep her private life out of her therapy sessions, but when asked about her own private heartache, she gave a long, poignant answer about long-lost love. It turned out to be a monologue from the Bette Davis three-hankie movie *Now, Voyager.* Dr. Tracy wasn't just being whimsical, though she's as chronically, unapologetically unconventional as Fish, as flamboyant in flouting the official rules of the profession. Her flamboyance had a point: to make fun of people who let their own emotions push them around. Tracy wants patients to face facts, and no fact has ever fazed Tracy.

Tracy may seem crazier than her patients, but her maddest strategy may be her best: the personal "theme song" to give one mental strength to do what must be done. Rejecting Ally's suggestion (the show's theme song, which Tracy thinks is "terrible"), Tracy tells Ally to try again. Ally proposes to go with "Tell Him," by the Exciters. Later, "Wedding Bell Blues" and a hallucinatory set of Gladys Knight's Pips help Ally along.

What's the secret of Tracy's success? She gives firm answers to silence Ally's doubt and confusion. And when a hallucination gets out of hand—the dancing baby starts getting aggressive—Dr. Tracy knows just what to do: "Kick his ass!" In a show largely devoted to matters of head and heart, Dr. Tracy Clark is a kick in the pants.

Vonda Shepard

ALBUMS

By 7:30 (1999)

"By 7:30"

"Mercy"

"Clear"

"Sail on By"

"Confetti"

"Cross to Bear"

"This Is Crazy Now"

"Baby, Don't You Break My Heart Slow"
(with Emily Saliers)

"You and Me"

"Venus Is Breaking"

"Newspaper Wife"

"Soothe Me"

"Souvenir"

Songs from Ally McBeal Featuring Vonda Shepard (1998)

"Searchin' My Soul"

"Ask the Lonely"

"Walk Away, Renee"

"Hooked on a Feeling"

"You Belong to Me"

"The Wildest Times of the World"

"Someone You Use"

"The End of the World"

"Tell Him"

"Neighborhood"

"Will You Marry Me?"

"It's in His Kiss (The Shoop Shoop Song)"

"I Only Want to Be with You"

"Maryland"

It's Good, Eve (1996)

"Maryland"

"A Lucky Life"

"Grain of Sand"

"The Wildest Times of the World"

"Like a Hemisphere"

"Naivete"

"Long-Term Boyfriend"

"Every Now and Then"

"Mischief and Control"

"Hotel Room View"

"This Steady Train"

"Serious Richard"

The Radical Light (1992)

"Searchin' My Soul"

"The Radical Light"

"100 Tears Away"

"Wake Up the House"

"Clean Rain"

"Dreamin' "

"Good to Yourself"

"Love Will Come and Go"

"Out on the Town"

"Cartwheels"

Vonda Shepard (1989)

"Don't Cry, Ilene"

"He Ain't with Me"

"Baby, Don't You Break My Heart Slow"

"Hold Out"

"Looking for Something"

"I Shy Away"

"I've Been Here Before"

"A New Marilyn"

"Say the Words"

"La Journée"

"Jam Karet (Time Is Elastic)"

When Vonda Shepard wrote her song "Naivete," which says, "I was born in a cardboard box, New York City, 1963," it wasn't far from the truth. Her bohemian folks were poor enough that they really did carry her around in a cardboard box. How did she get to the Bar in the Cage/Fish & Associates building? Practice, practice, practice—hours a day on the piano, according to her dad, Richmond, an acting teacher who moved the family to southern California when Vonda was a tot. She began her career as a singer-songwriter in her teens, got a job in Rickie Lee Jones's band at twenty, and recorded her first solo album in 1987. Vonda's original problem was, she was a post-twenty-year-old singer-songwriter in the school of Jackson Browne at the dawn of grunge. She had talent, she had promise, she looked like the down-to-earth offspring of a fashion model (which she is). She had champions with silver tongues: *Entertainment Weekly's* Chris Willman wrote this of the little-known Shepard: "[P]iano-based, baby-faced, supple-voiced singer-songwriters rarely get any better than this . . . the surprise is in the gorgeous harmonic sophistication of her original ballads."

Alas, with the change in musical tastes, her timing was all wrong—no guitars in shards, no needles on her tracks, no big sales for her first two CDs. Shepard borrowed money to make a third CD, *It's Good, Eve,* and hauled a keyboard not much smaller than herself to perform for crowds in rooms the size of her living room. Then David E. Kelley and his wife, Michelle Pfeiffer, discovered that one thing they both loved was an unknown singer named Vonda Shepard. Kelley hired her to give Ally an inspired theme song, "Searchin' My Soul"—and it helped that rock-folky Shepard, unlike lots of folks in Hollywood, still has a soul to locate. Shepard's down-but-not-downhearted tunes give Ally's thoughts a lyric voice. Now Shepard's got a gold record and an audience of more than 18 million. Her own introspective ballads alternate with her rousing revivals of classic tones that reflect Ally's mercurial moods. After a decade in undeserved obscurity, Shepard's tune "Baby, Don't You Break My Heart Slow" is a hit, rerecorded with Indigo Girl Emily Saliers.

Q: You appear as a character on *Ally McBeal*, the singer Vonda in the Bar. But you have a larger role—one of your songs helped inspire the whole show.

Shepard: David Kelley talks about me as being the voice of Ally—she'll be saying something, and my lyric will take over that matches her thought. I'm sort of her subconscious, in a way.

Q: Can you cite a classic moment of a meeting of the minds between you and Ally?

Shepard: I think my favorite early one was when she was walking down the street in the pilot and "The Wildest Times of the World" came on—it goes, "Ain't it funny how you're walking through life and it turns on a dime"—and you can feel how she feels.

Q: Does Kelley write a show with a lyric of yours in mind ahead of time?

Shepard: That sometimes does happen. In the show "One Hundred Tears Away," there's a minute and a half of that song played at the end of the show when she's walking down the street, and one of the coproducers told me that he was locked in his room for several hours blasting that song. So I was pretty flattered to hear that. It doesn't mean the episode is going to be about my song in it, but some emotion is triggered in his work.

Q: Long ago, in his first minute of abrupt fame, James Taylor wrote a song, "Hey Mister, That's Me up on the Jukebox," about how weird it was to hear his innermost feelings broadcast to the mass market. How do you feel about having your heart exposed via one of the most famous characters on TV?

Shepard: It makes me feel that I have a purpose and that my feelings are justified, because there's someone else out there who has them, too. Even if it's only a fictitious character!

an
INTERVIEW
with
Steve Robin

Steve Robin is the <u>Ally McBeal</u> producer who is responsible for clearing rights to the many songs heard on the show, among other duties.

Q: Have you ever had to switch one song for another at the last minute?

Robin: Absolutely. There have been numerous occasions where David has scripted a song and the clearance has been denied the day before we were either going to re-record it or shoot it. When schedules get tight toward the end of the season, clearance is a major concern.

Q: Can you name one song that got switched in a particular scene?

Robin: There was a scene in an episode last season where we wanted to use a Sarah McLachlan song called "I Will Remember You."

Q: It's on the album *Mirrorball*.

Robin: It was also on a CD sampler that Fox gave us as a reference for film and TV use. We were therefore under the impression that they owned the publishing and master and that the song was clearable. Vonda cut a version of the song and it was edited into the show. It wasn't until the last day of mixing, the day before network delivery, that we found out Sarah McLachlan owns her own masters and won't

allow re-recorded uses of her songs. She cleared her original recording, but that was it.

Q: Why couldn't you just use that recording?

Robin: Vonda's voice works as the show's musical voice. Sarah McLachlan's recording is amazing, but on *Ally McBeal*, we usually stick with Vonda's recordings. So we began scrambling for a song that worked with the scene. I remembered a song on Vonda's first album called "Looking for Something" that worked lyrically for the scene with Lisa Nicole Carson's character, Renee. She was pining over a former boyfriend, just sitting in a chair in her living room looking at pictures. The lyric is "I've been looking for something all of my life." That whole song worked well with the issues Renee was dealing with at that point. We cut it into the show, showed it to David. He approved it and we went with it.

Q: I keep seeing the phrase *needle-drop*. What is that?

Robin: On the occasions David doesn't ask Vonda to re-record a song, we use the original recording. David uses the term *needle-drop* so we all know he wants the original master used.

Q: Why does Kelley re-record old songs?

Robin: Primarily because Vonda is the musical voice of the show. But I also think that he

doesn't want to attach the viewers' previous feelings about a song to his story. People sometimes associate a song with a certain time and place and I think Vonda's voice helps to keep the viewer in the story and in Ally's world.

Q: But using old songs is a great idea. Kurt Vonnegut once wrote about a character who builds a life from the lyrics of popular songs— and we all do it.

Robin: Yeah. David seems to be really lyrically driven. And he's aware that music has a profound effect on people. He scripts 99.9% of the music in the shows. Of the 175 or so songs we've done, there have been maybe five that someone else has suggested.

Q: Was there a debate about the show's theme?

Robin: No, not really. I had been a fan of Vonda's music for several years and remembered liking "Searching My Soul" off one of her earlier albums. I brought the song into the cutting room during the pilot and played it for David, Jeffery, and Jonathan. They all liked it, but David felt it was a little too slow for a main title. About a week later, Vonda and her manager invited us to a live rehearsal where Vonda was working with her band. We asked her to play a faster version of "Searching My Soul";

she did, David liked it and said go with it. A week later we were at Conway Studios with Vonda and her band cutting a new one-minute, rocked-up version of the song that became our main title theme.

Q: Dr. Tracy feels the same way about personal theme songs. Faster, faster!

Robin: Exactly.

Q: What about theme songs for characters?

Robin: Well, "Tell Him" was originally Ally's. That was the very first song we ever recorded with Vonda for the series, back in the pilot. Cage's has just been Barry White, all down the line. I think there was a Marvin Gaye song maybe the first season, but Barry White has certainly taken over. I mean, "You're the First, the Last, My Everything" is Cage's theme song. And Ling got her "Wicked Witch of the West" theme that she's always arriving to.

Q: Somebody told me that back in *L.A. Law* days Kelley had a whole disquisition about how that was the greatest movie ever made, *The Wizard of Oz.*

Robin: It seems to be one of his favorites. References to it show up in most of his series.

If you look at *L.A. Law* or *Picket Fences* or *Ally*, he's always reached into *The Wizard of Oz* somehow. The *Picket Fences* pilot circled around that movie.

Q: How does the song-recording schedule go each week? It's not the only thing you do.

Robin: Just one of my chores. It only occupies about two days of the first week of prep. We get a script, I look at the songs, and I have a conversation with David about the tone, as to how he wants the songs to be recorded, I then go into the studio with Vonda, usually for two days. Sometimes one day. If it's three songs we can do it in one, if it's more than three songs, we do them in two days.

Q: Vonda's voice is amazingly prominent. Why does Kelley use her so much?

Robin: She's got a real soulful voice and David really likes the connection that she gives—the lyrics and the music—to his stories.

Q: The needle-drop old recordings work in one way, triggering memories, but Vonda makes it more spontaneous and live.

Robin: Absolutely. Vonda works with a four-piece band, so our songs are usually a little more sparse than the original recordings,

which I think allows them to work more subtly with the dialogue and story.

Q: What's your favorite song on the show?

Robin: This season Vonda re-recorded some Roy Orbison music that sounded amazing. I thought her version of "Crying" was fabulous, it really shows off her range. The most fun songs for me were "Secret Agent Man" and a silly one called "Gimme Dat Ding" that Peter MacNicol's character John Cage was dancing to.

Q: Now, there's one more member of the Ally music team we haven't mentioned.

Robin: People get the impression that Vonda is the only one who does music for the show, but Danny Lux does a huge amount of music for us. We had a sequence where Cage and Fish were in a rap club and kind of dancing to this rap scene, and he wrote that song. And he's a composer—he does all the underscore for the show. And actually, he just won an award from BMI for doing that.

ON THE SET
of *ally mcbeal*

*As cranes busily erect multiple build-
ings to house David E. Kelley's burgeon-
ing TV empire on dozens of acres in
Manhattan Beach, California, the cast
and crew work on an equally ambitious construction project: an episode
of* <u>Ally McBeal</u>.

This one is called "Sex, Lies, and Politics," which could serve as a subtitle for the entire series. This particular story centers on a senator who courts conservative votes by scapegoating a bookstore for selling smutty books, but like any episode of the show, it's about sex in general, the wriggly nature of truth in court (and in courtship), the politics of society at large, and the microcosm of the office family.

"It's a show of ideas," producer Jonathan Pontell murmurs softly, almost whispering, because a scene is being shot nearby. There's reason to keep your voice down: Peter MacNicol is off in a corner rehearsing a long speech. "What David does so beautifully is just taking an idea and exploring it from so many different facets," Pontell says. "In Act I you're on one side of the argument; in Act II

you're on another side; in Act III you go back to the other; and in Act IV you're sitting there wondering what the jury's gonna come back with."

"An *Ally* case reminds me of what Henry James said," I tell Pontell. "'In political discussions I'm always of the opinion of the last speaker.'"

"That definitely applies," says Pontell.

"A lot of writers use their scripts as a way of editorializing and getting their own opinion out," says special effects man Mike Most. "But I think David really doesn't care which side you come down on, he just wants to make you think. He's not out there to say, 'I feel this way and you should agree with me because I'm right.' He puts both sides out there, and you decide. That's the brilliance of it. There never is a black or white answer in a David Kelley script. The obvious conclusions are never the right ones." Sometimes the point is simply the irony of the law: Fish has to advise one client that he can't go for an insanity defense, the reason being that his murder attempt failed; he actually would've been better off if he'd managed to kill the guy.

Whether he's commenting on matters legal, social, or emotional, Kelley always does it through the medium of characters whose motives, however peculiar, always proceed with logical integrity. "I think of his characters as being sort of on a palette," says Pontell, "and he's a painter, and depending on what he wants to say, he can say it through these different characters."

Kelley also has a palette of physical spaces—the sets the characters inhabit. The Unisex bathroom and the Bar look far tinier than they do on the show, whereas the attorneys' offices look much bigger. Snooping around looking for clues to characters, we find on Cage's desk a Japanese sand rock garden, a Zen fountain, a windup Graf Zeppelin on wheels, a Silenta 4000 air purifier, a cappuccino machine, and little sculptures resembling atoms. Fish has a little futuristic Bang & Olufsen phone and the Investor's Business Daily opened to the section, "Stocks in the News." The backdrops of Boston glimpsed through the windows look remarkably realistic. You can see the people at

their desks through the windows of skyscrapers across the street—even though there is no street, only 18-by-70-foot photo murals hanging from the ceiling a few feet away. The "buildings" flutter slightly when crewmen walk by.

Ally and Renee's apartment is enormous: a loft with a giant fireplace flanked by spiral staircases leading to bookshelves. They could sublet their kitchen and still have plenty of room to ramble. Notes on the fridge bespeak the single life: A picture of a cow saying, "Holy cow, are you hungry again?" A scribbled note: "Gripe of the day—no life! Long workdays, bad food, no snowballs yet, no coffee!!! Getting up early, court sucks, men who grope and bite me."

Books they're dipping into speak to the inner life they cultivate when not watching *Hush, Hush, Sweet Charlotte* or gorging on chocolate ice cream; *Birds of America*, by Mary McCarthy; *A Marriage Made in Heaven*; Michael Crichton; Plato; Sigmund Freud's *Civilization and Its Discontents;* Stephen King; and half a dozen volumes of Nietzsche next to *The Bridges of Madison County*.

On the wall, there's a big print reading, "In the Room the Women Come and Go, Talking of Michelangelo."

Time to tiptoe out and into the office of production designer Peter Politanoff. "When you see Ally's apartment in person, it's very large, but the way we tend to shoot it with longer lenses, everything actually looks much smaller," says Politanoff. "A wide-angle lens will separate everything, a long lens will tend to pull everything more together. We never shoot those wide shots that show the entire apartment. It's just the style of the show. I guess it's that intimacy."

Politanoff is proud of Ally and Renee's new digs. "The original one was your really typical Beacon Hill apartment, small, boxy, rigid, very traditional. I'd always lobbied for something a little bit more over the top. My concept in designing is that it's aspirational (something an ambitious young legal professional might aspire to) but not unattainable." Politanoff used to design *Miami Vice*, where couches cost $10,000 and unattainability was the point. "*Miami Vice* was about the look of the show and the music. There was no story line." His designs for Ally quietly accommodate the complex stories and support the characterizations. "If Calista were living in something decorated with Louis XV antiques, you're going to have a tough time relating to that environment, so consequently you're going to have a tough time relating to the character." The apartment is done in terra-cotta, ochre, and blueberry hues; the office in kiwi mango and a French blue accentuated by lavender; the courtroom in tony shades. "I like to work with values darker than skin tones, so it makes the flesh tones much richer."

After Ling told Fish she couldn't stand the "newness" of his town house, Politanoff gave it a "mild deconstructivist attitude: galvanized metal, stained wood, brushed steel." In Fish's apartment hang several Politanoff pieces. Peter's work can be found in several galleries in Los Angeles.

The bright, grinning Rorschach blots on Dr. Tracy's wall may also wind up for sale in the real world. "You probably missed Dr. Tracy's smile therapy ink blots," says Politanoff. "After about four

hours of doing ink blots, I'm sort of getting sort of silly with them. And then I'm thinking, wait a minute—smile therapy! And so I do the Happy Face to moderate Cage's reactions to trying situations. You have to know about Cage's smile therapy to get that." In fact, newcomers to the show may be puzzled when Cage (or, occasionally, Ally) reacts to upsetting remarks with a broad smile. It takes an educated fan to recognize the "smile therapy" grin as a Dr. Tracy–taught technique. Such in-joke details serve to bond viewers with the characters. "It's sort of training and selecting an audience. This is a nonlinear show. It jumps all over the place, and it rewards extreme attention."

Dr. Tracy's happy-face inkblots fit into the overall color scheme of the show. "I did these in different colors, so they're basically like an Andy Warhol sort of thing," says Politanoff. "A lot of the themes in the sets are retro themes. Their apartment, some of the furniture and accessories are thrift shop '60s items. And in general last year when we did fantasy sequences, I would always try to go for sort of op art images."

There's a dog outside the Ally set, but her artful furniture is in no danger: The pooch is on a leash held by a crew member, who says, "We're taking a moment." The dog has a job in this episode: Ally, feeling guilty about kissing Billy, has hallucinations that people on the street (including the pope) are calling her names, and then a dog piddles on her leg—which proves not to be a hallucination. "I think that's Calista's real dog," says somebody on the lot. Jane Krakowski, who plays Elaine, isn't sure which dog has the piddling cameo role. "We're a very dog-oriented place. Everybody brings their dogs to work, and Webster, who is Calista's dog, has sort of become the mascot of *Ally McBeal.* I think that David wrote it in that it was going to be Webster, but apparently Webster couldn't lift his leg on cue. So that's the story I heard—that they had to get a stunt dog. Calista's dog needs more training."

Getting dogs to hit their marks is the least of the challenges of today's episode. In the setup scene, John Cage tells his colleagues that the bookstore-versus-the-moralizing-senator case will be settled out of court; suddenly, the senator's lawyer decides to take it to court after all, leaving Cage one day to prepare. The panicked Cage resorts to several courtroom ploys, among them a blowtorch that releases a giant fireball, followed by a full-scale musical routine.

The blowtorch involves a collaboration between Mike Most, the visual effects specialist, and John Cazin, the physical effects coordinator who worked as a key pyrotechnician in detonating the innovatively multicolored flaming spaceships in *Contact* and *Starship Troopers*. "You'll see this huge flame come out of a really small blowtorch," says Cazin. "I'll do a 10- to 15-foot fireball in front of a black screen, we'll film it, Mike will scan that, and we'll stick it in. I get to play with my pyrotechnics and Mike gets to play with his computers. It's like a lyricist and a composer working together."

And working fast. Given the tight schedule, these guys are playing with fire. "Exactly!" says Cazin. "I get paid to play! We just got the script for this episode. With television, in the best-case scenario we have eight days or nine days of prep for an episode coming up." Adds Mike Most cheerily, "In features they have fourteen months and $10 million to do it."

But films are increasingly driven by elaborate effects, while on *Ally McBeal*, effects are quick hits that exist strictly to enhance character and serve the story. No matter how cool an effect is, if it doesn't play, it doesn't stay. For instance, at one point, Dr. Greg Butters and Ally caught each other's eyes, and a couple of effects scenes were concocted. "There was supposed to be a moment

where their lips grow and kind of get closer," recalls Most, "and then we changed that to another shot where their tongues come out and touch each other. And it just got dropped altogether. Mostly because it worked just as well, if not better, to just have them look at each other and Calista take a little smiling moment to think about it, and then just come up with the line that follows: 'My New Year's resolution is less fantasy, more reality.' And we didn't actually have to play the fantasy for the line to work. It actually worked better without it." Idiosyncratic as it is, Ally is reality programming.

"Logistically, it's real big," says producer Mike Listo. "The scene that we're finishing now, the 'Music Man' scene, the tone is a real big challenge. I mean, it's obviously a fantasy show, but you try and do some of these crazy things and not make them look ridiculous. It's sort of like classic musicals—people don't ordinarily burst into song and dance, right? But sometimes they do."

What's about to happen, Listo explains, is that John Cage will lead the jury in a number from Meredith Willson's famous musical. "He finds out that while they were sequestered, they watched *The Music Man*. So he parallels the sermon

that he's trying to pull off with the song that Robert Preston sings—'Trouble in River City.' It's kind of a commentary about censorship and bluenosed attitudes and a guy making it look like he's helping the community when he's just going for political gain."

Just as Kelley asked the effects department to come up with a working prototype of a remote-controlled briefcase in three and a half days—they obliged—his scripts require constant scrambling by all concerned, and about five shows are usually in various stages of production at any one time. "We do a lot of scenes in a small amount of pages," says Listo. "That's a rehearsal and a lighting setup every time there's a scene, and very often it takes the same amount of time to light three-eighths of a page as it does to light six pages. It's very dense for TV. David really is amazing with pace."

The velocity of the production is intense, which matches the energy level of Kelley, who is among the most prolific scribblers of scenes, weavers of ingenious story lines, and jugglers of acting ensembles in the history of the tube.

Kelley has said his writing actually improves as each season goes on, writing and rehearsal time gets tighter, and the pressure increases. "It kind of ignites it," Bellows says. "You get to a kind of a rhythm. It all assembles itself; as it gets faster, it gets smoother in some ways." On the set, the second everyone gets their pages, they're off on a mad dash to devise ways to meet the challenges Kelley has dreamed up for them.

On the courtroom set, everyone's on the alert. Peter MacNicol, who plays Ally's senior partner John Cage, got his script unusually close to the day it was to be shot, and the "Trouble" routine presents a challenge that his character might find "troubling."

MacNicol, a seasoned stage and screen star and director of several *Ally* episodes, is just the man to reprise Preston's virtuoso solo, but it's a bit more difficult in this context. Cage's spiel has to mesh with his cross-examination of a bluenose senator who's out to close down a bookstore and with his sly appeal to the jury to compare the senator to the pool hall–hating philistines of Willson's play. Cage is famous for being able to conduct a jury to sing his legal tune.

Only this time, Cage also has to blend his supremely assured rat-a-tat chat with a group of musicians who leap up to accompany him in court. The full musical score will be added later, and MacNicol has to coordinate his speech and movement with a "click track" played into his eardrum via what's called an "earwig," a little plastic gizmo that's inconspicuous on camera.

"Well, you've got trouble my friends, right here, I say trouble, right here in River City!" says MacNicol, with impeccable rhythm. "Well, sure I'm a billiard player, certainly mighty proud to say it, I'm always mighty proud to say it. This bookstore was your pool table, wasn't it, Senator? Your opportunity to convince the folks in River City they had big trouble."

Spotty audio cues on the electronically glitchy "earwig" throw off MacNicol's verbal groove. Also, the monologue is written for a flexible beat set by the actor—and part of the humor is the extreme variation in syllable counts from line to line. That's tough to accommodate to the inflexible metronome of orchestration to be added later.

"Did you ever take and try to find yourself an ironclad lead from a three-rail billiard shot?" MacNicol asks the jury. "@*%#!" We couldn't hear where the line diverged from the click track, but MacNicol could. This outburst is only mildly angry, but it's out of character for Cage.

MacNicol takes a moment, re-fuses with his character, and addresses the actors in the jury box in a conciliatory Cage-esque manner. "I profaned. I apologize. It was unacceptable." A few more takes and he nails it. On the show, Cage will appear as he always does: infallible, uncanny, apt to lapse into song and dance or detonate a fireball as if it were the most natural thing in the world.

MacNicol makes it all look so easy—he makes weirdness seem normal. But getting there isn't easy, for him or the large cast whose concatenating contretemps and abundant acrobatics have made the show an Emmy-winning comedy, one of the stranger and more ambitious ones in history.

The "Trouble" scene is done, fated to lose one of its elements in editing—a brass band that popped up to accompany Cage in the courtroom. Now the whole cast of attorneys gathers around the conference table for the setup scene. In marked contrast with the elaborate musical sequence, this scene appears to be little more than a bunch of actors sitting around waiting. Many of the most striking elements will be added later. Courtney Thorne-Smith's head is, at present, of normal size. Everyone knows that after the effects guys are done, her head will expand hugely and then contract to the sound of a deafening heartbeat, which represents Ally's guilt over having kissed Billy. Ally's intolerably noisy conscience is about to force her to jump up from the table and race out of the room.

On the set, the actors perform in tight-ensemble style, alert to the camera and each other's every glance. "It's like osmosis," explains Greg Germann, who plays Fish. "We're all learning from each other and finding our rhythm and style. It's a tricky show, because David's walking a line: If we go too far in one direction, it becomes a little bit broad, and if we go too far in the other, it becomes a soap opera. So we want it to be funny and kind of heightened, but we also don't want to lose the audience as far as being something that people identify with. There is a real style to the show: It's real nutty and real fast and facile, and all of us are coalescing."

When Calista Flockhart jumps up and runs, she takes about three steps and halts just out of camera range, squandering not one erg of energy. She knows those three steps conveyed the racing panic the scene calls for, and her face is calm. Off camera is no place to indulge in heavy-duty method-actor emotions. Flockhart saves it all for the screen, and she's got Ally's moves down to a fine art.

"I'm beginning to think she's a little more weird than the strange little man," Lucy Liu's Ling coldly announces. MacNicols's Cage flashes a broad smile denoting irritation and wounded pride. Later, Ally snappishly tells Billy that they've simply got to tell Georgia. "Tell her what?" says Billy. "Her head is about to explode and the pope is stalking me!" Ally shouts.

Tension mounts on camera, but between takes, everyone snaps out of tense-focus mode and into hang-loose mode. A smiling Liu plops herself down in Greg Germann's lap, and they make wisecracks with an easy informality that Fish and Ling may never attain. MacNicol is the picture of joshing serenity.

"It's like a family," says Thorne-Smith. "I think that what people respond to in the cast is that we genuinely like each other so well that if, you know, I'm working on a case with Nelle, I can be mad at her in that point and it doesn't feel like everything is going to fall apart. You know the characters are able to be incredibly honest with each other and say to each other what the audience is probably thinking about the characters, and still be OK."

Does the ensemble owe its family feel and its close-order-drill efficiency to the grueling work schedule? "Oh, absolutely," says Thorne-Smith. "How often is it that you're sitting around a table with people for fourteen hours? And of that we're actually filming for only two hours. So that's ten hours of sitting there, and every time you're sitting next to somebody else. So it's like some weird EST group where you're getting to know each other in strange circumstances."

So many scripts, so little time—yet so few frayed nerves in evidence. What's the secret of happiness for the Ally cast? Ping-Pong diplomacy between

takes plays its part, testifies Gil Bellows. "Not everybody plays, but let's see, I do, and some of the crew, and Greg plays. Ping-Pong is just a good focus thing. Somebody hits the ball at you as hard as possible, and you just try to get it back on the table. And fifteen minutes later, you put your coat on and you go inside and you sort of do the same thing with David's scripts. It's fun."

The Ping-Pong may be ruthless, but once the camera is on, the competition is apparently more collegial than cutthroat. "I've had many jobs where you kind of protect what you're going to do so carefully, because you can't trust the other actors to respond to what you're doing," says Thorne-Smith. "It's typical of the stress of TV. But David has a lot of faith in his cast, and we have a lot of trust in each other. So when somebody does something, you can react safely."

On the *Ally McBeal* set, expect no mercy at the Ping-Pong table. And when the work starts, expect the best.

the case of the missing
ATTORNEY GENERAL

U.S. Attorney General Janet Reno played a crucial part in the breakup of Fish and Whipper, but when Sharon Jetton in the casting department sought an actress to play her, the look-alikes simply didn't look like Janet Reno. "We didn't even have anyone really close," says Jetton.

"It was Jeffrey Kramer who said, "Let's get Linda! She's tall," says Linda Gehringer. Gehringer had worked for Kelley's crew on _L.A. Law_; she was the woman who dies in the dishwasher in the pilot of _Picket Fences_; and she worked on _The Practice_. Gehringer also played the bookstore owner in the Ally episode "Sex, Lies, and Politics." But her Janet Reno makeup job was so transforming it fooled her closest colleagues. "I was rehearsing a play this summer," says Gehringer, "and my cast came in and they were all talking about the Janet Reno episode of _Ally_ the night before, and I said, 'That was me!' They died!"

Gehringer's Reno impression even fooled some of Reno's colleagues in the nation's capital. "I made 8-by-10s of a head shot the makeup artist took, I gave one to David Kelley and one to my husband. My brother-in-law is a national judge, and he wanted a copy of it because he married us, so I wrote on it, 'I never would have gotten married if it wasn't for you.' So now in his office in Washington, he's got it on his desk. And people come in and go, 'I didn't know she got married!'"

season ONE

TITLE	EPISODE #	FIRST AIRED
PILOT	101	09/08/97
COMPROMISING POSITIONS	102	09/15/97
THE KISS	103	09/22/97
THE AFFAIR	104	09/29/97
ONE HUNDRED TEARS AWAY	105	10/20/97
THE PROMISE	106	10/27/97
THE ATTITUDE	107	11/03/97
DRAWING THE LINES	108	11/10/97
THE DIRTY JOKE	109	11/17/97
BOY TO THE WORLD	110	12/01/97
SILVER BELLS	111	12/15/97
CRO-MAGNON	112	01/05/98
THE BLAME GAME	113	01/19/98
BODY LANGUAGE	114	02/02/98
ONCE IN A LIFETIME	115	02/23/98
FORBIDDEN FRUITS	116	03/02/98
THEME OF LIFE	117	03/09/98
THE PLAYING FIELD	118	03/16/98
HAPPY BIRTHDAY, BABY	119	04/06/98
THE INMATES	120	04/27/98
BEING THERE	121	05/04/98
ALONE AGAIN	122	05/11/98
THESE ARE THE DAYS	123	05/18/98

PILOT

written by David E. Kelley, **directed by** James Frawley

THE BRIEF: Harvard Law alumna Ally McBeal gets fired by her fast-track firm after a senior partner puts the moves on her. Her classmate Richard Fish hires her for his new firm—where her Harvard ex-boyfriend, now married, happens to work. Ally tackles her sexual harasser in court, copes with the creative chaos of Cage/Fish and Associates, and tries to break the spell of old emotions.

Be careful whom you kiss when it's your first kiss—that's the lesson Ally learns when we meet her in the first episode's opening shot. Gazing out her office window, Ally flashes back to her first kiss, with Billy Thomas, at age twelve. "It was too much—I actually felt my whole body tingle."

At Harvard Law School, Ally was still kissing Billy. But Ally made Law Review and Billy didn't, so he transferred to Michigan. "So basically...you're putting your career between *us*," Ally snaps. Billy says nothing, but his shamed face says it all. (Actually, not quite all—there may be a secret or two hiding in

that silence. Stay tuned. Every moment in Ally's life is capable of coming back at her at any time, and nobody's heart is a simple two-dimensional object.)

Billy winds up clerking for the Supreme Court. Ally gets a great job with a big Boston law firm. Grimly, her walruslike senior partner, Jack Billings, starts to grope her in the hall. She blows the whistle. Billings gets the boot. Wily Billings claims he's got OCD (obsessive-compulsive disorder). To prove it, he starts pawing every woman in his path, so he can sue the firm under the federal Disabilities Act.

Ally winds up getting sacked because the firm loses less money if she goes. As she carries

her files outside, she bumps into her Harvard acquaintance Richard Fish. "You're looking fabulous!" Fish says. "I know, I just got fired for it," Ally replies. No harassment here—Fish wants nothing but money and fun. To him they're synonymous.

Fish thinks it would be fun (and lucrative) for Ally to work with him at Cage/Fish and Associates. She meets Elaine Vassal, her insubordinate, inordinately nosy secretary—and Billy, her new colleague. Ally flees into her new employer's bathroom.

And finds Fish is in there. Cage/Fish has a unisex bathroom. Fish asks if it's going to be a problem for Ally to work with Billy. "Because if it is, well, I can't do anything about it, but I'd be happy to sympathize." Fish really means well. As long as he can do whatever he wants, smoke cigars, and chase women's wattles, he's happy. And he wants everyone in his firm to be happy, too.

Ally strives to keep her feelings for Billy strictly above the neck, but hormones and history subvert her at first. All he has to do is say, "Coffee?" and Ally's flashing on them naked, splashing in passion in a giant foaming Starbucks cup. In Ally's world, caffeine and lust are intimately intertwined. Billy, exhibiting classic transparent male emotional denial, says he's glad Ally's joined them—"Not as an ex-boyfriend, but as a lawyer who appreciates a talented addition to the firm."

Ally have a past. Ally is unreasonably—but understandably—stunned that Billy has a wife. Everyone confronts everybody else about the romantic yearnings the firm is rife with. Fish has the answer to smooth everything over for all concerned—his favorite word to drive inconvenient feelings away: "Bygones!"

But Ally's drama has just begun.

👫 OPPOSITE (top and bottom): Ally flashes back to her young love with Billy. ABOVE: She meets her new colleagues, former Harvard classmates Billy and Fish. RIGHT: Ally reacts to the news that Billy's now married.

Four arrows spring from an invisible crossbow into Ally's left ventricle.

Ally loses her first case. *Man Made Magazine*'s editor ran a horny nun's lurid account of sex with a kinky minister. Open-and-shut First Amendment case. But the disgusted judge rules against her. Fish is shocked. Billy tries to blame the judge. "Don't you stick up for me!" Ally demands. She's a big girl, she can pick herself up when she falls.

Now it's Ally's turn to be shocked by Fish. She walks in on him hiring, for a fat fee, the pig Jack Billings. "Let's face it," Fish chirps, "being so brazen, he sort of represents everything I stand for." Outraged, Ally is smart enough to express her objection in fiscal, not moral terms: If Fish hires Billings, Cage/Fish will be liable for sexual harassment claims. "He can't stop himself, remember?" Ally seethes.

"I'm assuming he made the whole obsessive-compulsive disorder thing up," Fish says.

"Completely. But you didn't hear that," Billings chortles.

"Didn't have to, I've got it on tape," Fish says, whipping out a concealed tape recorder. Billings is busted. "It's not just winning, it's winning ugly that matters," Fish gloats.

All's not calm and bright at Cage/Fish, though. It dawns on Georgia, Billy's wife, that Billy and

SONG LIST:

"Neighborhood" ♪

♪ "Baby Don't You Break My Heart Slow"

"Maryland" ♪

♪ "Hold Out"

"Lucky Life" ♪

♪ "The Wildest Times of the World"

"Tell Him" ♪

♪ "Psycho Theme" *

"Drowning in My Own Tears" ♪

♪ "Mischief and Control"

"Hemisphere" ♪

♪ "Searchin' My Soul"

*Danny Lux provides the dramatic underscore for all episodes and occasionally rescores well-known instrumental pieces.

compromising POSITIONS

written by David E. Kelley, **directed by** Jonathan Pontell

THE BRIEF: It's a big week for flesh mortification at Cage/Fish and Associates. Cage, Billy, two judges, and Ally's date are exposed for embarrassing acts of public lust.

Ally gets to meet her new boss, John Cage—and defend him for soliciting a prostitute. "We could argue she just came out of nowhere and attacked him with her esophagus. Seriously," Fish suggests. In court, the instant Ally begins her defense of Cage, Billy crashes through the door, whispers in Judge "Happy" Boyle's ear, and Boyle dismisses the charges.

Billy isn't saying how he pulled off this miracle.

That night, Fish makes Ally go to dinner with Judge "Whipper" Cone, his sexagenarian sexpot girlfriend, and Ronald Cheanie, a big new client the firm's courting.

They all debate prostitution and sexual politics. "Have you ever used your sexuality to gain a business advantage?" Cheanie asks Ally. She says no—but it

dawns on her that by assigning Ally to be Cheanie's date, Fish is using her sexuality to woo a new client. "I'm involved in the very thing we're having a conversation about," Ally thinks. "I'm basically a call girl." For this she went to Harvard Law?

En route to the restroom, Ally catches the rather pious Cheanie lip-locked with Whipper. At home, Ally asks her roommate, Renee, her closest chum and, as assistant district attorney, the occasional foe of Cage/Fish, if she should tell Fish. Renee says the messenger always gets shot—let some other busybody tell him about Whipper's illicit kiss.

So Ally asks her assistant, Elaine, the busiest body in Boston, for some gossip assistance. Elaine wrongly guesses that Ally is asking how Billy got Cage off, so she tells her about Billy's bachelor party, where a hooker entertained all comers—including Billy and Happy Boyle. Ally confronts Billy, who actually defends the double standard. "Women don't have the same sex-drive thing," Billy claims. He points to his zipper. "This makes men stupid." He puts his hand on his heart. "This makes women stupid."

👨👩 **LEFT:** The women at Cage/Fish cast a cool eye on male escapades. **OPPOSITE (top to bottom):** Ally's vision of "Happy" Boyle at Billy's bachelor party; Billy facing Ally's wrath about his bachelor party; Fish grazing Whipper's wattle in ecstasy.

"I can't believe I'm hearing these things coming out of your mouth," Ally hisses, "but considering the places it's been, maybe I shouldn't be shocked." Even though she's still in shock over Billy's marriage, Ally is rattled by any assault on the institution of marriage—especially since she could have wound up as the bride betrayed by that bachelor party.

Fish asks Ally to clinch the Cheanie deal by going out with him again. She goes but feels guilty, as if she's "being unfaithful to love itself." At dinner, Ally tells Cheanie she saw him kissing Whipper. Cheanie admits he did wrong but chalks it up to the same anger Ally felt that night about getting set up on an involuntary double date. He wanted to get even with Fish.

All this pro-marital morality appeals to Ally, and she kisses Cheanie on the way home.

At work, Ally finds Billy on the verge of confessing his bachelor-party badness to Georgia. In the nick of time, Ally diverts the conversation, shuts up Billy, and saves Georgia from needless, marriage-damaging humiliation.

But the two other guilty parties make poignant confessions to Ally. Whipper admits she should have slapped Cheanie instead of smooching back—and would have twenty years ago, but at her age, the flattery overcame her. Cage amazingly changes from pig to penitent in Ally's eyes by saying his hooker thing was a one-time folly caused by loneliness. "Whatever a woman's idea for an evening of passion might be, I rarely find myself in the picture. And sometimes I find myself with my judgment compromised."

Ally refuses to give up on the possibility of lasting love. "I like to take that with me to bed at night. Even if I'm going to bed alone."

SONG LIST:

"Pearl's a Singer"

"Grain of Sand"

"Leave It to Beaver Theme"

"Searchin' My Soul"

the KISS

written by David E. Kelley, directed by Dennie Gordon

THE BRIEF: Ally goes on her first real date with Ronald Cheanie, and he confuses her by not kissing her on the lips. Ally and Georgia represent an anchorwoman who got fired for losing her looks and is suing the TV station for sex discrimination.

Ronald Cheanie and Ally have a date, and the crucial question of the good-night kiss is more vexing than usual because they've already shared an impulsive kiss. Ally tells Renee that it wasn't a real kiss: "I didn't have to do any kissing back. My lips just held their ground." But Ally knows Cheanie probably considered it a kiss and will expect another, and she's been reading this book called *The Rules*, which advises women never to kiss on a first date if they ever hope to get married.

At the end of the delightful date, Cheanie solves her dilemma in the worst possible way. Just as she's about to modify The Rules slightly, thinking to herself, "I can give him a *little* kiss, nothing slutty in that," Cheanie dodges

her proffered pucker and gives her a quick peck on the cheek.

"We were dancing close. Most men would've asked to sleep with me. What he did was *rude*!" Ally complains to Renee. Not that she would've consented, but she's insulted. "I'm a sexual object, for God's sake. He couldn't give me a little grope?"

In court the next morning, Ally is equally appalled by the behavior of the station that fired veteran TV anchor Barbara Cooker, her client. The newswoman won seven Emmys and a Peabody, but it's nubile bodies the station seems to value in newswomen. "Only 6 percent of the eighteen to thirty-four-year-old group would care to sleep with her," reads an official memo about Cooker. "Basically, the only men who get a rise out of her are no longer capable of rising."

Defending the station is Jack Billings, who sexually harassed Ally at her former law firm. His arguments are ingenious. He

makes Cooker admit that she'd gotten her start by replacing an older, more qualified news-woman. "Good looks and youth cut in your favor fifteen years ago, didn't they, Ms. Cooker? Isn't that wretched hypocrisy?"

Cheanie tells Ally that her powerful, questing personality intimidates him. Throwing The Rules right out the window, Ally snaps, "If you want some Stepford girl with her own apron set, fine, she's out there waiting to rub your feet. If you want *me*, go for it, 'cause I'm—I'm—I'm—I'm *it*!"

Ally is going with her gut instincts, but it's a risky business. Cheanie dumps her. In court, she makes a ringing

indictment of the anchor-woman's employer: "The finest journalist they had, and they cut her loose because not enough people wanted to see her naked." Billings is so spooked, he offers to settle the case for $400,000 and no admission of guilt. Ally says no, and Ms. Cooker goes with Ally's instinct.

The jury vindicates Cooker with a $930,000 judgment

against the station. Ally celebrates by going on a double date with Cheanie (who's evidently back on again) and Billy and Georgia, feeling good that she's healthy enough not to resent them.

"Who says I'll end up alone?" she muses. Watching the dancers but feeling less jubilant, Ms. Cooker sits at another table—alone.

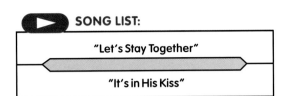

OPPOSITE (left to right): Ally's close encounter with Cheanie; a day in court. ABOVE: Billy's reaction to Georgia and Ally as co-counsel.

the AFFAIR

written by David E. Kelley, **directed by** Arlene Sanford

THE BRIEF: Ally gives the eulogy for her favorite law prof—who had coincidentally been her secret lover. The memory of her old flame winds up turning Ally's affair with Cheanie to ashes.

James Dawson, Ally's and Billy's memorable professor for Constitutional Law, takes up jogging and promptly drops dead. Mrs. Dawson asks Ally to give the eulogy, unaware of Ally's five-month affair with the deceased years ago. "I know you and my husband were close," says Mrs. Dawson, unaware of the irony.

Cheanie is hurt when Ally gently rebuffs his offer to attend the funeral. He thinks it's because she prefers Billy's company. "Even though you're no longer a couple, when you feel about to hit bottom, he's still the best cushion in town,"

Cheanie says bitterly. Ally can't confess the tsunami of adulterous memory that's washing over her, nor can she deny her deeper intimacy with Billy. Cheanie doesn't know all, but what he does suspect is on the money.

At the wake the night before the funeral, Ally reminisces painfully over Dawson's coffin. Then she turns, and her eyes meet those of Dawson's daughter. Ally flashes back to the last time their eyes met, when the girl went with her daddy to the zoo and met Ally.

One look and the girl had known her dad was in love with Ally. Catching the look in her daughter's eyes locked on Ally's, Mrs. Dawson is hit with the same revelation.

The widow calmly confronts Ally in her office. Her husband had left her briefly, but Mrs. Dawson had presumed it was for a faculty member. "But it

BELOW: (flashback) Ally and her law professor.

LEFT: Ally after speaking at Dawson's funeral.
BELOW: (fantasy) Ally suffers from foot-in-mouth disease.

her office. For old times' sake, they dance—with a strange, charming chasteness—to Johnny Mathis, singing "You Belong to Me," along with the recording. They get the words all wrong, but it's all right.

was you." Mrs. Dawson has one question: "The man I knew—*did* I know him?" Not only has she lost her husband, she's lost confidence that his love was ever real. Was he a man or just a mask?

Then, as Ally sprints to Billy's office for advice—almost colliding with Cheanie—she shouts at him, "No! No! I don't have to 'let you inside' me—it's *dangerous* in there!"

Ally asks Billy which would hurt the widow less: to be told that Mr. Dawson was just meaninglessly womanizing with Ally, or the truth, that he felt the biggest tragedy of his life was not spending it with Ally. Billy advises her not to burden the widow with the unbearable truth.

Mrs. Dawson rescinds her request for Ally's eulogy. But nobody tells the minister, so he calls her up to the pulpit. On the spot, Ally wings it with angelic grace, giving an awkward, bizarre, yet touching tribute to Mr. Dawson as a man who loved his wife and kids above all else in life. "You thought you really knew him?" she says. "You did."

Cheanie ends their affair. Billy knows she'll be staying late to work off her grief, so he drops by

SONG LIST:

"Maybe I Know"

"You Belong to Me"

87

one hundred TEARS away

written by David E. Kelley, **directed by** Sandy Smolan

THE BRIEF: Ally quarrels with a woman at the supermarket over the last can of Pringles. Ally trips the woman, is also accused of shoplifting, and winds up facing a hearing to determine her mental fitness to practice law.

Ally's supermarket show-down with a fellow shopper earns her a pair of handcuffs, a mug shot, and a hearing before the Board of Bar Overseers. They've suspended her license. "Ms. McBeal," says her chief inquisitor, Mr. Pink, "you trip people in supermarkets, you steal spermicidal jelly, you punch people in the streets. I personally saw you acting very erratically on a pulpit at my friend's funeral."

"There's an explanation for all of it, every last bit!" Ally protests.

But Pink's not listening. He's pals with Jack Billings, the woman-harassing old boss whose butt Ally kicked in a law case. This whole hearing against Ally is really political payback.

Back home, Renee coaxes Ally to confess what the spermicide was doing in her pocket. She wasn't really shoplifting it, she was simply embarrassed to be seen with it and planned to pay at the register. But Ally's not dating anyone, and Renee wants to know who the spermicide was for.

It was for Omar Sharif, the character in *Funny Girl* who shows up at the stage door and sweeps Fanny Brice off her feet. Omar Sharif, Ally explains, is her symbol for "the guy who just walks in from another world—the guy who is *looking* for my door....With one look, we know

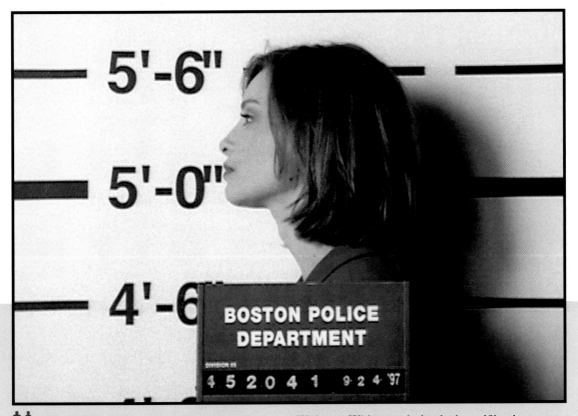

 OPPOSITE: The scene of the crime. ABOVE: Mug shot: The attorney stands accused.

we were meant for each other, like Barbra Streisand and Omar Sharif. Except instead of singing about it, we make passionate love! Girls have dreams like that sometimes."

Meanwhile, there's the nightmare of Ally's board hearing. Mr. Pink calls Elaine to testify about Ally's shaky state of mind. "Did you ever tell anybody she was 'two-thirds of a Rice Krispie: She's already snapped and crackled, and she's close to the final pop'?"

"Sometimes I say things just to make people think I'm a wordsmith," Elaine confesses.

At the final hearing, Billy gives a passionate defense of Ally's emotional approach to life and warns everyone not to surrender what she represents. Judge Whipper, who had turned Ally in, recants. "She stands guilty of being female, young, attractive, and how *dare* she be aggressive?" says

Whipper. Whipper admits she herself has been part of Ally's problem. "In the old boys' club, not all the predators are boys."

The Board can't bear to hear any more crazy testimony and officially declares Ally sane enough to be a lawyer.

SONG LIST:

♪ "100 Tears Away"
"Mischief and Control" ♪
♪ "Look What They've Done to My Song, Ma"
"Walk Away, Renee" ♪
♪ "I Wanna Love Him So Badly"
"Every Now and Then" ♪

the PROMISE

written by David E. Kelley, **directed by** Victoria Hochberg

> **THE BRIEF:** Ally has to juggle two cases in one week: John Cage is arraigned for prostitution; an ice-cream company sues for infringement of copyright. Ally interferes in the love life of her opposing counsel in the ice-cream case.

Exulting over her new piano, Ally plays "Goodnight, My Someone" from *The Music Man*, singing it along with Renee. On the lyric, "sleep tight, my love," Ally keeps hitting the wrong key on *love*.

"I can never get that note right," Ally says.

"Tell me about it," says Renee. She adds, "This is a sad song. It's about a lady who's got nobody so she's gotta sing to an imaginary someone every night. It's about a lady—"

"—just like us," Ally says disconsolately.

"I hate pianos," Renee says.

This experience no doubt increases Ally's irritation at the office the next day when she finds the men ogling a dishy mail-delivery girl en masse.

"You can give them law degrees, dress them up, but in the end? Neanderthals," says Ally.

"When a male of the species looks at that, he should become *Homo erectus*," Fish says.

Ally handles the case of an ice-cream firm suing another for use of its name. Harry Pippen, the obese opposing counsel, is said to "move like continental drift." Harry is so big, he might actually influence it. When he has a heart attack in the courtroom hallway, Ally's mouth-to-mouth CPR resuscitates him.

Harry tells Ally he's never felt a kiss like Ally's kiss of life, so he cancels his imminent wedding to the also overweight Angela. Pained, Ally is forced to tell Harry that he is definitely not her "someone." It's not just that she wants to protect his feelings—she's forced to advise him not to pursue the girl of his dreams, and that's contrary to her raison d'etre.

So Harry asks Ally's advice. Though a fine woman, he says, Angela never made his heart bounce. "Do you think it's wrong to marry

someone . . . not because she's the one, but . . . because she's the *only?*" Harry asks.

Ally says we've got to keep our promise to love and hold out for that someone who will make our heart bounce.

Her next case throws icy water on Ally's romantic notions. Sandra Winchell, her client, is an attorney who became a prostitute for dispiritingly realistic reasons. All the good men were married anyhow, Sandra testifies, and they were trying to seduce her, proving they weren't so good after all. "Fidelity, marriage—men just aren't built for it," Winchell says.

"Objection!" shouts Ally. Oops! She's not supposed to object to her own client, even if the woman does talk like that Neanderthal Fish.

John Cage gets Sandra acquitted by arguing that prostitution laws are hypocrisy because movie stars simulate sex for cash, and plenty of women say no unless a man has dough. Ally asks Cage if he really believes that all women sell sex to get ahead. Cage says he only made that argument "because I was paid to."

Angela confronts Ally, attacking her for talking Harry into leaving her at the altar. "Sometimes when you hold out for everything, you wind up

with nothing," Angela says. But Harry comes to his senses and proceeds down the aisle with her.

Unwinding at the Bar, Cage reveals that he's no advocate of chill romantic realpolitik, like Sandra. "The world is no longer a romantic place," he tells Ally. "Some of its people still are, however. Don't let the world win, Ally McBeal."

SONG LIST:

♪ "I Only Want to Be with You"

"Ask the Lonely" ♪

♪ "Goodnight, My Someone"

the ATTITUDE

written by David E. Kelley, **directed by** Michael Schultz

▶▶

THE BRIEF: Ally is smitten with a legal colleague of Renee's, and also by a rabbi who won't grant Ally's client a divorce even though her husband is in a coma.

Visiting Renee in the court-house, Ally loses her cool when the hot district attorney Jason Roberts walks across the hall toward them. Ally blocks the elevator door to give him time to get on and is knocked into the other closing door and flung to the floor.

"You can sure fall hard," Jason says, helping her up.

"You have no idea," Ally replies. Renee gets off on the first available floor to give Ally maximum time alone with Jason. Ally has twelve seconds to find out if she'll be seeing him again. The theme from *Jeopardy* plays in Ally's head, and just before the *bing!* Jason asks her out.

Lovestruck, Ally stands in the elevator watching him walk away, and the doors whomp her back onto the floor.

But on the date, Jason falls in her esti-mation. He drops big dollops of salad dressing on his chin while eating and, incredibly, misses it when he goes to wipe his mouth. Here sits a man with future written all over his face, and it's ruined by salad dressing all over his face. Ally never forgets a salad-dressed face.

Ally's legal obstacle is Joseph Stern, a recalcitrant rabbi who won't let her client, Karen Horwitz, remarry because her hus-band's in a coma. He was hit by a bus before they could obtain a formal Jewish divorce decree, called a "get."

"These people want to be married. This is a really silly rule. Seal the deal," Ally says.

"The Torah decreed this strict rule to give would-be adulterers the strength to resist," Stern says, sternly.

"What if your wife had a vegetable for an ex. You wouldn't be married. Ever think of that, Mr. Scholar?"

"I'm not married."

"And you wonder why!"

Stern is charmed by Ally's irreverence and asks her out. The way to this rabbi's heart is through his funnybone.

Ally and the rabbi may or may not have a stomped wineglass in their future, but she figures what the hell. "Instead of waiting for Mr. Right, I'm going to take chances on Mr. Not Likelys."

👤👤 OPPOSITE (top to bottom): Cage prepares for court; Georgia, Fish, and Billy react to the news that Georgia's former employer has agreed to settle her lawsuit against them to the tune of $311,000. ABOVE: (fantasy) The drop of dressing on Jason's chin becomes magnified in Ally's imagination.

▶ **SONG LIST:**

"This Guy's in Love with You"

"*Jeopardy* Theme"

"Going the Distance" (*Rocky* Theme)

"These Are My Mountains"

drawing the LINES

written by David E. Kelley, **directed by** Mel Damski

▶▶

THE BRIEF: Ally and Georgia blackmail a millionaire into voiding his prenuptial agreement, Caroline Poop tries to blackmail Cage/Fish with a harassment lawsuit, and Billy's memories are triggered by the sight of Ally and Georgia sharing esctasy over morning cappuccino.

The Cage/Fish coffee machine is broken, so Ally brings in take-out from Starbucks. She gives Georgia a sensual-sensitivity lesson on how to milk the most exquisite bliss out of that first cup, and soon they're both moaning with pleasure. Billy glimpses them and suddenly misses his sex life with Ally. It seems he and Georgia never gaze into each other's eyes the way he and Ally used to.

Ally and Georgia's friendship deepens as they team up to help Marci Hatfield, dumped by her husband for a new mistress. He's worth $18 million, but her prenuptial agreement limits her to $600,000.

Ally and Georgia demand more. "Who will your children side with if your womanizing comes out?" Ally asks Mr. Hatfield. Defending marriage is her forte, but she feels slimy for using children as leverage.

She's crossed a moral line. So has Billy. "We gotta draw some lines," she tells him. He's got to stop discussing his sex life with Ally, and she promises to stop the morning coffee orgasms in the office.

👨👩 OPPOSITE (top to bottom): The first sip of cappuccino honed to a fine art; Billy and Fish demonstrate the expressive potential of the human tongue. ABOVE RIGHT: Elaine retains Caroline Poop to sue Cage/Fish. BELOW: (fantasy) Ally guiltily hallucinates herself as a slimy lawyer. Flockhart did the scene while colleagues murmured, "I'm so sorry," and poured on her head five gallons of chocolate syrup, honey, and ketchup, to give it the red tint of motor oil.

Elaine devises a foolproof method of getting attention: She retains the aggressive and intimidating Caroline Poop to sue Cage/Fish over the mail-girl incident, claiming that the men's ogling of the mailroom delivery girl constitutes a hostile work environment. Poop threatens a walkout by the women in the firm, led by Elaine. "The publicity would be taps for this firm," says Poop. "By the way, John Cage's little arrest for soliciting a prostitute need not be a *huge* issue."

That's blackmail! Why, that's…well, that's exactly what Cage/Fish is doing to Jason Hatfield. Then Fish crosses another line: He has a private detective snap Hatfield nuzzling a young blonde. The pictures would enrage his mistress and buttress his wife's case.

"What do we do with these?" Ally asks dubiously.

"We extort, that's what we do," says Fish.

Hatfield caves and gives his wife $2 million. Fish defies Poop's blackmail, however, and the women abandon Elaine's walkout strike. Everybody dances a bad week away down at the Bar. "It's really gracious of you to forgive me on such short notice," says Elaine. Fish smiles—either she is forgiven, or he's glad her coup is quashed.

Battle lines are undrawn, and conga lines seem imminent.

▶ SONG LIST:

"The Only Love I Ever Had"
"It's My Party"
"The Boy from New York City"

95

the DIRTY joke

written by David E. Kelley, **directed by** Dan Attlas

THE BRIEF: Ally and Renee have a dirty-joke—telling contest, and Cage/Fish is sued by the famous mail-delivery girl.

Renee startles Ally at a crucial scary moment while Ally is watching *Whatever Happened to Baby Jane?* and Ally screams. "Cruelty is funny to you? Pain?" They get on the subject of Julie Andrews and dirty jokes—Ally's high school classmates voted her Most Likely to Become Julie Andrews, and sensing this prissiness, the men at Cage/Fish always stop telling dirty jokes when Ally walks in.

So Renee encourages Ally to tell the men a dirty joke. As an example, Renee tells her favorite:

A guy finds a girl on the beach. "She says, 'I'm twenty-one years old, I have no arms, no legs, and I've never been kissed.'" He kisses her. She cries again. "I'm twenty-one years old, I have no arms and no legs, and I've never been screwed.' And with that, he bends down, picks her up, and throws her into the ocean and says, 'You're screwed now.'"

Ally's disgusted. "A woman has no arms and legs and you make fun of her sex life." Renee mocks Ally's prudishness. Ally bets Renee that if she told her joke in front of their friends at the Bar, nobody would laugh. If they do, Ally will have to get up and tell her own dirty joke.

Jennifer Higgins, the voluptuous delivery girl at Cage/Fish, sues the firm for creating a "hostile work environment."

LEFT: Renee tells her rude story. **ABOVE:** Is it true Twins have more fun? **OPPOSITE** (top to bottom): (fantasy) Ally as the limbless woman in Renee's joke. "*This* they think is funny"; Fish and Ally deal with the Jennifer situation.

"How's she gonna prove Fish had formal notice of the hostile environment?" Ally wonders. "Subpoena his penis?" Still, work-environment law is so new and elastic, everyone's afraid Jennifer might win. And Elaine's lawsuit had demanded that Jennifer be fired, which could be construed as hostile.

Ally is half-sympathetic to Jennifer. "Part of me thinks this girl does have a case. Another part . . . all these harassment laws overprotect us. Makes us seem like victims."

In court, all Ally has to do is ask Jennifer one question: "So when Elaine filed her lawsuit, that's when you felt the hostility?" Jennifer says yes. The case turns on a precise point of law. Jennifer has tied her hostile-environment claim to Elaine's lawsuit—and lawsuits have immunity. Ally saves the day. Jennifer loses the case.

But Ally loses the dirty-joke bet. Renee's joke slays 'em, and Ally's joke bombs. Rabbi Stern explains that dirty jokes need to have a hostile edge to be hostile to be funny.

In the end, Fish apologizes to Jennifer. "The women here are really angry at me and the other men. Not you. And we are to blame. I'm glad you're still working here."

SONG LIST:

"Falling" ♪

♪ "I Started a Joke"

"The Sound of Music" ♪

♪ "The Way You Do the Things You Do"

boy to THE world

written by David E. Kelley, directed by Tommy Schlamme

THE BRIEF: Whipper makes Ally do Christmastime work as a public defender to try to save a transvestite prostitute with a lovely spirit. Fish sues to fulfill his runt-intolerant uncle's last request.

Ally is in high holiday spirits trimming her tree from a stepladder. In her world, when her emotions are elevated she's apt to be physically elevated, too.

She falls off the ladder onto the tree, clinging like a desperate gecko. Renee walks in. "It's come to this. You're humping the tree."

Judge Whipper is short on public defenders and assigns Ally to reach out to Stephanie Grant, a transvestite hooker, "the most fragile person living in the harshest of worlds." To beat the rap, Ally goes for a transvestite fetishism plea. She gets an expert to testify that Stephanie may suffer from "gender dysphoria," another reason not to bust him for soliciting.

This hurts the sweet kid's feelings. "You mean, like I'm sick." He left Ohio for Boston because everyone called him sick. But for him it's Ally's long shot or jail, and everyone knows what happens to boys like him in jail.

To build the defense, Ally has to ask him whether, when he wears women's underwear, he ever touches himself. "I know it's hard," Ally says. "You have to trust me, Stephanie, if I'm to get you off." The two inadvertent puns make Ally's face fire-engine red.

Stephanie swiftly becomes the main man in Ally's life—makeup adviser, genius seamstress, and best gal-pal—and is redeemed from the streets by a job at Cage/Fish, where Elaine, all sisterly, warns him the men are all pigs.

Fish is devastated by the death of his intolerant uncle, who irrationally loathed short people. Fish wages a successful court battle to permit a celebration of his uncle's beloved bigotry by having Randy Newman's "Short People" performed at his funeral, most upliftingly.

Renee teases Ally about all the men she's been kissing lately: Cage under the mistletoe, perhaps the rabbi—who knows who else. "I'm the hot one here and it's your lips getting all the Chap Stick."

Ally says demure is in. "You scare men."

"Scare men, yeah," says Renee. "I scare them stiff."

Everyone's jolly holiday mood is shattered by a phone call. Stephanie has been found murdered in

ABOVE (top to bottom): Ally's early consultation with Stephanie Grant; Fish's solitary vigil at his uncle's tomb. OPPOSITE (top to bottom): Ally mourning the murdered Stephanie; Ally, overwhelmed by Christmas.

SONG LIST:

"Christmas Tears"

"This Christmas"

"Soothe Me"

"Jingle Bell Rock"

"Christmas Don't Be Late/The Chipmunk Song"

"Let It Snow"

"Short People"

"Hark, the Herald Angels Sing"

the Combat Zone porn district by a john enraged upon finding Stephanie wasn't a real Jane.

While Fish makes a secret solo visit to his uncle's grave, exposing his soft heart to no one, Ally fulfills Stephanie's last wish: She fixes his makeup in the morgue, so he can exit this life as pretty as he wanted to be.

SILVER bells

written by David E. Kelley, **directed by** Joe Napolitano

THE BRIEF: Ally takes the case of two women and a man who want to stretch the definition of marriage to include trios. Whipper and Georgia make painful discoveries about their own relationships.

Ally's new clients are James, Mindy, and Patti Horton. They have three kids: two by James and Mindy and one by James fertilizing Patti's egg implanted in Mindy. Ally's job is to make honest women of both Mindy and Patti by forcing a court to recognize the arrangement as a legal marriage.

"Why can't we look at this as a kind of same-sex marriage with a heterosexual thrown in to chaperone?"

Ally ventures. Whipper cracks that Ally is just using a lame argument to hide her lack of belief in her case.

All three Hortons don't sleep together. "There's nothing kinky—I guess the women just take turns being too tired," Ally reports. "The penis is not a share toy!" Renee objects.

Mr. Horton brags about their family. "Conventional? No. But we're happy, devoted to each other. The kids live in a home where there's love and trust and security. How many in this room can make the same claim?"

Not Ally, Georgia, and Whipper, who gun him down in a fantasy sequence.

Mindy, the first wife, testifies that her husband's affair with Patti actually reheated his cooling passion with her. Georgia is alarmed to realize that Ally's arrival has done the same for her union with Billy—more caring, more sharing between the sheets. But Georgia resents that Ally's presence has had any effect on her relationship with Billy. Ally isn't pleased by her effect on their marriage either. "It's certainly not my plan to break up your marriage, but I'm not thrilled to be the best thing that ever happened to it."

Whipper yearns for the intimacy of marriage. Fish asks Whipper what's so important about marriage anyhow? "It must mean something, Richard, if you're so afraid of it." Later he confesses the hard truth: His parents were so mutually abusive that he finds marriage abhorrent. He uses major age difference as a shield against commitment. He calls it "the guardrail."

After Whipper rules against legal bigamy, Mindy reveals that she hates the three-way lifestyle. She was just trying to hang on to her family. Whipper and Fish try to hang on for one more Christmas office party. He sings

her a song: "More Today Than Yesterday." He's a remarkably good singer but a lousy committer. Everyone dances, everyone is alone, but they are alone together.

👨👩 OPPOSITE (top to bottom): Fish serenades Whipper; (fantasy) Ally, Georgia, and Whipper have the same reaction to James Horton. RIGHT and BELOW: The Cage/Fish Christmas party.

SONG LIST:
"More Today Than Yesterday" ♪
♪ *"I Saw Mommy Kissing Santa Claus"*
"Let's Get It On" ♪
♪ *"Going the Distance"*
"Santa Claus Is Coming to Town" ♪
♪ *"Please Come Home for Christmas"*

cro-MAGNON

written by David E. Kelley, **directed by** Allan Arkush

THE BRIEF: Ally and Renee take up sculpture; upon discovering that the male model, Glenn, is unusually well-endowed, Georgia joins them. Ally dates Glenn. In court she defends a hunk who stood up for the honor of his date. Cage/Fish, minus Ally, bond at a sports bar, smoking cigars and watching a prize fight.

Ally and Renee attend sculpting class. Their model is the supernaturally "gifted" Glenn. Noticing their fixation, the instructor asks, "Everything okay here?" "Well," says Renee, "I might need a touch more clay." When they tell the guys that size doesn't matter, are they being truthful?

It all put Ally in a decidedly receptive mood, as proved by her behavior while defending nineteen-year-old Clint, who punched a guy for insulting his date's virtue. "Just looking at this kid makes me horny," Ally thinks to herself, appalled by her feelings. She can't even stop herself from grabbing Clint's posterior in court.

Ally and Glenn go out on a date. She admits that if a guy impugned her chastity at a party, she'd be peeved if her date punched the offender but disappointed if he didn't.

"So you like a little Cro-Magnon in your man," Glenn says. "Some," Ally replies.

They play "Heart and Soul" on Ally's piano. "Bottom," she says, voluntering to take the bottom melody line. "Top," he says, and the weight of innuendo rolls them off the piano bench onto the floor in front of the fireplace.

Their passion is intercut with scenes from the increasingly violent prizefight the guys at Cage/Fish paid fifty dollars to see on pay-per-view. The guys, including Elaine, watch, holler, and puff cigars, as Georgia watches in disbelief.

Later that evening Ally emerges from the shower satisfied and solo, having sent Glenn home. The Dancing Baby appears, and taking Cage's advice, instead of ignoring him she dances jubilantly with him. If you can't beat him, join him.

Glenn was fine. But when the famous dancing baby hallucination shows up, Ally saves the last dance for him.

ABOVE: Renee enjoys her sculpting and the model.
OPPOSITE: Ally and the Baby dance the night away.

▶ **SONG LIST:**

"Hooked on a Feeling"

"The Wildest Times of the World"

"I Could Have Danced All Night"

"Heart and Soul"

"Intermezzo" *(Cavalleria Rusticana)*

the BLAME game

written by David E. Kelley, **directed by** Sandy Smolan

▶▶

THE BRIEF: Ally's one-night stand returns to haunt her when Glenn, the sculpture class model, reappears. The firm tries to cash in on the crash of Transatlantic Flight 111. Ally and Renee take vengeance on Glenn by giving him "the penguin." In each case, who's to blame?

In a Freudian dream, Ally and Georgia go down in a plane crash. Ally bobs up on her seat cushion, alone in the ocean (naturally), but poor Georgia is beheaded. Ally subconsciously wants Georgia dead for stealing Billy—or so Renee and Ally are convinced—but Georgia reassures Ally that the dream is really just about the case they're working on—the 100 percent fatal Flight 111.

Meanwhile, Glenn, the inordinately well-endowed model Ally had a one-night stand with, unexpectedly walks by one morning at Starbucks. Supposedly he was safely out of the country, and his sudden appearance prompts Ally to fantasize beheading him with a machete. But when he asks her out again, she feels

trapped and consents. Later, Renee asks Ally what she's so angry about, since the micro-affair was her idea. Ally says she never would've done it if he hadn't claimed he was about to vanish from her life. "He used a line! Flashed me a little gather-ye-rosebud look, and I bit his hook-line and swallowed his sinker!"

Awkwardly, Glenn overhears this. "Don't you have a *plane* to catch?" Renee hisses, nicely fusing the double meaning of airplanes in the episode: death and the fear of emotional attachment and abandonment. Glenn protests that it wasn't a line—his trip fell through—and he's the one who feels manipulated. "Let's face it, you could've asked me to spend the night." Now Ally really feels there's no escape from a second date.

Back in court, Cage/Fish faces a tough time proving who's to blame for Flight 111. There's no evidence the airline was negligent. "Don't bring the law into this!" Fish says. "If somebody's dead, there's money." Cage/Fish brings out a miracle witness, John Hoverless of the National Transportation Safety Board, who chalks up the crash to mechanical failure. Suddenly it looks like there's cash in that crash.

But opposing counsel Larry Ballard notes that there's no evidence of mechanical failure, just the opinion of Hoverless, whose credibility he proceeds to terminate: "Did you ever claim to be abducted by aliens?"

"I had a vivid dream once," Hoverless stammers. "I adjusted my position on the alien thing."

Ally realizes in horror what her crash dream really meant: She's afraid of falling for Glenn. But after their second torrid encounter, she offends him by presuming that he's prone to bouts of volcanic midday romance. "I feel like some kind of boy-toy," he says. Ally does get wrapped up in her own one-woman emotional maelstrom, and Glenn opens her eyes to his hurt feelings: He's a lowly snowboarding nude model with a complex about fast-track career women. So he dumps her, while the entire restaurant taunts her by singing "Na Na Na Na, Hey, Hey, Goodbye."

Humiliation doesn't bring out Ally's best side. She talks Renee into asking Glenn out and luring him into "the penguin," a ploy in which a girl convinces a guy to drop his pants and waddle toward her like a penguin—whereupon she leaves him publicly exposed and hops into a getaway car driven by her girlfriends, all guffawing at him.

Ballard convincingly defends the airline against Cage/Fish by critiquing society: "If we get cancer, we sue a doctor. If a hurricane hits, we sue the church, it was an act of God. Pain doesn't just happen. There's got to be somebody to blame."

Ally realizes she did the same thing: foisted blame onto Glenn. She apologizes, but the jury has less insight into blame games. Despite zero proof, they award $1.1 million to the crash victims.

👨👩 **OPPOSITE:** Furious that Glenn reneged on his promise to leave the country, Ally hallucinates his beheading. **ABOVE:** "The penguin."

SONG LIST:

"Hooked on a Feeling"
♪ *"Going the Distance"*
"Baby, That Is Rock 'n' Roll"
♪ *"Na Na Hey Hey Kiss Him Goodbye"*
"Tell the World How I Feel
♪ *About 'Cha, Baby"*

BODY language

written by David E. Kelley, Nicole Yorkin, Dawn Prestwich, **directed by** Mel Damski

▶▶

THE BRIEF: Ally and Renee unhappily serve as bridesmaids, which raises all kinds of personal issues. Ally represents a woman who wants to marry a convict serving a life sentence. Fish's major crush on Attorney General Janet Reno sparks slapstick comedy and casts a poignant new light on his and Whipper's love.

B eing single is never more miserable than when you're trapped in preposterously unflattering bridesmaids' dresses, open to ridicule for appearance and lifestyle. The bride only married the jerk of a groom because she hit thirty and got desperate. "If I ever get that desperate, just drop a big rock on my head," Ally tells Renee. The bouquet is tossed, Ally does a slo-mo football lunge, whomps the other women aside, and grabs that bouquet. In fantasy, Renee drops a boulder on her head.

In reality, the two cozily toast marshmallows over the bridesmaids' dresses burning in the fireplace. Renee says women are brainwashed from day one by stories about Snow White, Cinderella, the Little Mermaid, and Pocahontas being saved by "getting the guy." Ally vows never to wear another bridesmaid's dress. "I swear, I'd sooner go out in public in my pajamas."

Ironically, Ally takes on the case of Janie, also thirty, who's desperate to marry Michael, a convict doing life for bombings and hijackings. Judge Smart says it's the warden's call to permit or forbid the union. "Oh, right, let's have the warden decide! To him the Constitution is a big ship. If two people love each other, the courts should stay clear," Ally argues.

Rules are rules, the warden says. No marriage unless there's a child or one on the way. And no conjugal visits for unmarried prisoners. Catch–22. Plus a Catch–23: no conjugal visits for maximum security prisoners, period.

But there's no law against turkey-baster babies. Janie happens to mention she's ovulating, so Ally and Georgia grab a plastic container and head for the penitentiary to get a sperm sample from Michael. Fish thinks Janie's marriage is a great plan: "He almost literally wears the ball and chain, and not only will he not be having sex with other women, he won't be having it with you. In a sense, you really *are* married."

Although devoted to Whipper, Fish has a chance encounter with the Attorney General. Whipper catches him chatting up Janet Reno in a bar, fingering her wattle. Fish claims it was firm business. "I have no doubt your business was firm!" Whipper snarls. Fish and Whipper share a moving reminiscence about their past. He reminds her that she was the one who wanted to keep the relationship a safe arm's-length affair. Whipper reminds him that he's forgetting what happened next: They both fell in love. Whipper and Fish reconcile.

Stopped by police on their way back from the prison with Michael's sample sealed in its container, Ally and Georgia have a hard time explaining where they've been, what they're carrying, and where they are going.

After all that, Janie decides not to conceive. But the judge consents to the wedding anyway, forcing Ally to break a vow to help Janie make hers. She buys a bridesmaid's dress to replace the burned one. It's hideous, too, because all bridesmaids' dresses are as hideous as brides are beautiful.

But Ally still has a promise to make good on. She swore she'd sooner go out in her nightie than don another bridesmaid's dress. So as good as her word,

Ally dances in her pajamas before all her smiling friends as the snow begins to gently fall.

👫 OPPOSITE: (fantasy) Renee's reaction to Ally catching the bride's bouquet. ABOVE (top to bottom): Fish touches Janet Reno's wattle; Whipper's reaction; into the Dumpster goes Fish.

SONG LIST:
♪ "The Ride of the Valkyries" (Götterdämmerung)
"Don't" ♪
♪ "For Your Love"
"Going the Distance" ♪
♪ "When You're Smiling"

ONCE in a lifetime

story by David E. Kelley & Jeff Pinker,
teleplay by David E. Kelley, **directed by** Elodie Keene

THE BRIEF: The flip side of Ally's theme song, "Tell Him," is that if you're never gonna love him, you've still got to tell him, tell him, tell him right now. Ally dodges this responsibility with her boss Cage. Ally and Billy represent a famous painter who wants to marry a woman six decades younger—in order to honor his late wife.

As Ally struggles to communicate to Cage in some way less painful than actually telling him that their romance isn't in the cards, Cage's colleagues give him calamitous courtship advice that makes matters worse (though it helps us know the characters better).

Fish thinks Cage is being too shy to win Ally. His oddball tactics may win in the courtroom, but in courtship you need more than hypothalamus isometrics. "Women need to feel dominated even when they say they don't," claims Fish. Georgia walks by just in time to see him give Cage a love lesson that begins, "You feel my dominion and you want to surrender to it!"

Instead of telling Cage how she just doesn't feel, Ally tries to turn him off by talking like a makeup-obsessed imbecile. Pumped up on Barry White's unstoppable seduction music, Cage clamps one of Elaine's patented vacuum kisses on Ally and literally knocks her off her feet. "I've been untoward," mourns poor Cage.

The next day, Ally accidentally knocks him over in the office, breaking his remote flusher. Then she breaks his heart by explaining that he's given her the dreaded "ick"—a sense that their love is just not meant to be.

This week's client is Seymore Little, an aged, important American painter who's suing to force his legal guardian—his son—to permit his marriage to Paula,

an art student sixty years his junior. He gave her a $300,000 boat, which makes Ally suspect gold-digging. "I smell a rat in the wedding cake, and it's you," Ally tells Paula.

Little is stubbornly devoted to his art—and to his late wife, Gail, with whom he shares heart-to-heart chats every blessed day. That's why his son, Sam, had him declared incompetent and in need of a guardian—Seymore can't stop talking to his dead wife, out loud and in public. "There are some loves that just don't go away," Sam explains to

Ally and Billy. "I wouldn't expect you to believe that." Ally and Billy exchange glances, and a huge elephant representing their own relationship appears in the room.

Seymore's son offers Paula the whole $800,000 in Seymore Little's account in return for dropping the lawsuit. Startlingly, Paula doesn't want the money. She wants a sham marriage strictly so that she can seize legal guardianship from Sam and give Seymore what he wants above all: a gallery to exhibit his obses-

sive paintings of Gail. Sam fears this would sully Seymore's legacy. "Loving somebody forever—that's some legacy," Ally counters.

In the final scene, Vonda sings an affecting version of "The End of the World" as Seymore gazes at a painting of Gail, Billy slow-dances with Georgia while mooning about Ally, and Ally weeps about the loss of love—not just hers, everybody's.

OPPOSITE (left to right): Elaine demonstrates the vacuum kiss; Cage clutches his remote flusher. ABOVE: Cage in sync with Barry White.

SONG LIST:

"Since I Fell for You"

"Can't Get Enough of Your Love, Babe"

"The End of the World"

"Going the Distance"

"You Belong to Me"

"Hooked on a Feeling"

forbidden FRUITS

written by David E. Kelley, **directed by** Jeremy Kagan

THE BRIEF: The firm defends a U.S. senator being sued for stealing another man's wife. Georgia confronts Ally about her ongoing crush on Billy.

Billy and Ally are amazingly in sync when they lead a meeting about Mr. Bepp's case versus Senator Foote, who married the former Mrs. Bepp. Billy and Ally finish each other's sentences seamlessly as if they were two parts of the same soul. Everybody is impressed. "Have you two been passing notes in class?" Fish asks. Georgia is awed by their teamwork and terrified by their revived intimacy.

Georgia springs a truth-or-dare question on Ally: If she and Billy were alone on a desert island and no one could ever find out, would they have sex? Ally has the sense to say no way. Georgia suspects she's lying. Georgia says there's only one way to resolve the intolerable tension: Ally should spend a night with Billy. "Just get it out of your system. . . . Go ahead, take a night, take a weekend. But find out!"

Renee knows she can't endorse Georgia's offer, but she's listened to Ally obsess over Billy too long not to be curious

about what would happen. "How often do you get forbidden fruit served up on a platter?" she says to Ally. Ally virtuously declines to bite Billy's fruit, but she does have one regret: back when she was with Billy, Ally's sexuality was just developing, and she wishes Billy could know what a red-hot lover she's become.

"Ally, I'm your roommate," Renee scoffs. "We have thin walls. . . . I make more noise breakin' in a new shoe!"

"I'm fantastic in bed!" Ally retorts—just as Georgia is walking in to apologize for her rather shocking offer. It's an awkward moment.

Ally feels equally awkward walking into court to defend the homewrecking senator. Here she is, a strong advocate of marriage, standing up for adultery and shattered dreams. The attorney of the cuckolded Mr. Bepp says that marriage has no sanctity if society doesn't recognize the difference between courting someone who's single and someone who's married.

Ally goes on to tell the court (and Georgia and Billy) that, single or married, the couple meant to be will wind up together: "Stick laws between them, stick a court, a judge, an old girlfriend, they'll still find a way to be together." Thanks to Ally, the senator is exonerated.

Ally celebrates by gorging on ice cream with Renee. Ice cream is to her what champagne is to Fish—in victory she deserves it and in defeat she needs it.

Then Ally goes to bed alone, as Vonda croons a sad slow version of "You Know He'd Rather Be with Me." A girl can dream, can't she?

OPPOSITE (left to right): The Dancing Baby becomes a spear-hurling Cupid as Ally's biological clock ticks on; dinner meeting discussing Fish's strategy in Senator Foote's case. RIGHT: Cage and Ally slow dance in court to Nat King Cole's "He'll Have to Go," demonstrating the irresistible force of a love song. ABOVE: (fantasy) Ally drowning in her sea of troubles—one of the toughest tricks the special effects team ever pulled off.

SONG LIST:

♪ "Going the Distance"

"Someday We'll Be Together" ♪

♪ "Hooked on a Feeling"

"Hidden Persuasion" ♪

♪ "He'll Have to Go"

"She'd Rather Be with Me" ♪

"I have a way with Freudian slips."

"It was so real."

"It'll be worth it."

"Everything's my business."

"We're women. We have double standards to live up to."

"I want, I want, I want."

"I am not a weakling."

"Did I just say that? Did I just say that, too?"

"I don't need a therapist, I have a roommate."

"You know what makes my problems bigger than everybody else's? They're mine."

"Today's gonna be a less bad day . . . I can feel it."

"Excuse me?"

"I have my dignity. Or at least it should look like it."

"I demand to know what part of me you are laughing at."

"If you can end your day dancing, then you can't complain."

"I practice innocence."

"Can't I just apologize to everybody and be excused."

"I can't call him—rule number five."

"I really hope he calls today just so I can hang up on him."

—ALLY McBEAL, *McBealisms*

theme of LIFE

written by David E. Kelley, **directed by** Dennie Gordon

THE BRIEF: Ally finally gives in to Cage and visits his one-of-a-kind psychiatrist. She also meets the best once-in-a-lifetime kind of guy since Billy: her new client, a doctor being sued for offending a patient with the operation required to save her life.

Ally tries to get her anger out by taking a kickboxing class with Georgia. Unfortunately, it only makes her feel like kicking people in addition to Georgia. Cage recommends his smile therapist. Ally refuses.

Ally is so stunned by her attractive new client, Dr. Greg Butters, that she falls down in his presence. When Ally falls in front of a man, it generally means that she's falling for him. The urgent dancing baby hallucina-tions he triggers are another clue. Still, she's a lawyer, and she does her job, which is to defend Butters against a lawsuit by Hanna Goldstein.

Hanna doesn't mind that Butters saved her life, but she's furious that he did it by putting a hog liver in her body. Hogs are revoltingly unkosher, and Hanna angrily contends that he could have kept her alive with a machine until a human liver was available. She accuses him of making a name for himself with an innovative therapy by treat-ing her like so much meat. How dare he say she's "compatible" with a disgusting hog?

Ally has been falling down a lot lately, even by her standards. When she trips over her own shoe in the office, she flings the shoe in fury, cursing the "stupid fashion people" who force women to wear topple-inducing foot gear. The shoe conks Cage's head, prompting him to proffer his therapist's card and provoking Ally to relent at last.

The therapist, Dr. Tracy Clark (Tracey Ullman), has Ally's number: "You got a little see-through baby ooga-chuckin' spears at you. You're a cracker!"

Dr. Tracy says that kickboxing Georgia is admirably therapeutic. "She's a beautiful, smart woman married to the man you love. Smack her! We don't deny human nature in this room."

What Ally really needs, Dr. Tracy says, is a theme song to cheer her up. Ally tries "Searchin' My Soul" (the show's theme). Dr. Tracy says it stinks. But she's excited by Ally's second choice: "Tell Him" by the Exciters.

Ally isn't excited at all to learn in court that Dr. Butters had a grant he would have lost if he didn't do a hog-liver transplant within the year. But he proves to be above suspicion, and Hanna loses the case. A blow is struck against antipig bigotry, and Ally remains lovestruck by Butters.

But there's one thing she still can't figure out. How come when he kisses her, a whole lot of steamy buildup culminates with a cool peck on the cheek? As we know, a peck in place of a hot kiss is a mortal insult to Ally (provided it's the right guy). Butters really looks like he could be Dr. Right, but something's wrong. What Ally needs now is to find out just what it is that's turning a potentially great kisser into a silly pecker.

SONG LIST:

♪ "Blue Danube"

"Hooked on a Feeling" ♪

♪ "Tracy"

"Tell Him" ♪

♪ "Young at Heart"

the PLAYING field

written by David E. Kelley, **directed by** Jonathan Pontell

THE BRIEF: Ally defends Greg, her love interest, from a lawsuit by child-prodigy attorney Oren Koolie. Cage/Fish represents a woman suing an employer who promotes only those women with whom he's had affairs. Ally bemoans the unlevel playing field of life and love, and does her best to make a man's world more to a woman's liking.

Images of the dancing baby continue. He's no longer dancing, but plays an aggressive game of street hockey. Ally's shrink, the sensibly daft Dr. Tracy Clark, asks if the hockey baby is any good. "I don't know, I don't watch hockey," says Ally. "I think it's cruel to the animals, dressing them up like that and making them skate."

Dr. Tracy prescribes violence for "Little Chuckie." Next time Ally sees the baby, she's to treat him like a hockey puck. "Kick his ass!"

Dr. Greg Butters gives Ally a ride to work. His concentration veers from the street to her eyes, causing Butters to run a stop sign and hit another car. Ally tries to fast-talk Butters out of trouble with some legal jujitsu, but it backfires.

Upon returning to work Ally opens her office door to face that familiar hallucination, the baby, and spin-kicks him. Only it isn't the baby. It's Oren Koolie, the attorney for the accident victim who is suing Dr. Butters. Oren, a

BELOW: On Dr. Tracy's advice Ally kicks what she thinks is the Dancing Baby, only to discover it is Oren Koolie, opposing counsel and child genius. **OPPOSITE** (top to bottom): Oren's settlement strategy—crying; the Baby is back and this time he's armed with a stick and a puck.

Fish walks in. Ally and Georgia assault his diverse insults to women. "Verbal spankings titillate," he says. Georgia throws her shoe at him, conking poor Cage instead.

Ally advises Dr. Butters to settle: $35,000 and Oren will walk. The case is settled. Just as Butters is inches from a clean getaway, Ally summons up the hallucinatory backup singers, her version of Gladys Knight's Pips, to boost her confidence and advises Butters to stay. He obeys. They dance.

At the Bar, Fish says, "Georgia, hey, dance? Level playing field on the dance floor, you know."

nine-year-old with a genius IQ, is practicing law until he is old enough to go to medical school in a couple of years. He cries for effect, then demands $125,000 for his client.

Cage/Fish tackles an ingeniously backward sex-harassment case. Eva Curry is suing her boss for promoting only women who have slept with him. "The women who choose not to exert that influence are penalized," argues Fish. "Res ipsa de facto quid pro quo, e pluribus penis."

When Ally won't give Oren Koolie's client $125,000, he hides under the table crying. Ally plops him tenderly on her lap and advises the friendless child genius not to be in such a rush to be a man. Oren is touched—and brings his offer down to $75,000.

Georgia had won a sex-harassment case against her old boss (who'd transferred her because she was beautiful). She tells Ally how angry she is that the boss gave up when she threatened a sex-harassment claim. "I wished I fought him on an even field"—not as the beneficiary of a law that implies women are somehow weaker than men. Ally discusses with Georgia the sex-role social codes that forbid her to speak first in her romantic relationships. "Who says I have to sit back and let *Greg* initiate? Who says I can't grab a bull by his . . . horn?"

SONG LIST:

♪ "This Guy's in Love with You"

"Hooked on a Feeling" ♪

♪ "Maryland"

"Where Peaceful Waters Flow" ♪

♪ "Dream Lover"

"Tracy" ♪

happy birthday, BABY

written by David E. Kelley, **directed by** Tommy Schlamme

THE BRIEF: Ally's twenty-eighth birthday is imminent; she defends a man who unpleasantly surprises a woman he's dating by sneaking into her apartment in the wee hours and tickling her foot to feed his fetish. Meanwhile, the mystery of Dr. Greg Butters's ambivalence is solved at last.

Renee is prosecuting Ally's touchy client Mark Henderson, a foot fetishist. Mark used to date the glum-eyed Cheryl Bonner, but he turned her blossoming affection to cold fury by tiptoeing into her apartment and caressing her pedal extremity at 3:32 A.M. He swears it's a misunderstanding: Cheryl had said she liked foot massages and romantic surprises, which she admits on the stand. When Mark found the door to her apartment unlocked, he thought she wanted his visit. After all, their third date had gone so well.

On the other hand, it is Mark's third foot-related offense. At home, Ally tries to sweet-talk Renee into giving Mark a break, as a birthday present to

Ally. No deal. So Ally plies Renee with a foot rub and plea-bargains Mark's sentence down from a jail term to counseling, as Renee moans in foot-rub ecstasy.

But Ally is not at all ecstatic when she invites Greg Butters up to her room after a sizzling good-night kiss and he mysteriously refuses. This is thwarting Ally's life plan: At twenty-eight, she expected to be curled up with a husband reading *What to Expect When You're Nursing AND Trying Big Cases*. Instead she's representing nut cases and curling up with an inflatable doll.

At the Bar, as a surprise birthday gift for Ally, Elaine has arranged for Butters to serenade her with a love song in front of all her friends. He's a sexy singer, and Elaine is sure Ally will soon need "the Bounty quicker picker-upper."

But Renee ruins Ally's night by impulsively leaping to the stage and turning Greg's solo into a darn near R-rated duet. Back home, Renee pleads for forgiveness. She admits she's an exhibitionist who never met a spotlight she didn't like but swears she'd never cut into Ally's romantic action.

Greg arrives, asks Renee to go to her room, and gives Ally a bombshell announcement: He's transferring to a big new job at an emergency room in Chicago. That's why he's been so reluctant to get their affair going. He asks if he can still take her out for a birthday dinner. "I think you've blown out enough candles for one birthday," Ally replies.

Ally discovers that Cheryl is only suing Mark out of heartbreak: She thought he might be The One at last, her last chance. So when his love turned out to be perversion, Cheryl was

devastated. Yet Mark insists Cheryl truly tickles his fancy and begs for another chance. They forgive each other's trespasses and go out for coffee. A prelude to passion.

Butters tries to woo Ally at the last-minute, but she says, "I'm not a *que sera* kind of girl." Ally rebonds with Renee—two single girls alone together again—and Vonda strikes up an upbeat version of "Que Sera, Sera."

OPPOSITE: Renee checks out the dance floor situation. ABOVE: Greg prepares to drop a bombshell on Ally—he's leaving Boston.

SONG LIST:

♪ "Happy Birthday"
"It's Not Unusual" ♫
♪ "Falling" ♪
"I Am a Woman" ♫
♪ "Mischief and Control"
"Love Me" ♪
♪ "Don't"
"Tell Him" ♪
♪ "Charm You"
"Whatever Will Be, Will Be
(Que Sera, Sera)" ♪

the INMATES/ AX murderer

written by David E. Kelley, **directed by** Michael Schultz

THE BRIEF: In this special two-part episode, two worlds collide. The denizens of Cage/Fish and Associates meet the folks from *The Practice*.

Do not adjust your sets. Ally's pals are entering a strange new world where the stakes are high and the lawyers' brows are permanently furrowed. They are entering the alternate world of . . . *The Practice*. And of course the attorneys on *The Practice* think they're the ones who've stumbled into the Twilight Zone.

Fish defends a French bistro for firing a heterosexual waiter. Not only is there no law protecting heterosexuals from discrimination, as there are in many states for homosexuals, but Fish thinks the restaurant has a completely legitimate interest in satisfying its clients' demand to be served by ultra-cultivated snobs.

Billy engages Donnell and Associates as co-counsel in a murder case. Marie Hansen has allegedly killed her husband with a hatchet while in a blackout. Her psychiatrist informs the attorneys that she has undergone a past-life regression revealing that she thinks she's Lizzie Borden.

The women of Cage/Fish go gaga over Donnell. Ally finds she likes the guy, a lot, and Donnell shows signs of feeling the same. But Billy is mortified by the eccentricity of his colleagues compared with the savvy, combat-hardened troops Donnell commands. How can he explain John Cage, for instance, who mentions that he once had a cousin who was convinced she was Helen Keller in a prior life. "Happiest person I ever met. She'd walk around saying, 'I can *see*! I can *hear*!'"

Ally defends her firm and its warm if wacky ways. She tells Bobby Donnell, "Our long-term policy is probably to bounce our kids on our knees."

She asks if he wants kids—hey, can't blame a girl for asking—and suggests that "for the sake of their innocence, you might want to cling to your own."

Renee gets on the wrong side of the law of love and the law of the land when she picks up fellow attorney Michael Rivers. She lures him to her apartment, seduces him with her come-on attitude, and then, when he won't take no for an answer, kickboxes him out of the ballpark, breaking his neck.

As the paramedics wheel Michael away on the gurney, Ally reams Renee for her teasing style. "You can lead a man by the penis, but it's the wrong way to tame him," says Ally. This time Ally's going to be the one defending her roommate in court.

OPPOSITE (left to right): Fish fingers the wattle of Camryn Manheim from *The Practice*, putting his digit in danger; Fish admires himself on the TV news. ABOVE and BELOW: Renee decks her date, and tries to explain her actions to the police.

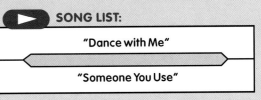

▶ SONG LIST:

"Dance with Me"

"Someone You Use"

being THERE

written by David E. Kelley, **directed by** Mel Damski

THE BRIEF: Georgia and Billy are stunned by the prospect of an unexpected pregnancy—and Ally is both stunned and under-standably, unreasonably jealous. Renee's date that got out of hand and landed her grabby man in the hospital now lands Renee in court.

Georgia drops a pregnancy test kit in the Unisex. When Fish walks in, Ally snaps it up and hands it to Georgia behind her back.

The test result weighs heavily on Ally's mind, but she's got a more pressing problem. Michael Rivers, who pawed Renee, got clobbered, and came to with a broken neck and facing a paramedic, is in court painting himself as the assailee, not the assailant. Ally and Cage will have to work wonders to save Renee.

Renee was "oozing sex," Rivers accurately says, dropping "sexual entendres like bread crumbs," leading him on to her apartment for "coffee" (read sex). He claims he was just matching her move for move when abruptly "she goes into kickbox overdrive."

Cage fights back with every eccentricity in his arsenal to slow the momentum of Rivers's all too persuasive testimony. He uses a clicker to state objections. He "stands corrected" in noisily squeaky corrective orthopedic shoes. He's outrageously sarcastic. "She sent mixed messages," Rivers says. "Mixed?" Cage replies. "As in 'No!' 'Don't!' 'Get out!'?"

It's not looking good for Renee, and then it gets worse. Glenn, Ally's nude model boy-toy and the victim of Renee and Ally's "penguin" routine, takes the stand and tells how Renee lasciviously lured him to drop his pants in the snow, then drove away with Ally in a getaway car, laughing at him. The women aren't laughing now. Renee's prosecutor asks Glenn how Renee asked him out. "She said she liked one-night stands even more than Ms. McBeal," Glenn says.

Cage pulls his oddest head-scratcher of a tactic yet. He lets Ally call Renee to the witness stand, then suddenly jumps up and says he's not going to call her after all, since the prosecution has such a weak case. Renee sits back down. Later, Renee throws one of the fits she's all too good at throwing. In a rare burst of anger and strategy explanation, Cage hisses that he pulled that trick because Renee is a hostile witness who would only strengthen Rivers's case, and that juries get suspicious of defendants who won't take the stand—but they won't blame her if her lawyer won't let her testify. Plus, Cage needed a chance to say her accusers had a terrible case. "Because they have a wonderful case, and if we chose to put on a defense, we might reveal that we don't have one."

Uh-oh.

Billy and Georgia have their own uh-oh moment over an apparently positive pregnancy test. Ally fantasizes a projectile piercing her belly. Cage counsels Ally to allay her pain by picking a new theme song, the silliest possible melody, to trivialize the trauma. She chooses Trini Lopez's "Lemon Tree."

Ally runs into Glenn in the elevator and, to the comic astonishment of an elderly couple, quarrels with him, shouting, *I don't date guys for giant schlongs, Glenn!* "Who pulled my pants down in the middle of the road and gave me a penguin?" he retorts.

Ally and Renee have a quarrel that isn't funny. Ally calls Renee on her self-serving self-defense plea. "This sex-as-power thing?" Ally snaps. "It isn't fun. You have a problem . . . and you need to get it, Renee." Renee explains the roots of her neurosis in a rough girlhood incident.

Renee anxiously awaits her verdict, and Georgia awaits the pregnancy test result. Renee dodges the bullet, and Georgia misses the stork.

OPPOSITE: Cage prepares his closing argument. ABOVE: Glenn testifies about getting "the penguin." BELOW: Ally reacts to news of Georgia's possible pregnancy.

SONG LIST:

"Wedding Bell Blues"

"I'll Be There"

"Going the Distance"

ALONE again

written by David E. Kelley, **directed by** Dennis Dugan

THE BRIEF: Cage faces his toughest case yet, more impossible than Renee's kickbox date. In the course of it, he faces an even tougher personal travail: the case of the long-lost love.

Vincent Robbins robbed a bank years ago and went to jail. For eighteen years, he patiently and unobtrusively collected spare rubber bands, knitting an afghan to conceal his hands while he wove the rubber bands into a trampoline big enough for the large old man he'd become in prison. At last, just one month before he was due to be released at age seventy-two, Vincent finished his masterwork rubber-band trampoline.

So he jumped, higher and higher, until he cleared the wall in an exhilarating arc of freedom more joyous than anything in *The Great Escape*. Once over the wall, Vincent fell to earth and sprained his ankles. They caught the visionary old duffer with ease.

Unless Cage can spring him by legal means, Robbins will go behind bars for another twelve years and certainly die in sad captivity. Cage has one day to work this miracle.

"Pinch your nose, get it to whistle, take a moment, make your feet squeak," implores Vincent's desperate attorney. "My client needs somebody to pull a rabbit out of a hat. I'm told you can do it." Cage is troubled.

Then he gets more trouble. The lawyer trying to keep Vincent in prison is his best friend Hayley from law school, whom he's loved from afar even though she has never given evidence of anything beyond platonic affection for him.

Vincent isn't an ideal client, mainly because he's so idiosyncratically idealistic. He just couldn't bear confinement, and he just had to fulfill the promise of his rubber-band invention. He tells the judge he was wrong to have robbed the bank. "But as an American, I had a *constitutional right* to use a revolver while doing so!" says Vincent, patriotic in his own mind.

Cage movingly wins the unwinnable case by pulling a kind of emotional switcheroo. He poetically compares the old man's quest for a flight to freedom—the quest that sustained him behind bars for so long, the dream of his life's sole soaring achievement—to the dream of a "certain man" Cage knew who was secretly in love with a woman who was his best friend, although he never dared to tell her. That man wishes he had learned the lesson of courage from Vincent Robbins.

Hayley, a brisk, sunny, basically warm yet oddly remote eccentric, is visibly moved to realize that Cage is speaking of his own unconfessed passion for her. He isn't the soul mate she's seeking.

Vincent goes free, but Cage ends the episode in the solitary confinement of unrequited love.

▶ **SONG LIST:**

"I'm in Love Again"

"Ain't That a Shame"

"Alone Again"

OPPOSITE: Vincent makes a jailbreak on his prison-made rubber-band trampoline. ABOVE: Vincent knits rubber bands for the trampoline. BELOW: Richard Fish on marriage: "A person would never even buy a car if he were told he'd have to drive it for life—it's silly."

THESE are the days

written by David E. Kelley, **directed by** Jonathan Pontell

▶▶

THE BRIEF: Ally puts her crush on Bobby Donnell to the kiss test. Georgia and Billy reheat their romance. Cage defends his cousin for playing Cupid with a paddle. A janitor tries to switch hearts with his billionaire boss.

Bobby Donnell (of *The Practice*) asks Ally to help with a bizarre case: Brian Michaelson, CEO of MicroWorld, is dying, soon to leave his kids fatherless. His best pal is Bernie Gilson, once a homeless man living on a grate, whose demeanor so impressed Brian that he befriended him and hired him as MicroWorld's janitor. Bernie wants to trade his healthy heart for Brian's faulty one. Both men have hearts of gold.

"Why would any sane man swap his good heart for a sick one?" the judge demands. Sad-eyed Bernie says it's because his life has never amounted to a hill of dust-mop dust. "I can die never having done anything. Or I can die giving life to a person I love. Imagine giving children their father."

Meanwhile, Cage's cousin Alan Farmer is arraigned for whacking five couples with a canoe paddle to jolt them into truer love. "Nothing bonds like a little crisis," Farmer says. He may have provoked three marriages. "I'm an apostle of love," insists Farmer.

Ally snaps out of her fantasies and plants a big kiss on Bobby's lips. "I have a great imaginary world," she explains. "Sometimes I just need things to happen for real."

Billy and Georgia realize that their romance has worn down to a ritual seventeen-minute clutch each Tuesday and Saturday. "I feel like we're becoming this little corporate Stepford couple," complains Billy. So what does he want Georgia to do, strut around the house naked? Well . . . yeah!

Cage loses his paddle-happy cousin's case.

The judge demands that Ally decide on the heart-swap case, and she rules against it. Brian

and Bernie take it in stride—they exit bickering lovingly, like true brothers. Bobby calls a time-out on his brewing affair with Ally. She feels as if he's put her "on layaway." If only the last love-thwarted year could be erased from her life.

Cage consoles her with what his mother used to say: "If you think back on and replay your year… if it doesn't bring tears, either of joy or sadness, consider the year wasted."

Back at the office, Georgia, stark naked except for some sexy red pumps, walks in on Billy, and Ally walks in on them in flagrante. Ally bids them a good night, walks outside, flashes back on her year, and finds it very full indeed.

SONG LIST:

"Just One Look"
"Fools Fall in Love"

"Neighborhood"

OPPOSITE (left to right): Ally between her clients, the MicroWorld zillionaire and the janitor who's all heart; "Happy" Boyle delivers a stern opinion on tooth decay. ABOVE: Cage with his cousin and client Alan, who conks lovers' skulls for their own good. ABOVE RIGHT and BELOW RIGHT: Elaine and Georgia develop a sudden taste for Bobby Donnell.

"Bygones."

"Tell me . . . what kind of lie works here?"

"Speak not from strength but from estrogen."

"'Problem' is a bleak word for 'challenge.'"

"It's not my style to care about others,
but what's going on?"

"That would be funny if it weren't so humorous."

"Ouch. That would hurt if I cared."

"Good news should never go uncelebrated."

"Love. You can't bank on it."

"Tonight is a night for you to feel good about yourself."

"Under the robe besides a phenomenal body is a good judge."

"I'm nothing if not redundant. I also repeat myself."

"Love . . . it's an equation. A 'me,' a 'you,' derives a 'we.'"

"The trick is to fast forward through the
lousy parts of life."

—RICHARD FISH, *Fishisms*

secrets of
the UNISEX

"It's supposed to be a private place," says
Gil Bellows about the Unisex bathroom,
"but there is no private place on
Ally."

"The challenge was trying to decipher what the Unisex was, number one," says *Ally McBeal* production designer Peter Politanoff. "When the script first came out, we asked, 'David, what is a Unisex bathroom?'" He said, "Oh, it's like the one we have at Fox." And the one that we have at Fox is your typical shared bathroom, which is a stall, a urinal, a sink, and a lock on the door. But that's not very funny. So I thought, well, I had heard that David writes a lot for the bathroom, and he'll write a lot of silly scenes in the bathroom. And I had heard about *Picket Fences* and some of his other shows where there's a lot going on in the bathroom. So I thought, obviously no urinals, because that would make everyone uncomfortable. But what if they were all stalls, and what if you had men and women sitting next to each other? So I did a sketch, submitted it to him and he loved the idea. And it became the talk of TV.

"The point of its size was to keep it intimate. If it's small, then they have to bump into each other. There has to be some anxiety. There has to be some angst about going to the bathroom. It's a private place, but all of a sudden it became thought, if they faced each other, and the wall were cut out so you could actually have a conversation while someone's looking in the mirror and looking at someone standing across from them, then that tended to work very well."

"It's actually a pretty difficult set to work in because it's pretty small," says producer Jonathan Pontell, "but it was a brilliant idea. Just think if another writer created it. You need places to go when you're doing a scene; most writers would write it in a lounge or a coffee room or something like that. But David writes a Unisex bathroom—it just gives you such possibilities of things to do. While you're playing the scene, you also have the concept of people being there that you don't know are there—that's just wonderful. It's sort of a private zone; it is, but it's not. It's a yin and yang. The possibilities for the human discomfort are multiplied."

very public. When Cage jumps over into Fish's stall, it's presented as if there was nothing unique or special about it. It's presented as if it were commonplace—every workplace has one of these. And the little circular mirrors are very helpful in composition, in terms of how you interact when say you have four to six actors in the scene. Put two on one wall, two on another? That's not too terribly interesting. Then you have to shoot into mirrors to see someone on the other side; if you put them all on one wall then it's all very linear. So I

A to Z

Acute Courtesy Disorder: The "illness" affecting Ally and her future client Hannah Puck, who threw her best friend in a Dumpster for stealing her boyfriend. ("Story of Love")

Adorability and Shyness: What Cage wants his "courtship smile" to convey to others. It's important to distinguish this smile from his "smile therapy" smile, a technique taught by his therapist, Dr. Tracy. Later, he discovers his inner Barry White and realizes that adorability and shyness are not the quickest way to a woman's heart. ("The Playing Field")

Albert, Marv: Cross-dressing sportswriter whose unfortunate stumble into the media spotlight makes any joke about cross-dressers much funnier. Rabbi Stern uses Marv as an example of the importance of cruelty to lewd humor. ("The Dirty Joke")

Alien: She-monster in Sigourney Weaver sci-fi horror classic, which Ling changes into briefly in her coworkers' transitory hallucinations. ("Angels and Blimps")

Andrews, Julie: Loathed by Ally because in high school she was voted Most Likely to Become her. She didn't, though. ("The Dirty Joke")

Apologize: What Cage repeatedly does, particularly in court, after he's said something especially outrageous for manipulative effect. And if you believe he's sincere in saying "I apologize," you've just been manipulated by the master.

Apostle of Love: How Alan Farmer defines his life's work. He is defended by Cage (his mortified cousin) on a charge of whomping lovers on the head with a miniature canoe paddle to encourage them to stop quarreling and start loving each other more. He tries whomping Bobby Donnell when he hesitates over sweeping Ally off her feet, but it doesn't work. ("These Are the Days")

Asparagus Diet: How you can tell someone (say, Ally) is hiding in a Unisex stall with his or her feet up. ("Fool's Night Out")

Ass-holy: When Billy apologizes—sincerely—for having been "holy" in criticizing Ally for having sex with Glenn, Ally says he was actually being "ass-holy." In fact, Billy was basically being jealous—Glenn's inordinate manhood made Billy's wilt. ("The Blame Game")

Automatic Seat Warmer: One of Elaine's inventions to make toilets more user-friendly. The automatic seat-flipper gets Ally in cold water.

Bagpipe Biscuit: Renee's term for Cage, who weirdly plays the bagpipe and is nicknamed "The Biscuit." ("The Attitude")

Bar Dancing: Dancing in order to be seen, the way it happens in the Bar. Distinguished from "real dancing," that is, losing oneself to the music. Slow dancing is presumably a subcategory of Bar dancing, only with a more restricted range of vision. ("It's My Party")

Barbie and Ken: The Mattel dolls to which Renee compares the youthful Ally and Billy. They soon prove to be more complex than Barbie and Ken. ("Pilot")

Barbie and Midge: The Mattel dolls to which Michael the convict lasciviously compares Georgia and Ally. ("Body Language")

Barbie and Skipper: The Mattel dolls to which Caroline Poop derisively compares Georgia and Ally. Ally tells Georgia it could have been worse—Poop could have compared them to Barbie and Midge. ("The Dirty Joke")

Bashful Bladder: An affliction the Unisex rest room sometimes gives Ally, making her ask her coworkers to turn on the faucet, thereby masking sounds that would otherwise embarrass her. With this prim attitude, imagine how she feels later on when she gets her butt stuck in the toilet and has to have handsome firemen break the porcelain to set her free. ("Drawing the Lines")

(My) Big Lofty Goals: The reason lots of men try to date Renee, in Renee's opinion in "Cro-Magnon." Compare Elaine's resonant phrase for delivery girl Jennifer Higgins's breasts: "big alabaster buoys."

Big Sorry Swoop, the: Ally's angry term for men's attempts to apologize after hurting her feelings. "Men are so good at swooping in with apologies the day after. First the pain, then the Big Sorry Swoop." Ally's being unreasonable, but she's got a point: Men want to be bad, then get credit for being good.

Bottom-Feeding Scum Suckers: A term most people associate with criminal attorneys, as Fish tactfully tells criminal attorney Bobby Donnell. ("The Inmates")

Bounty Quicker Picker Upper: What Ally would need when sultry-voiced Dr. Greg Butters crooned her a tune, according to the unapologetically earthy Elaine. ("Happy Birthday, Baby")

Bowl, a Fresh: Cage's preference in a rest room.

Boxing: A sport detested by Georgia and beloved by Elaine, Billy, Cage, and Fish. Fight Day is the only day when cigars are permitted at Cage/Fish. ("Cro-Magnon")

Boyfriend Test: What Glenn unfairly bypasses by telling Ally he was leaving the country soon to go snowboarding, thus exempting him from the usual high standards of the Boyfriend Test and falling under the looser rules of the One-Night-Stand Test. ("The Blame Game")

C

Cappuccino: The steamy stimulant is a pulse-quickening symbol of all that is sensual. If Ally sips cappuccino anywhere near a man, it's an erotic red alert, especially if she spills it on him.

Cardiopulmonary Resuscitation: Technique that Ally uses to save a much larger man's life and that Fish uses to heroically bring Stefan the frog back to life as a comatose potential vegetable (and, ultimately, a meat dish, as Ling points out). ("Worlds Without Love")

Chagrined: How Cage feels when he emerges from the Unisex without his pants on or asks Ally for a date with his pants unzipped ("Silver Bells") or suffers any analogous mortification. Closely related to the words "troubled" and "flummoxed."

Chickens: They make Cage faint from nausea. Elaine makes sure everyone knows this embarrassing fact. ("The Inmates")

Christmas Fatigue Syndrome: Whipper's ailment circa December 15, when it occurs to her that another year has gone by and Fish steadfastly refuses to propose. ("Silver Bells")

Climbing Jack's Beanstalk: Elaine's term for Ally's lovemaking with Glenn the Nude Model, who has, as Elaine decorously puts it, "a trunk like Dumbo." ("Cro-Magnon")

Cracker: A crazy person. One of Dr. Tracy's favorite words.

Cruella: Nickname of Laura Payne, who stole Hannah Puck's boyfriend and winds up flung into a Dumpster by Hannah, who packs the strength of a dump truck into the chassis of a Pinto. ("Story of Love")

D

Da Da Da Da Da: To the tune of "John Jacob Jinkleheimer Smith," the syllables Cage hums to ward off anxiety. Often a prelude to the stuttering, compulsive repetition of places and names associated with New York. It's a habit that catches on with Cage's friends when they're feeling flummoxed.

Dancing Twins: Two identical guys with reliably bad fashion sense and good spirits, always willing to dance with any woman or women at the Bar. They make no demands, never duck commitment, never impose hard choices. Alternate Definition: The strange writhing terpsichorean hep cats Cage and Fish become when Nelle and Ling take them to a rough dance club and they degenerate beyond cool.

Date High: The giddy thrill Georgia tells Ally she misses now that she's happily married and something she's nervously considering getting from old flame Ray. ("Just Looking")

Death and Adultery: The two sure things in life, according to Ally. ("The Affair")

Distort the Law Beyond All Common Sense: A lawyer's job, according to Ally. ("Body Language")

Doll, Inflatable: When Dr. Greg Butters eludes Ally's erotic clutches, she comforts herself by taking the doll to bed. In "Happy Birthday, Baby," when Greg goes AWOL to an ER in Chicago, Ally pops the doll's stupid male head with an angry bounce of her bottom. Mysteriously, an inflatable male doll is glimpsed in later episodes.

Doogie Munchkin: Ally's nickname for the nine-year-old attorney Oren Koolie. ("The Playing Field")

Double Promise Keeper: A bigamist. Renee's term for Ally's client Mr. Horton in "Silver Bells."

Dumb Stick: Ling's term for the penis.

Dumpling: One of Fish's terms of endearment for Ling, in keeping with her strict instructions to call her "anything food." Variations include "macaroon," "pumpkin," "sugar," "honey," "bacon bits," "crouton," and (when Ling is in growl mode) "toast." ("You Never Can Tell")

E

Ear Twist: How Renee persuades Ally to double-date with Renee's pal Ben and his fathomlessly awful friend Wally, a man far beyond the reach of smile therapy. ("You Never Can Tell")

Easement on Her Left Breast: An offer Fish's secretary made, if only Fish would give her Fridays off. ("Compromising Positions")

Eleven: Number of times Ally phoned Greg after an apparently final spat. ("Only the Lonely")

Enigma: What Cage tells Renee he is. "You're a cute little enigma," she replies. ("Drawing the Lines")

F

Fa La La La La: The Christmas version of Cage's habitual warding-off-anxiety chant "Da da da da da." He utters it while asking Ally to the Christmas dance. ("Silver Bells")

Five Seconds: Length of time Ally considered Georgia's angry permission for Ally to bed Billy once more, just so all three of them could be sure, once and for all, whether Ally and Billy are meant for each other. ("Forbidden Fruits")

Flammable: A characteristic of Elaine's amatory perfume, according to Ally—a charge hotly denied by Elaine in "Drawing the Lines." Evidently Fish feels flammable on occasion in the Unisex—he's sometimes spotted emerging from a stall with a just-extinguished match.

Follicle Swelling: A disorder that strikes Cage whenever people bicker around him. ("Theme of Life")

Full Vertical Scan: What Ling got from a union worker, making her sue for sexual harassment. ("You Never Can Tell")

G

Glandular Pulls: What Cage reluctantly feels for Nelle, whom he'd rather safely covet from a safe range. ("You Never Can Tell")

Globby Glutes: Georgia's term for the "fleshy, jellylike" buttocks of Jack Billings, Ally's first boss, who falsely claimed to have an obsessive-compulsive disorder that forced him to grab women's buttocks, including Ally's, in "The Kiss." The opposite of "great glutes," which Dr. Tracy is untroubled to find Ally admires in a globless young man to the point of distraction.

Goo: Cage doesn't want "to goo" Ally by kissing her. He secretes excessive saliva and is troubled by the gooing potential thereof.

Gooey Creamy Italian Dressing: The substance that transforms dreamy D.A. Jason Roberts from Ally's love object du jour into the antidote to desire. ("The Attitude")

Gorbachev: The scarlet blotch–challenged Russian leader whom Ally believes she resembles after Elaine's "Pimple de Minimis" treatment. ("The Attitude")

H

Hair Tickle: Ling's caressing, maddeningly sexy massage technique involving only her long tresses on Fish's naked quivering chest. ("Pyramids on the Nile")

Handshake: How the stunned Billy and Georgia celebrate a positive pregnancy test. A bit stiff—if it had been Ally, she would've done handsprings. Later, Billy and Georgia loosen up. In fact, Georgia's looser fashion look alarms Billy. "Evening wear," Georgia calls her remarkably high-slit dress. "Yeah, as in lady of the evening," Billy protests.

Hard L: A way of pronouncing Ling's name that infuriates her, causing her to demand that people cease and desist with this pronunciation—and causing people to say it that way as often as possible, just to peeve her.

Horizontal Way of Life, Completely: The life Ally and Billy would lead if stranded on a desert island and nobody could ever find out. In "Forbidden Fruits," Ally assures Georgia that Ally and Billy would never even touch each other on a desert island. In a deserted office, maybe, but on a desert island, never.

Henderson the Rain King: Ally's favorite book, by Saul Bellow. She identifies with the hero, who goes around saying, "I want! I want!"

Hip Flexors: Portion of Ally's anatomy that got her stuck in the toilet, according to the handsome fireman who frees her. ("Just Looking")

Hitting the Sexpot: What Fish thinks a man has accomplished when a woman (say, Nelle) invites a man (say, Cage) to her place to cook him dinner. Ally agrees that this is what such an invitation signifies, and history proves her right.

Horny Toad: Another of Ling's names for the dumb stick: "There's nothing dumber than the Horny Toad." ("It's My Party")

I

Ick, the: That telltale sensation that one has no future with a particular man. Not necessarily an expression of disgust. For instance, Cage gives Ally "the Ick," but she loves him and knows they're kindred spirits.

Impulse Control Therapy: A kind of therapy Ally has never undergone. ("100 Tears Away")

In Victory I Deserve It, in Defeat I Need It: Why Winston Churchill and Richard Fish say they drink champagne daily. ("Compromising Positions")

J

Jugglee: One juggled by a love object while said love object concerns herself with the love object she prefers to the jugglee. A status Cage does not want. ("The Blame Game")

K

Kiss: "There's more intimacy, more emotion, more connection in a kiss than in any other physical act, and we wanted to stay right there in that, that . . . place." Ally, explaining why she just kissed Billy instead of going further. ("Sideshow")

Knee Pit Thing: The dangerous erotic maneuver Fish taught Cage, which makes Nelle scream—and not in ecstasy. ("Only the Lonely")

L

Language of Loneliness, the: Ally's native tongue, according to Fish, which qualifies her to mediate between minister Mark Newman and choir singer Lisa Knowles, who leads the congregation in bitter pop songs to avenge getting dumped by Newman. ("Fool's Night Out")

Laugh Track: Deafening tape-recorded cachinnation that Dr. Tracy Clark plays when her patients say something so naive that her own guffaw isn't enough to scorn it with laughter. ("Theme of Life")

"Lemon Tree": An ironically sweet Trini Lopez song that Cage's therapist teaches him to bring to mind to dull the pain of rejection by Ally. By associating Ally with the lovelorn lyrics of the ridiculous tune, Cage finds he can trivialize and detoxify the pain she represents. ("Being There")

Lesbians: In "The Dirty Joke," the sexual subculture Georgia erroneously fears that people—specifically Caroline Poop—think she belongs to because her voice is low. In "Pilot," women Ally respects but resents being assigned to smile at in order to land them as clients. In "The Playing Field," Fish claims lesbians teamed up with ugly women to initiate sexual-harassment legislation in America. And what Ally sometimes pretends to be to discourage conservative suitors who give her the Ick.

"Let's Get It On": Marvin Gaye song used by Cage to pump him up for maximum romance.

Lick Each Other's Tonsils: Ally's idea of how to while away the time with Dr. Greg Butters. ("Theme of Life")

Little Chuckie: The "dancing baby," as referred to by Dr. Tracy Clark. ("The Playing Field")

Little Huggy Bastard: The "dancing baby," as referred to by Ally. ("Forbidden Fruits")

Little Mr. Helmet Head: Ally's term for the dumb stick.

Lizard Lappers: Women with thin, dry lips, which Fish hates. ("Civil War")

Long John Silver: Elaine's name for Glenn, the nude sculpture model.

Lottery Ticket: What Ally compares her purchase of spermicide to when Billy rather annoyingly points out she's got no man to buy spermicide for in "100 Tears Away." Also, what two-ton attorney Harry Pippen compares his courtship of Ally to in "The Promise."

Lucky Underwear: What Ally wears for a date with Ray, prior to getting stuck in a toilet whose whooshing she finds embarrassingly pleasurable. ("Just Looking")

M

Michael: A name with sometimes porcine associations (though many Michaels are innocent). Michael is Renee's date-rape assailant, whom she kick-boxes in "The Inmates." Another Michael, a convict, pig-gishly asks Ally to model for him so he can go produce sperm to artificially inseminate his wife in "Body Language." The "big, fat hog" whose liver was implanted in the ungrateful Mrs. Goldstein by Dr. Greg Butters is also named Michael in "Theme of Life."

Millie: Nelle's beloved hamster gobbled by an Argentine Horned Frog in the trauma of her childhood, explaining her revulsion for frogs hopping out of toilets onto her. ("Story of Love")

Ms. Grab-the-Opposing-Counsel's-Butt: Ally's affectionate name for Georgia in "The Kiss." Let the record reflect that in "Cro-Magnon," Ally also grabbed a man's butt in court, her nineteen-year-old client Clint Gill, prior to kissing her teenage client Jason Tresham at Fenway Park. In "The Real World," Dr. Tracy sees nothing so abnormal about that—but then, she's a Menudo groupie.

N

Naked Nude Buttocks: The part of Whipper that Ling remembers vividly after walking in on Whipper nude in Fish's apartment when Whipper was making a last-ditch attempt to win Fish back. ("Worlds Without Love")

Naked Nude Woman Lighting a Fire: Whipper, as described by Ling, whose seduction technique involves lots of candles. ("Worlds Without Love")

99.6 Percent: How close Ally is to being over Billy near the end of her first year with Cage/Fish and Associates. ("Alone Again")

Nose Whistling: An affliction Cage has turned to his advantage, by using it to distract opponents in legal proceedings.

O

Orange: Among the skin colors U.S. law forbids discriminating against. A woman in "Happy" Boyle's court invokes this law, having gotten orange skin, possibly by eating too many carrots. ("Happy Trails")

P

Peck: Beyond intolerable if it's done by a man Ally wanted a full-on kiss from, like Cheanie. Dr. Greg Butters pecks both her cheek and her lips, indicating hesitant interest.

Penguin, the: The peculiar routine Ally and Renee have twice pulled on a man they want to get even with. It is an extreme measure involving luring him onto a deserted road on a chilly night, wooing him into dropping his pants to his ankles, and getting him to waddle toward one as one's friends observe via infrared binoculars while laughing. ("The Blame Game")

Penile Psychic: What Ling claims she is. ("Sideshow")

Perverted by Principle: What can happen to the legal system when nobody listens to Fish. ("The Blame Game")

Piece of Cute Meat, a: Ally's term for Cheanie, in defense of her right to kiss him, since a man would do the same thing if the situation were reversed. ("Compromising Positions")

Pillar of Dignity: What Cage promised Fish he would be when they started the firm, leaving it to Fish to be the shark/hammer/ass.

Pimple-Diminishing Needle: Elaine's device for shrinking—not popping—blemishes. Used before Ally's date with D.A. Jason Roberts in "The Attitude."

Pimple de Minimis: Elaine's quasi-legal term for a pimple after treatment by the pimple-diminishing needle. ("The Attitude")

Pips: Imaginary backup singers Dr. Tracy Clark urges Ally to conjure up whenever she needs confidence. It works. Try it at home, folks! ("The Playing Field")

Platonic Friendships: The best, according to Cage's lost law-school love Hayley, who, when they have a chance courtroom reunion, tells him her best relationship ever was her sexless one with Cage. And what's nonpareil about platonic friendships? "They don't disappoint." ("Alone Again")

Porcelain Skin: A shining attribute possessed by Cage's occasionally naked date Nelle and also by the toilets Cage so loves—which Fish thinks is no coincidence. ("Making Spirits Bright")

Potosin: What Ally wants a couple of shots of prior to giving birth, at her earliest opportunity.

Prostitute: A professional woman employed on occasion by Billy, Cage, "Happy" Boyle, and Dr. Carpenter. The careers chosen by the transvestite Stephanie and Whipper's pal Sandra Winchell, a former lawyer. What Ally sometimes fears the law turns one into, in a metaphorical sense.

Protective Evidentiary Retroactive Vici: The meaning of the legal acronym "PERV," as Fish tells Mark Henderson the foot fetishist, after Mark overhears Georgia call him a perv. "Vici" means "I conquered" in Latin, a quote from Julius Caesar. Fish claims it means the firm intends to win the case for Henderson. ("Happy Birthday, Baby")

Q

Qualified to Satisfy You: How Cage feels while singing Barry White. ("Only the Lonely")

R

Red Sox World Series Win: The thing Fish is waiting for to propose to Whipper, or anyone in "Body Language." In "Angels and Blimps," an event that would be a clear sign from God that He exists—but that would deprive us of the essence of God, the hope against hope.

Res Ipso de Facto Quid pro Quo E Pluribus Penis: Fish legal rule, roughly meaning: "Even if sexual-harassment laws clearly don't apply to my client, who was neither harassed nor offered any quid pro quo promotion, we should win because it's a male boss and if you squint and look at it really, really perversely, you can detect a faint resemblance between my client and the harassment victims the law *does* protect. Plus I really, really want to win." An extrapolation from the principle "Res Ipso Retainer." ("The Playing Field")

Res Ipso Retainer: Fish rule meaning "money talks," and any case involving same—even one without merit—has a cause of action worth acting on by Cage/Fish and Associates. ("Theme of Life")

Rude: What Ally feels Cheanie is in neglecting to grope her on a first date; what Georgia and Billy are for having a positive pregnancy test (false, as it turns out) when Ally isn't even married yet; what Greg is for bringing a date to a fake party Ally arranged purely to make Greg jealous of her date, a hired male escort.

Rudolph Red: Ally's facial shade upon being accused by Renee, Elaine, and Georgia of having had sex very recently. ("The Blame Game")

S

Seven: How many grandkids Ally and Billy envision themselves having. ("Sideshow")

$700: The price of missionary-position sex with lawyer-turned-lady-of-ill-repute Sandra Winchell. Deducted from his taxes by her client Dr. Carpenter as "stress therapy." ("The Promise")

Seventies Slut Rock: In Ally's opinion, the genre of music Elaine exemplifies while singing onstage at the Bar with the Ikette-like back-up group in "Silver Bells."

Sexual Object: What Ally says she is, dammit, when a man she wants doesn't treat her like one. ("The Kiss")

Sharif, Omar: Barbara Streisand's swain who comes out of nowhere and sweeps her off her feet in *Funny Girl*. Ally's metaphor for the man she's buying spermicide for, even though she has nobody to buy spermicide for. ("100 Tears Away")

Shark/Hammer/Ass: What Fish promised Cage he would be when they started the firm, leaving it to Cage to be the pillar of dignity. ("Compromising Positions")

Shoe Sniffing: Something Fish likes, though not nearly as much as wattle caressing.

Shoe Throwing: Something Georgia and Ally do when they get angry.

Sideless: What Ling calls herself when no one will take her side. ("Just Looking")

Sleep Over: When Ally and Renee spend the night in the same bed in their apartment. Signifies a rough time for the admirable supportiveness between Ally and Renee.

Smile Therapy: Cage's treatment to avoid a gloomy facial appearance. He claims (accurately) that some evidence suggests that the mere fact of flexing smile muscles tends to improve moods. Thus, when Cage is smiling, it is usually because something has upset him terribly and he's desperately trying to suppress emotions that cause most people to frown, or worse. The bigger the smile, the worse Cage feels. ("Body Language")

Smudge Plum: Makeup Ally shallowly claims to be deeply interested in when trying to convince Cage that she's not worth loving and that he should turn his bedroom eyes elsewhere. ("Once in a Lifetime")

Soot Gambit: Fish's little stratagem to trick women such as Attorney General Reno into permitting him to caress their wattles unawares. He tells them they have soot on their necks, and sometimes they buy it.

Southern Compass: Fish's word for a dumb stick. ("Only the Lonely")

Soybean: One of Fish's food names for Ling ("You Never Can Tell"); food that caused an allergic reaction in childhood apparently making Cage hallucinate Pinocchio ("Making Spirits Bright")

Spit the Hook: In Fish's lexicon, to dump a girlfriend if you're a guy or a law firm if you're a rich client.

Squat and Gobble: Strip joint featuring men. ("Just Looking")

Stand to Be Disparaged: Something nobody at Cage/Fish and Associates will do when caught in an embarrassing act. Cage coined the phrase.

Stepford Girl: Ally's phrase for women less difficult than she is.

Stink Sticks: Ally's word for cigars.

Stupid Fashion People: The sinister, all-powerful people who force women to wear ridiculous shoes, causing them—specifically, Ally—to fall down all the time. ("Theme of Life")

T

Thanksgiving: A horrible holiday. What's worse? "Knowing Christmas comes next," according to Ally. ("You Never Can Tell")

Thirty: In "Body Language," the age at which a woman will marry a jerk out of panic. Also, in "Happy Birthday, Baby," the age when one's face starts to crack. When Ally was fifteen, she'd look at people who were thirty and think, "Die, already!"

Thirty-five: The age after which Cage feels bold enough to take matters—that is, Nelle—in hand.

3.2 Times a Month: How often Georgia and Billy make love—always on Tuesdays and Thursdays. Until she starts greeting him in the nude wearing very pricey shoes. ("The Affair")

Twenty-eight: A horrible age for a birthday, because it's two years from thirty. ("Happy Birthday, Baby")

Two: Number of good men per state, according to a magazine article Ally read.

Two Cartons of Vanilla Ice Cream: Ally's antidote to the upsetting news that the sight of her teaching Georgia how to turn morning coffee into a quasi-orgasmic experience reminds Billy of what orgasms with Ally were like and of the painful fact that he and Ally used to gaze into each other's eyes during sex but he and Georgia don't. In another episode, Renee muses, "Who needs a man when we've got ice cream?"

Two-Thirds of a Rice Krispie: Elaine's definition of Ally as a candidate for the laughing academy: "She's already snapped and crackled—and she's close to the final pop." ("100 Tears Away")

U

Unpure Sexual Thoughts: What Ally has about her sweet, emotionally mature teenage client Jason Tresham, who gets to first base with Ally at Fenway Park. ("The Real World")

Uppity Breasts: What Ally accuses Elaine of having. ("Drawing the Lines")

V

Vacuum Effect: Elaine's practiced technique for removing excess saliva from a man during a kiss without anyone being the wiser. ("Once in a Lifetime")

Vietnam: What even the most nutritious vegetable can turn into if stuck between your teeth without vigilant dental care, in Judge "Happy" Boyle's opinion. ("These Are the Days")

W

Wacko: What Billy calls Ally when he's mad at her; what Dr. Tracy thinks all her patients are, but hey, it heats her pool. The word, however, offends Dr. Peters, the therapist for ax murderer Marie Hanson—perhaps because he's wacko, too.

What Women Want: "Not only are we wired to want what we can't have, we're wired to want what we really don't want," says Ally to Whipper in "Worlds Without Love." Then again, Ally says in "Sideshow," "I don't want what I want and I want what I don't want. And to complicate it even more right now, I don't know what I want or don't want."

World's Naughtiest Confessions: Father O'Riley's future show on Fox (right between *The Oral Office* and *Deadliest Car Crashes*), which will consist of his tapes of what people said to him in confession. Ally is one of his stars. ("Worlds Without Love")

Z

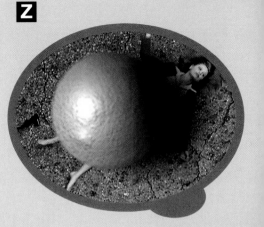

X

Y

Yappers: The theory that talking about heartbreak makes you feel better was, in Cage's opinion, "made up by a bunch of yappers." When Hayley breaks Cage's heart, the last thing he wants is to talk about it with Ally, the last woman who broke his heart. But he appreciates her yapper's sympathy. ("Alone Again")

Yoda: What some called Judge "Happy" Boyle behind his back. ("Happy Trails")

Yuletide Catnip: How Renee refers to Cage at a dance party at the Bar. It must be the mistletoe talking. Mistletoe has great powers in Ally's world.

season
TWO

TITLE	EPISODE #	FIRST AIRED
THE REAL WORLD	201	09/14/98
THEY EAT HORSES, DON'T THEY?	202	09/21/98
FOOLS NIGHT OUT	203	09/28/98
IT'S MY PARTY	204	10/19/98
STORY OF LOVE	205	10/26/98
WORLDS WITHOUT LOVE	207	11/02/98
HAPPY TRAILS	208	11/09/98
JUST LOOKING	209	11/16/98
YOU NEVER CAN TELL	206	11/23/98
MAKING SPIRITS BRIGHT	210	12/14/98
IN DREAMS	211	01/11/99
LOVE UNLIMITED	212	01/18/99
ANGELS & BLIMPS	213	02/08/99
PYRAMIDS ON THE NILE	214	02/15/99
SIDESHOW	215	02/22/99
SEX, LIES, AND POLITICS	216	03/01/99
CIVIL WARS	217	04/05/99
THOSE LIPS, THAT HAND	218	04/19/99
LET'S DANCE	219	04/26/99
ONLY THE LONELY	220	05/03/99
THE GREEN MONSTER	221	05/10/99
LOVE'S ILLUSIONS	222	05/17/99
I KNOW HIM BY HEART	223	05/24/99

the REAL world

written by David E. Kelley, **directed by** Jonathan Pontell

THE BRIEF: The firm defends a woman who, at thirty-seven, fell in love with a sixteen-year-old boy. Now he's a smart, sensitive, adorable eighteen, and he incites several women to urgently consider issues of romance and the tyranny of time. Cage and Fish hire a new attorney, the icy blond bombshell Nelle Porter, not a popular choice with the women.

It's tough to say which is more provocative, the firm's case or its new employee, the hot young lawyer Nelle Porter. Like Cage, she's been hailed in *Boston* magazine as a rising star. She's also the most stunning physical specimen anyone at Cage/Fish has ever laid eyes on. When Cage says "she's got serious porta-

bles," he refers to the big-bucks clients she'll bring to the firm and also to the fact that whenever he looks at her, he hears the "bomp-bomp-bomp, bomp-bomp-ba-bomp" opening bars of "You Can't Hurry Love."

Elaine explains to Ally, "Richard's looking for a rain-maker" (as Cage has also been described.) "She looks like she makes sleet," Ally snaps. Her nickname is "Sub-Zero Nelle."

Nelle may frost Ally, but the case of Laura Jewell and Jason Tresham has her all steamy—and she's not alone. Probably every woman in the courtroom responds to Laura's plight. There she was, a divorcée dining alone, and her charming teenage waiter asks why she's so sad. From her demeanor, Laura seemed more than just lonely, Jason testifies. She seemed to know too much: "That some people find love permanent. And some are just meant to be alone."

This hits Ally hard, as when Laura muses that "things die in men as they get older. They lose the essence of the very thing a woman wants most...simple intimacy. He made me feel as if I were flying and falling all at once." Jason isn't just a symbol of young virility. Laura and the wise-beyond-his-years Jason describe a brief relationship of tender mutual fulfillment without a hint of exploitation. It ended with no regrets on either side.

Ally has impure thoughts about Jason—they've even had premonitory dreams about each other. She asks Dr. Tracy and Renee for advice. They point out that for Ally, true love signifies what she and Billy knew in their youth. "This kid can be some kind of lifeline to innocence," Renee says. "Ally, for you puppy love is the best kind just because all men are dogs."

Jason understands. "It was some kind of reunion with fun you had before," he says perceptively. "Got you to first base, anyway," he jokes. They kiss good-bye. Love need not be permanent to be true.

 OPPOSITE: Sub-Zero Nelle. LEFT: Dr. Tracy advises Ally. BELOW: Renee prosecutes Ally's clients. BOTTOM: Fish and Cage at the end of the day.

When men age, they start putting career pragmatism ahead of romance.

"I just want to remember a little," Ally says.

Laura's prosecutor, Renee, derides the double standard: If Laura's and Jason's sexes were reversed, it would be a slam-dunk conviction. "When a man cheats, he's a bum, but a woman, she's just bridging her little Madison County." Cage counters by defending the lovers and referring to the love affair presented in the film *Summer of '42*, and the jury votes with its heart. Later Cage tells Ally that his passion for Nelle is worth it even if he loses.

Jason, who also feels it's better to have loved and lost than never to have loved at all, wins Ally's heart by sneaking her into Fenway Park after hours, where they reenact Carleton Fisk's immortal 1975 home run. "They lost the seventh game," Ally reminisces, "but still. . . ." Ally gently refuses Jason's romantic overtures.

▶ **SONG LIST:**

"In the Real World"
"You Can't Hurry Love"

"Tonight's the Night"
"Just What I Needed"

they eat horses, DON'T THEY?

written by David E. Kelley, **directed by** Mel Damski

▶▶

THE BRIEF: Radio/TV shock jock Harold Wick is sued by Nelle's client Ling Woo for creating hostile, sexually charged work environments. Cage defends a restauranteur being sued for serving horse meat. The plaintiffs found it delicious until they found out what it was.

Into the firm swoops a new beauty: Ling Woo, Nelle's first big client. Ling is taking on toilet-mouthed radio personality Harold Wick, and it's a legal long shot. Ling manages a steel plant "dominated by male workers with the IQ of meat," as Nelle puts it. If the plant's owner had been subjecting employees to Wick's crude woman-bashing show via loudspeakers on the job, he could easily be sued. But Woo—whose brusque manner makes Nelle look like America's Sweetheart—is suing Wick because the men she supervises listen to him in their *off* hours and then come to work and behave badly. Nelle says Wick is "contributing to an atmosphere of gender bias."

Cage takes a meaty case. Joseph Handy's eatery serves horses as cuisine, and two nauseated diners are suing. "Couldn't you just say 'neigh'?" Cage asks the diners. But they'd ordered in French. Secretly the case troubles Cage, a devoted Mr. Ed fan. He asks his client Handy about the venerated status of horses in our culture. "What if Elizabeth Taylor ate her horse in *National Velvet*?"

"Are you sure she didn't?" Handy retorts.

Nelle walks in on Cage in his office preparing his summation. "Have you ever had horse meat?" asks Cage. "Thanks, but I've already had dinner," Nelle says. "I'm free Thursday night. How about Thursday?" Cage inadvertently gets a dream date with Nelle, but it's clear who's holding the reins as this relationship goes out of the gate.

More shocking than Wick's shock-jock program is the judge's ruling on Ling's case. Buying Nelle's argument that products like cigarettes are being held responsible for their impact, he says, "Bottom line, when it's foreseeable that the product you put out there can cause harm, liability is right around the corner. Lawsuits have already been brought against Hollywood movies. The talk show—it's likely to be next."

👫 **ABOVE:** Georgia and Cage defend the equine-cuisine king Mr. Handy. **BELOW:** Ally appears on Wick's shock-jock radio show. **OPPOSITE:** Cage contemplates his childhood stuffed animal, a horse named Frawley; Cage copes with old emotions.

Then comes another shock: Ling drops the case and proves she's got more legal horse sense than Fish and company. She knows they'd lose on appeal and won't get a dime, so she hits Wick where it hurts. He'd made an offensive joke to the firm's women about having just taken Viagra, so Ling tells the media that she's dropping the case because—she strongly implies—Wick is impotent. Ling knows Wick can't prove reckless disregard for the truth, and because he's a public figure, he has no libel case. Mortified by Ling's dirty tactics, Ally agrees to be a guest on Wick's radio show.

Cage wins the Handy case by noting that horses have no rights. "The Constitution doesn't start out 'We the horses.'" Plus, if horse meat is outlawed, burgers will be next, and burgers are an American institution.

Everybody celebrates with a dance at the Bar. "You can't deny you're having fun," Fish says to Ling, lusting.

"Yes, I can," says Ling. But she can't. She's smiling. Nelle and Ling are now full-fledged members of the firm's family.

SONG LIST:

♪ "Will You Marry Me?"
"What Kind of Fool Do You think I Am" ♪
♪ "Mr. Ed Theme Song"

FOOLS
night out

written by David E. Kelley, **directed by** Peter MacNicol

▶▶

THE BRIEF: Ling sues the nurse in the office where her sister went to have breast implants. The firm tackles the dilemma of a minister whose dynamite choir singer is singing the blues instead of the hymns she's supposed to be singing, because she's angry that the minister has dumped her. Ally learns a stunning fact about Billy and Georgia's past.

Ling has come up with another perverse lawsuit, and it's a doozy. Her sister got breast implants that didn't work out, and Ling wants to sue—not the doctor who performed the operation, but the nurse whose beautiful breasts the doctor falsely suggested were the result of his implant surgery. In fact, the nurse's breasts were all natural. The incompetent doctor went bankrupt, and since the nurse has family money, Ling wants to go after it.

"You're suing a woman because her breasts are real?" says the irritated Georgia.

"When you say it in a tone like *that*, of course it's going to sound silly," says Ling.

Ling's unpopularity among the firm's women is getting worse. Elaine rather naughtily suggests that Ling's bad mood could have a simple explanation: "Maybe her gynecologist pulled the wrong tooth."

Fish gets an emergency call from Newman, his minister friend. Newman had an affair with Lisa, the best singer in his choir—the one who sang "Short People" for Fish's uncle's funeral. He broke up with her, and now she's singing lovelorn songs like Al Green's "I'm So Tired of Bein' Alone" in church, songs of heartbreak and rebuke directed right at the minister, who won't talk to her about why he dumped her. Newman is afraid of firing her because it would look like retaliation.

Ally and Renee attend a service and stand up for Lisa's songs, which ring true. They're tired of bein' alone themselves. But when Lisa angrily follows Newman's sermon on world peace with the Randy Newman tune about the A-bomb that goes, "Let's drop the big one now," Ally admits that Lisa has some personal issues to resolve. Newman explains to Lisa that he realized that she could never be the passion of his life, giving her a painful sense of closure.

In talking it over with Lisa, Ally gets a jolt of the same emotion. It dawns on her that Billy didn't transfer from Harvard to Michigan just for career reasons—he went to shed Ally. "He met somebody who was at Michigan—he met you," Ally tells Georgia. It's all true. Ally feels that her dream of ideal love—based on her memories of Billy—was a fraud all along. That may not be quite fair or factual, but it's intensely how she feels.

The lawyers and Ling compare her sister's implanted breasts with the nurse's au naturel pair. Unable to bear the nonsense anymore, Georgia calls a halt to the case. Ling is furious. Nelle tells Ling that she's provoking fights to make her unpopularity less painful. Fish tells Ling he does the same thing and asks her out. She starts to thaw and become more human—or at least more Fishlike.

Ally walks home alone.

👫 OPPOSITE: Choir member Lisa sings songs of rebuke to Reverend Newman, the minister who dumped her. ABOVE RIGHT: Fish and Cage in deep discussion. BELOW: Purely for professional purposes, Billy makes a close inspection to determine whether breast implants can be distinguished from all-natural breasts.

SONG LIST:

♪ "Maryland"
"You Can't Hurry Love" ♪
♪ "What a Friend We Have in Jesus"
"You're the First, the Last, My ♪
♪ Everything"
"Tired of Being Alone" ♪
♪ "Political Science"
"Fools Fall in Love" ♪

it's MY party

written by David E. Kelley, **directed by** Jace Alexander

THE BRIEF: Elaine's boyfriend George Madison, a Baptist who serves as editor of a women's magazine, is fired because a Southern Baptist Church advocates the subordination of women to men. Even though Madison doesn't share this view, his publisher won't stand for being associated with such antifeminism. Madison catches Ally's eye. A judge rules against Ally's skirt.

Elaine introduces the firm to her best catch yet, magazine editor George Madison, and to her best invention yet, condoms with slogans on them. She gives personalized samples to everyone, with an apt saying for each: Fish ("Bygones"), Nelle ("Caution: Frostbite"), Cage ("Enjoy the Moment"), etc. Elaine's says, "Come Here Often?" and her boyfriend George gets two: "Been There" and later "Reinstate Me" (George is suing to get reinstated as editor).

The pained look on George's face when she presents him with lewd-logo condoms is bad news for Elaine. So is the look on Ally's face when she spills the foam from her cappucino on George's tie. Infatuated, Ally watches him walk away.

But the case goes well. "How can you have an editor of a feminist magazine who believes a woman's place is in the home?" demands the publication's attorney. Ally says George advocates total equality. "And if a Klan member tells me he personally has nothing against blacks, forgive my cynicism," says the publisher, Catherine Hollings. The judge rules that she's infringing religious freedom. George gets his job back. And the judge tells Ally, who's defied his ban on miniskirts in the courtroom, that she'll go to jail if she doesn't apologize.

"You're a pig," Ally tells the judge. But if she's about to spend the night in jail, she'll miss the big party she'd planned for her colleagues at her apartment. Nelle speaks up for Ally, protesting "the myth that a sexually attractive woman can't have credibility." Ally won the case, after all! Does her skirt silence her argument? Nelle lets her Niagara Falls–like hair down and flings a few clothes off in a restrained rhetorical striptease. "It's bad enough the legal profession is still an old boys' club—why should we have to come in here looking like old boys?" Nelle demands.

Nelle has saved the day—and night. Ally's party has a bad patch when the chat turns into a bitter and character-revealing debate about sex-role stereotypes. Fish pitches woo to Ling, who takes command by giving him a first kiss he won't forget. Everyone starts to dance, everyone's happy.

And then, while Diana Ross sings "Someday We'll Be Together," Ally's eyes lock on George's across the floor. Lyrics are invariably significant on this show. Will Ally and George wind up together?

SONG LIST:

"Just My Imagination"
"Someday We'll Be Together"
"Maryland"
"Superfreak"
"Please, Mr. Postman"
"Going the Distance"
"Double Shot of My Baby's Love"
"Desert Flower"
"Neither One of Us"
"War"

OPPOSITE BOTTOM: Ally's defiantly short skirt lands her in jail. **ABOVE:** Ally discovers that George and Elaine are a couple. **TOP RIGHT:** Ally defends herself in court. **RIGHT:** Ally in the kitchen at her party.

"*The world is no longer a romantic place; some of its people still are, however, and therein lies the promise. Don't let the world win.*"

—JOHN CAGE

story of LOVE

written by David E. Kelley, **directed by** Tom Moore

THE BRIEF: Ally inadvertently acquires a client who's being sued for dumping her best friend in a trash bin after the girl stole her boyfriend. Ally is of course on the verge of stealing Elaine's boyfriend. And Cage's beloved pet tree frog meets with a horrid fate in the Unisex.

Ally tries to help a girl crying in the street; the girl snarls that she's crying because her doctor just diagnosed her with "acute courtesy disorder," which peeves Ally so much she gets in a fight with her. Both wind up in jail. Ally volunteers to represent the girl, Hannah, to avoid being sued by her.

Elaine's intended, George Madison, visits the firm to get help setting up a new magazine he's launching. He asks for Ally; Elaine steers him toward Richard or Nelle instead because Ally doesn't handle that kind of work. He sneakily goes to Ally anyway. Elaine starts to get the scary picture.

So does Ally, especially when George confesses it's all a ruse—he really just came to court Ally. "You're Elaine's boyfriend, that's the end of story," says Ally. They barely miss being overheard by Elaine.

Hannah's friend Laura says she was never more mortified than when Hannah chucked her in the Dumpster.

"Suddenly she just grabs me by the hair," says Laura. "She's always been jealous of it."

"Oh, right!" says Hannah.

"She comes down on me like one of those pro wrestlers. Three broken ribs. She's picking me up, saying stuff like 'Time to take out the garbage.'"

"Your good friend . . . tells you she's in love with the guy she's seeing. Then *you* begin to see him," Ally cross-examines Laura. "That trash can she threw you into—did it fit?"

"For me to be even able to lift her shows I had to be on some adrenaline explosion," Hannah testifies. "She weighs at least twenty-five pounds more than me."

"*Objection!* My client would like that stricken," Laura's lawyer shouts.

Meanwhile, a more fatal violent event strikes the Unisex. Cage's pride and joy, his trained tree frog, Stefan, pays dearly for his habit of hanging around Cage's favorite toilet seat. (Evidently he shares his master's fondness for a clean bowl.) Stefan has been freaking out the firm's females in particular, and when he hops into the bowl to escape the panicky humans and Cage punches his remote flusher, poor Stefan is whisked away. They keep the news from Cage as long as they can, but ultimately there's nothing for it but a confession.

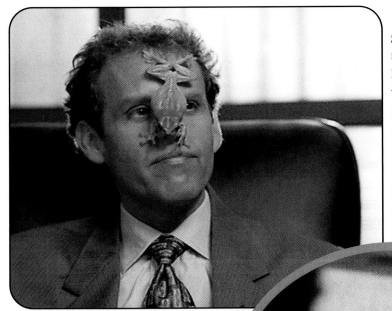

Stefan's death, gives Cage a replacement frog. "You're a kind person, Nelle," says Cage. So is Ally.

👫 OPPOSITE (top to bottom): Hannah and Ally's meeting has consequences for everyone; Ally and George lock eyes as Elaine looks on. LEFT and BELOW: Stefan the frog. BOTTOM: Cage consoles Ally.

Renee urges Ally to go for George. "Boyfriends don't get taken. People find each other. Sometimes there's a bump involved."

Elaine feels otherwise. "You can have any man you want, Ally. Please don't take mine."

Laura wins her case, and Hannah has to pay one dollar in damages. Laura gets the boyfriend. Hannah asks, "Can we get the court to order her to give him back?"

George begs Ally to go with her heart. He and Elaine aren't exclusive anyway, and they're just not meant to be. But Ally stays true to friendship above love. Nelle, who's most responsible for

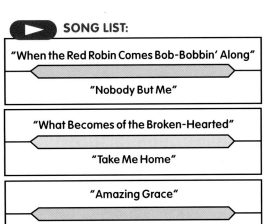

▶ SONG LIST:

"When the Red Robin Comes Bob-Bobbin' Along"

"Nobody But Me"

"What Becomes of the Broken-Hearted"

"Take Me Home"

"Amazing Grace"

153

worlds WITHOUT love

written by David E. Kelley, **directed by** Arvin Brown

THE BRIEF: Cage and Ally defend a nun who got the boot for dating a priest. Renee runs into her "Billy"—the love of her life, now married to someone else. Georgia has a close encounter with Cage's miraculously resurfacing frog, and Ling has a fiery faceoff with Whipper.

A pretty nun named Chrissa retains the firm to get her old job back after she's sacked for getting a man of the cloth— the saintly Father Peter— repeatedly unclothed. "Nuns

aren't supposed to have sex," Ally tells her. "Except, you know,...with other nuns." Cage agrees to take the case but has his doubts. "It would be a total Hail Mary [as in a desperate last-ditch play in football]."

Chrissa suffers on the cross-examination. "If a priest has sex with a boy, he gets transferred," Chrissa snaps. "Me they fire. At least my lover was of legal age, for God's sakes!" Cage protests that his opponent somehow hoodwinked Chrissa into this

inadvisable statement. "This man is an anti-Catholic papal bigot trickster!"

Poor Georgia hears bubbling while seated on the toilet. As she is standing to look, up pops Stefan, Cage's talented frog, landing on her nose. She hurls him at Nelle; they "Koufax" him back and forth until the unsuspecting Fish opens a stall, and splat! Poor Stefan slides slowly down the door to the floor, comatose. Cage walks in, but Elaine hides Stefan in her bosom and walks out. Later Fish brilliantly bamboozles Cage. "It's a miracle!"—Stefan has resurfaced, alive! In a coma, but alive!

Renee bumps into her old flame Matt. His marriage is rocky, and he wants to reheat things between them. Ally's vote is a big no, but we've never seen Renee this tugged and tormented by love.

Ally tries to talk Sister Helen, Chrissa's boss, into rehiring her. "It's not easy to leave a man. I assume

you've never been in her positions—*position*," Ally says. Worldly-wise, Sister Helen says she could forgive the sex but not the cover-up, and Chrissa only quit seeing Peter because he dumped her.

As she's leaving Helen, a conflicted Ally steps into the con-

fessional and tells the priest about the guilt she feels about her one-night stand with Glenn. "I often hear size doesn't matter," the priest says. "How was it?"

series, *World's Naughtiest Confessions*. Ally's confessor, too, alas.

The episode ends on a mournful note. Cage grieves—sincerely—over Stefan. Whipper deals with the sad reality that her affair with Fish is bygone at last. Most poignantly, Renee reflects on Matt, the lost love of her life.

👫 OPPOSITE LEFT: Cage is puzzled by Elaine's chest, which secretly hides his comatose frog Stefan. OPPOSITE RIGHT: Renee takes a sentimental journey back to her first love. OPPOSITE BOTTOM: Stefan on life support. ABOVE: Whipper takes Ally's advice and waits for Fish at his apartment. RIGHT: Ally turns white—her recent confession to Father O'Riley is destined for primetime TV.

"Unbelievable, you have no idea!" Ally replies. "I mean I *assume* you don't. Am I forgiven?"

Ally will also need forgiveness because she's told Whipper that she'd better make a surprise play for Fish real soon or lose him to his new romance. So when Fish at last gets Ling into his apartment, Ling is confronted with Whipper in the raw, lighting candles to set a romantic mood. Both women scream. In the morning, Ling tries to get Nelle to sue Fish for "intentional infliction of emotional distress. . . . I open a door and see naked nude buttocks!"

Nelle declines, so Ling goes shopping. Sister Helen rehires Chrissa. It turns out Chrissa confessed to Father O'Riley, who's been secretly videotaping confessions for his upcoming Fox TV

SONG LIST:

♪ "Crying"
"Looking for Something" ♪
♪ "Operator"
"A Love So Beautiful" ♪
♪ "World Without Love"

happy TRAILS

written by David E. Kelley, **directed by** Jonathan Pontell

THE BRIEF: Cage gears up for a serious kiss with Nelle. Ally is plagued with a karaoke-singing date who won't take a get-lost hint. The firm takes up the cause of civil rights for people of color—orange, to be precise.

Ally's morning starts off with a bad surprise, too. Ross "Fitzy" Fitzsimmons pops in with a fistful of flowers and asks Elaine where "Alison" is. "Bad date, last night, get rid of him quick!" Ally says, and dives behind a desk. Elaine says Ally's dead. "Is that her leg?" Fitzy asks. Elaine says it's a recent murder, the cops are en route with their chalk. Fitzy touches Ally's leg, eliciting a yelp of life. Desperate but resourceful, Elaine plants a big wet kiss on Ally to make Fitzy think Ally doesn't date men.

"I'm not falling for that lesbian trick," Fitzy says. "Do you think you're the first woman I've ever courted who's pretended to be either dead or gay?" Ally agrees to a second date, a karaoke experience she won't forget.

Cage drops in on Fish—while Fish is in a Unisex stall. "I'm fraught," says Cage. "You told me how Ling placed so much import on the first kiss. I'm concerned Nelle may do the same."

"John, you're in my stall."

"What were Ling's instructions, specifically?" Fish, a real pal, gives Cage some detailed kiss tips. "Look at us," Fish chuckles, "all this anxiety over a first kiss, in the bathroom like a couple of teenagers. Gay teenagers, my pants are down."

Nelle and Elaine enter the Unisex and overhear the lesson with great delight. The *Rocky* bells are of course the show's audio symbol of imminent triumph in life and love. When Fish says, "Bells—do you hear them?" Nelle and Elaine pipe up that they sure do. "It was wrong to have popped in," mutters a mortified Cage.

Ally's karaoke date with Fitzy comes to an equally dismal end, but he just won't admit defeat. In a fantasy sequence, he keeps clinging to a Dumpster. At last Fitzy does the Dumpster dive and Ally is free.

Walking Cage to his door, Nelle finally seizes the moment and gives him a major kiss. He struts his stuff down the street to the soulful styling of Barry White.

The case of the week involves a woman who lost her job for being orange. Maybe she ate too many carrots, maybe it's a sun reaction, but she's orange and out of a job. Judge Boyle muses that he'd always expected aliens to come demanding civil rights, but he'd figured they'd be green. "People sometimes think I'm an alien," he says. "Behind my back they call me Yoda. I try to rise above it." But the trial is interrupted by Boyle's sudden death.

Most of the firm's members, Stefan in tow, hear the bad news while at a Chinese restaurant. Cage, sensing Stefan's hunger, sends him to the kitchen for a snack fit for a frog. In Chinese Ling tells the waiter to get some lettuce for the frog. Much later, Ling and the waiter have a heated conversation, and she has an announcement: "The bad news is, Stefan is back. The good news is, he's delicious."

SONG LIST:

♪ *"Gimme Dat Thing"*
"Going the Distance" ♪
♪ *"Miss Gulch's Theme"*
"Puppy Love" ♪
♪ *"You're the First, the Last, My Everything"*
"Finale from Pippin" ♪

JUST looking

written by Shelly Landau & David E. Kelley, directed by Vince Misiano

THE BRIEF: Ling's mud-wrestling club is targeted by antismut activists. Elaine's new toilet-seat invention backfires, trapping Ally. Georgia wrestles with perilous emotions stirred up by an old boyfriend.

If Cage is sometimes "fraught," Ling is positively "overwrought." A group called MOPE (Mothers Opposed to Pornographic Entertainment) is trying to close down Ling's mud-wrestling club on the theory that it destroys the peace and quiet of the community with a lot of filth. There's no porn, actually—the women wear wholesome bathing suits. Fish assigns the women to represent Ling, while he and Cage infiltrate the club.

"I'm actually a good spy," Cage surprisingly divulges. "I briefly considered a career in the CIA. I have an ability to glide through a room unnoticed." He enters the mud club in a trench coat, to the tune of "Secret Agent Man," but soon he's as mud-splattered as Fish, who hops right into the ring with a lithesome wrestler named Jennifer.

Elaine invents a toilet-seat warmer ("I like a warm seat") that also has a remote control to flip the seat up and down, to prevent marital argu-

ments. Inevitably, Cage later hits his remote, flipping the seat up just as Ally is sitting down. Wedged inside the toilet bowl, she requires firemen to rescue her.

One further misfortune is that Georgia has fixed Ally up with her old boyfriend Ray, with whom she went out the week before she met Billy. The toilet contretemps embarrasses Ally, but she's also deeply concerned about Georgia's still simmering feelings for Ray.

"Sometimes I wonder . . . if we'd had *two* dates before you met him," Ray tells Georgia. "You ever wonder?" Billy walks in before Georgia can get an answer out.

Ling and Nelle debate whether Ling's club degrades women. "These women make nearly $100,000 a year!" Ling argues. "These Neanderthal drunken idiots hurl money at them. I'd defy anybody to go into that club and come out with a higher opinion of men than women." Ling's bottom line: "Sex is a weapon. We all use it. We tease, we tantalize. . . . God gave us that advantage by giving man the dumb stick."

Raymond is arguing MOPE's case. He cross-examines Ling: "Are you going to deny that women are being exploited in your club?"

"Women are exploited by the high heel shoe!" Ling says. "If anything, we should be glad to have my club, because *we* exploit *men*. In my club, the

In a tense finale, Raymond and Georgia get into an elevator alone. He stops the elevator and asks for one kiss—the kiss they never got to experience—"Under the heading that it will go nowhere." Georgia falters, then snaps the elevator back on. She is definitely a look-before-you-leap kind of person, and this is one big jump she's not ready for. She will learn, sooner than she suspects, how life-shaking a simple kiss can be. But is there any harm in just looking?

👨👩 OPPOSITE (left): Incognito, Cage infiltrates the mud-wrestling club. OPPOSITE (right): One of the club's wrestlers. ABOVE and BELOW: Trapped. Fire department to the rescue. RIGHT: Georgia is tempted by an old flame.

women basically control the dumb stick and take the men's money." The judge reluctantly rules that the club represents the community's standards all too well.

Ally, feeling defensive about Billy's interests and worried about Georgia's marriage, accuses her of carrying a torch for Raymond. Georgia basically replies that there's no harm done. "Billy going off to look at mud wrestlers—that would be less of an offense than what's going on here," Ally says.

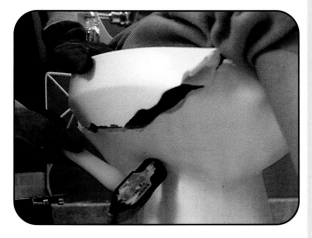

▶ SONG LIST:

"Secret Agent Man"

"Foolish Little Girl"

"One Fine Day"

"Hawaii Five-O Theme"

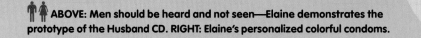
ABOVE: Men should be heard and not seen—Elaine demonstrates the prototype of the Husband CD. RIGHT: Elaine's personalized colorful condoms.

ELAINE, mother of invention

Elaine is not content merely to be the most efficient legal secretary in Boston; she wants to make her mark, for the purest possible motive: so that she'll be rich and famous, and men will line up to sleep with her.

In every situation, Elaine evinces an amazing can-do mindset. If there's a stage to be constructed to convert the office into a music hall for the Christmas show, she's got the drill and the skills for the job. If there's an office secret that needs detection and promulgation, she's got the firm's phones tapped and powerful directional microphones to snoop behind doors snappishly slammed in her nosy face. If Cage needs to solve his excess saliva secretion condition in time to kiss Ally, Elaine has the Vacuum Kiss technique, capable of turning any mouth into a slobber-removal device.

It is at the patent office, however, that Elaine most nobly demonstrates her inventive nature. Here are a few of her bright ideas to make the world a better place, or at least a better story.

THE HUSBAND CD

When Cage/Fish gets retained by Mary Halliday, who is suing her fiancé for standing her up on their wedding day, Elaine tries to soothe Mary's emotions by demonstrating with the Husband CD that she hasn't missed much. "I want you to know I share your pangs of loneliness," Elaine says, promising relief via her invention. This CD offers the entire soundtrack of a "fulfilling" marriage: the husband snoring every night by your side, flipping a newspaper's pages at breakfast, wheezing in decrepit sexual ecstasy at age sixty.

The Husband CD also offers alternate tracks, such as one titled "Him Listening to You the First Year" (a few seconds of silence) followed by "Him Listening to You Every Year After That" (the din of a football game). On one track, the audio bride can savor the sound of the virtual husband passing gas.

"Some of it's coarse," Elaine admits to a horrified Mary, "but it *is* a marriage."

ICE GOGGLES

Sick and tired of waking up looking sick and tired, particularly the morning after you get dumped shortly before your terrifying thirtieth birthday? Do tea bags pressed against your eyeballs fail to perk up your swollen morning face, which Elaine thinks is a particularly puffy, disgusting sight when you're retaining water? Then you need Elaine's Ice Goggles, which are ordinary spectacles, except that the frames are one-inch-thick packs of transparent ice. Elaine is a woman not only of passion but also of vision.

THE FACE BRA

Plenty of women fret about breast droop and sagging cheeks, but only Elaine has the insight to go beyond the pushup bra and the face lift. Voilà! The Face Bra employs a few well-placed wraps

of fabric to transform a woman's look from "Driving Miss Daisy" to "The Invisible Man." Strap it on and wrinkles are history. Not only does the invention prevent up-and-down wear and tear of delicate tissues but it minimizes blemishes by obscuring most of one's face with handsome bandages.

Hey, it doesn't look any sillier than Ally's and Renee's facial peels. And it accomplishes much the same thing: a tradeoff of humiliation today to keep the ravages of tomorrow at bay.

Elaine only calls it the Face Bra to get the concept across to investors. Once her infomercial is funded (by Ling), Elaine plans to start marketing it under the catchy ad line "The Mask—for women on the run."

THE COOL CUP

When Billy and Georgia experience a pregnancy that turns out to be a mirage, Elaine has a hot flash of inspiration. "Heat kills sperm cells," she says, with scientific accuracy. "With refrigeration, men can actually stay more virile." Most health authorities think it's enough to avoid tight underwear and excessive bicycle riding, but Elaine takes testicular heat minimization to its logical extreme in the Cool Cup, a conventional athletic protective jock strap equipped with a minifridge connected to the wall with an extension cord. She gets the reluctant Cage to model it in the office.

Elaine recognizes that the need for proximity to a wall socket might hinder some men's active lifestyles. But as soon as she gets funding, she'll finish the power pack that will free men to roam wherever Cupid calls.

Is that cool, or what? Cage thinks it's very cool. "Please turn it down some," he pleads in a still, small voice.

AUTOMATIC TOILET SEAT WARMER/ FLUSHER/FLIPPER

Not everyone shares Cage's obsession with a fresh bowl, but a toilet seat that won't give one's butt frostbite is something everyone welcomes, hence Elaine's remote-controlled gizmo to heat up the seat to any preset temperature preference. The remote wand also boasts an autoflush function and a seat-flip switch that gives women whose men always forget to put the seat down a high-tech alternative to murder. Alas, a misfire of the seat-flip feature traps Ally between the seat and the bowl, wedging her butt so firmly that firemen must be called to free her.

you NEVER can tell

written by David E. Kelley, **directed by** Adam Nimoy

THE BRIEF: Ling sues one of her employees at the steel plant for having impure thoughts about her. Ally represents Ling—unfortunately, with a bowling ball stuck on her finger. Cage freaks out over Nelle's improbable impure thoughts involving him. His colleagues try to help and only make matters worse.

Litigious Ling decides to take sexual-harassment law to a bold new frontier, suing one of her employees for "ooglement"—eyeing her at work—and for his thoughts. "He goes, 'Hello,' and he shoots me groin-motivated looks," Ling testifies. She can't fire him, because he's a union member. When his attorney asks if anyone else can attest to the "ooglement," Ling says, "They're all union, they stick together." Not only that, the man says her name, "Woo," in a way that she takes as a pun on the "post-coital 'Whew!'"

Fish usually likes an outrageous case, but this one's too out there even for him. In imploring her not to pursue an unwinnable lawsuit, Fish calls her "sweetheart." Ling orders him not to call her that, because she's obviously not sweet. Fish asks what endearment he can call her.

"Sugar. Or Honey. Pumpkin. Anything food," Ling instructs him.

Later, Ling walks in as Billy accuses Fish of taking Ling's silly cases just because he wants to sleep with her. Ling turns on Fish and demands to know if this is true.

Fish reassures her: "Bacon Bits, I'm *nice* to you because I want to sleep with you. I *kissed* you because I want to sleep with you.

But taking your cases? I do that only because you're wealthy and a potential cash cow for the firm to milk in perpetuity."

Nelle keeps pursuing Cage, who keeps eluding her. Billy warns Nelle not to hurt Cage, and Elaine tries to set a makeout mood in the Unisex by hiding in a stall with a boombox playing

👬👫 LEFT: Elaine attempts to make Ling more sympathetic to a jury—a neck brace. ABOVE: Nelle in "le Steward." OPPOSITE (middle to bottom): Elaine counsels Cage on love; Cage practices his dance moves. OPPOSITE TOP: Ally bowling, fingers stuck firmly in the ball.

*Episode number refers to the order in which they were filmed. In the book, we've chosen to list the episodes by airdate.

Barry White when Nelle and Cage think they're alone. Nelle warns Cage that she doesn't go for victims and her patience is thinning. Ling gives sympathy to Nelle, her soul mate. "It's a problem, being beautiful, Nelle. It's only the handsome men who ask us out . . . and handsome men are dolts. Life is unfair to us."

Renee drags Ally on a bowling double date with the preternaturally humor-impaired Wallace Pike, a man who's boring even by bowling standards. Trying out a bowling ball, seemingly a perfect fit, she finds she can't remove it. It's stuck! Wallace notes that fingers sometimes swell during menstruation. "Are you menstruating?" he asks helpfully. Ally can't have the ball sawed off, because it belonged to the late wife of the sentimental old guy who loaned it to her.

Falling down repeatedly thanks to the bowling ball, Ally loses Ling's case. "As long as men and women work together, there will be sexual energy in the room," Ally's opponent argues in court. "And this country is in the process of trying to outlaw every bit of it. *Enough* already." The court concurs. But Ally realizes that Ling prefers to lose—that way she can blame somebody else.

Finally free of the bowling ball, Ally is stuck with Wallace's unwanted affections. She arranges to have Wallace walk in on an Ally-Georgia make-out session. He murmurs his forgiveness and disapproval of homosexuality and heads for the right-wing hills.

Taking Elaine's advice, Cage gets manful and takes Nelle out for a firm spin on the Bar's dance floor. Too firm a spin—Cage yanks Nelle so hard they both crash to the floor. Cage has the passion, but when he falls, he falls hard—often physically. Is their affair down for the count? Stay tuned.

SONG LIST:

♪ *"Tell Him"*
"Gimme Dat Thing" ♪
♪ *"This Is My Song"*
"You Never Can Tell" ♪
♪ *"You're the First, the Last, My Everything"*
"You Are My Sunshine" ♪

making spirits BRIGHT

written by David E. Kelley, **directed by** Peter MacNicol

>>

THE BRIEF: The firm represents a man who's lost his job because he believes in unicorns. Renee gets in way over her head with her major ex, Matt. Cage makes repeated attempts to nab Nelle under the office mistletoe.

Ally gazes into a store window, musing on the reflection of happy couples brimming with Christmas cheer. This fades into Cage's reflection as he stares out his office window.

Cage's lonesome reverie is interrupted by Nelle, who looks sensational in an over-the-shoulder formal dress. Using his old CIA trainee skills, Cage hears the "You Can't Hurry Love" theme and attempts to creep up on Nelle as she stands beneath the mistletoe. "Any particular reason you're sneaking up on me like a cheetah?" she asks with a smile, fixing to kiss him—until they're interrupted by Fish with news of a crucial case.

Cage/Fish and Associates was founded largely on the business provided by investment coun-selor Sheldon Maxwell, and now they've got to get his job back for him. He was fired because he was fool enough to tell someone that he'd just seen a unicorn. Unicorns are gleaming white symbols of radiant, pure love—and Sheldon can sense that Ally has seen one, too. Unicorn seers are "lonely, with virtuous hearts," like the creatures themselves, Sheldon tells her. "They can only be approached by a person of pure spirit." And the unicorn's horn can lead you to love.

Or to big trouble. Ally walks in on Renee and her married ex, Matt, thrashing in the sheets. Later, Renee hopefully asks Matt to go with her to the firm's Christmas bash. But when he wants to keep their celebration in a private place, Renee realizes he's not ready to leave his wife publicly behind, so she painfully sends him packing.

Cage tries his mistletoe approach on Nelle again—unfortunately, just as Ling is walking in. Ling is all smiles, weirdly full of holiday spirit. At the instant Cage makes his move on Nelle, Ling cuts in between them, and instead of clutching Nelle, he inadvertently puts his hand on Ling's

chest. Ling shrieks, "You all saw it—he just sexually assaulted my left breast. It's gone numb!" (Gee, one would expect it to be Cage's hand that went numb in that encounter.) But Nelle points out the mistletoe, and Ling snaps back into her merry mood, kissing Cage.

Judge Whipper puts Sheldon back in charge of his $300 million financial accounts, casting a vote for hope against all reason. Ally, of course, keeps her faith in unicorns, and all they represent.

OPPOSITE (left to right): Cage contemplates mistletoe; unusual holiday cheer. TOP: Elaine's musical extravaganza. ABOVE: Ally sees her unicorn. LEFT: Ally contemplates a world without unicorns.

in DREAMS

written by David E. Kelley, **directed by** Alex Graves

THE BRIEF: Ally is summoned by her favorite teacher, Bria, to Bria's hospital deathbed, where she's enjoying blissful dreams of love with an imaginary man. Ally tries to get the doctor to put Bria to sleep—not death, but a deep, coma-like sleep state, so that her last weeks or months can be happy. Nelle begins to get extremely impatient with Cage's cowardly courtship.

B ria Tolson, Ally's high school teacher, has the perfect man in her life. Unfortunately, she only sees him in her dreams. Now that she's in her seventies and dying of Lou Gehrig's disease, she's seeing a lot of her phantasmal beloved, Henry Lane, but only when she drifts off. Waking up is always a disappointment.

"Don't grow old alone, Ally," Bria says. "It's not a good thing."

Bria's doctor happens to be—small world!—Greg Butters, Ally's on-again-off-again love. She launches a legal initiative to get the physicians to induce a coma for Bria, so that she can spend more time with Henry in a dream life where she's a healthy forty-year-old mother with a very attentive husband. Awake, Bria is perfectly aware that Henry is a kind of hallucination. "You think I'm crazy to want to live in that world," Bria says. "My God, wouldn't I be crazy not to?" Yet the court balks at putting Bria to sleep. Fish suggests taking her to a vet. At length, Whipper grants Ally's request for Bria's dreamy coma.

Meanwhile, Nelle bumps into Cage in the Unisex. It's almost midnight on New Year's Eve. They're alone. She drops her coat, notes that nobody is at all likely to come to the office at this particular hour of the year, and says, "You know what excites me a little? Public places." She starts to undo his tie.

Cage dives behind a stall door, hiding from her.

Nelle tells Ling her tale of woe. Ling tells Fish that Cage is gay. Fish objects that Ling won't sleep with him. Ling explains that she's putting him off because she doubts he's over "the big-haired blond naked nude buttocks thing [Whipper]," and she needs to keep him tantalized. Sex is too messy for her liking, she adds. "So if a woman doesn't want sex, it's OK, but if a man doesn't want it, he's gay," Fish says. "A medical fact," says Ling.

LEFT: Ling: "You're a man who thinks with his penis, for me to keep your interest, I've got to keep it alert." **OPPOSITE (top to bottom):** Nelle, dissatisfied with the pace of their relationship, lets Cage know he's headed for the Dumpster; Bria in her dream world of love.

Fish orders Cage to sleep with Nelle, who overhears the order. Cage confronts Nelle, who confronts Ling for blabbing. "The strange little man won't move on you, you became unfun and lousy company to *me*," explains Ling. Why should she be a victim of Cage's caution? Cage confesses to Ally that all he's trying to do is preserve the dream of happiness with Nelle from the probable disaster the real thing would entail.

Ling and Nelle take a steambath and discuss each other's love habits. "Compared to you, the *Titanic* struck heat," Ling tells Nelle. "Neither of us wants a man to go spelunking to our emotional core." They like Fish and Cage exactly because neither threatens to break through to real intimacy.

Vonda strikes up "Dream Baby," and Cage, Nelle, Fish, Ling, Ally, and Greg dance. In her sleep, Bria's foot taps to the beat.

▶ SONG LIST:

"Dream Lover"
"In Dreams"
"Dream Baby"
"Miss Gulch's Theme"
"You're the First, the Last, My Everything"

love
UNLIMITED

written by David E. Kelley, **directed by** Dennie Gordon

THE BRIEF: Ling files her oddest lawsuit yet and gives Fish the closest thing yet to actual sex. Ally and Fish try to stop a husband from annulling his marriage. And Cage and Nelle finally achieve consummation—of a peculiar sort.

An environmental group sues Ling to block her wetlands development project, so Ling countersues the environment—for causing her allergies. Since environmentalists have sued on behalf of the rights of trees, she advocates suing the trees right back. Ling softens her stance on denying Fish lover's rights and awakens him to the erotic potential of finger-sucking.

Ally takes a case that really sucks: Stanley Goodman, father of two children, is trying to annul his nine-year marriage because he suffers from "sexual obsessive-compulsive behavior" that made him mentally incompetent when he proposed. "Basically, I was crazy." Fish objects: "Your Honor, *any* man is crazy to get married."

Ally objects to Fish's objection. Later, she nails Goodman in her greatest close ever:

"People fall in love for all sorts of insanities and we don't legislate the reasons. But once they take vows . . . and once they start having kids, we take

that seriously, and we call it an institution. And for this man to be running around vaccinating any woman he can convince to play doctor; for this man to indulge his little affliction at the expense of his wife *and* his children; for this man to skirt financial and moral responsibility because he found a scuzzy lawyer and a scuzzier shrink to pronounce him disabled . . . ; for this man to say that he's addicted to love, addicted to sex, addicted to infidelity, lying, and cheating; for this man to come in here parading his penis like it should qualify for handicapped parking—how *dare* you subject this woman to this embarrassment? How dare you subject your kids to it? How dare you *live*, you giant *ass*?"

The courtroom erupts in applause.

Back at the office Cage does a seduction dance in Nelle's office, to his beloved Barry White. But when Nelle takes it all off, Cage runs from the room.

Ally makes Cage go explain himself to Nelle. Actually, he's noble, in a strange way. Despite his obsession with her stupefying beauty, she might never fall in love with him, and he might not fall for her. "You don't really get me, and I don't really get you," he says. A bit sharply—and justifiably—Nelle tells him that there is a woman who does get

him. Nelle alludes to Ally, and his infuriating waiting game has lost him Ally's heart, judging from the Greg Butters–besotted look on her face lately.

Nelle walks home alone, a bit glum, as a romantic snow falls. Greg and Ally dance in mutual enchantment.

SONG LIST:

♪ "Anticipation"
"Ooh, Child" ♪
♪ "Apples, Peaches, Pumpkin Pie"
"Could I Have This Dance" ♪
♪ "You're the First, the Last, My Everything"
"Love Serenade" ♪

🚹🚺 OPPOSITE (top to bottom): Ling shows Fish her finger-sucking technique: "Ever tried that before?" "After I eat chicken," says Fish, "but it's not the same." ABOVE: Laura Dipson, Executive V.P. for Women in Progress, tells Ally she's nominated for 1999 Role Model of the Year in the professional people category, but she'll have to change her look; (fantasy) Ally bites off Dipson's nose. RIGHT: Cage mourns the fact that he can't contend with his ultimate fantasy—Nelle getting naked for him.

angels and BLIMPS

written by David E. Kelley, **directed by** Mel Damski

THE BRIEF: Ling inspires a little boy to sue God—and her wild idea has some practical value. The firm takes on the case of a man who shot his wife's lover.

Ally, visiting Greg Butters at the hospital, runs into Ling, whose friend was a patient there. "I sent her flowers—she died, so I came to take them back." As Ally introduces her to Greg, Ling morphs into the Mother Alien from *Aliens*. Ling collides with a guy in a wheelchair on her way out and blames him: "Ow! Watch where you're going! It's bad enough you people get all the parking spots."

But Ling rises to the occasion when she meets Greg's patient Eric, age eight, bald as an egg from chemo and not long for this world despite his infectious joie de vivre. Eric wants to sue God for letting his father die and giving him leukemia. But it's Ling who suggests suing the church on behalf of God for refusing to chip in for the pricey experimental leukemia treatment his insurance company naturally won't pay for either. "Do you think there really *is* a God?" Eric asks.

"Of course there is," Ling says. "Who do you think these doctors walk around pretending to be, Moses?" But she warns Eric that he can't just loll around—he's got to be a fighter. Eric is spoiling for a fight.

Ally grabs Ling's arm and gets rid of her, but it turns out Ling is no amateur. She edited the Law Review at Cornell, Nelle tells Ally. Ling's idea: Eric's father was killed by a tree struck by lightning—an act of God. So they go after the house of God.

"Eric's parents contributed pretty generously to the church," Ling tells the church's thunderstruck lawyer. "I can make out an applied covenant of good faith under which we could argue a duty for the church to give back in Eric's need. He has cancer

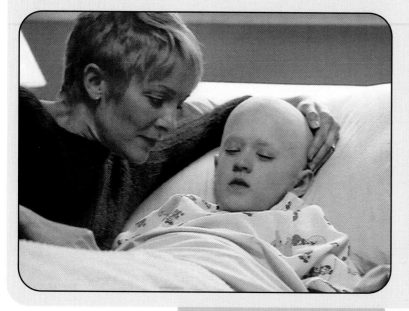

LEFT: Leukemia patient Eric Stall, who's suing God, gets comfort from his mom. **ABOVE:** Ally's new policy with Greg: "Less fantasy, more reality." **OPPOSITE:** Ally beholds the blimp and wonders, "Maybe God had men make the blimp just to remind people He's up there, 'cause every time I see one... I do think of Him."

and his father's dead . . . . As for why you'll settle, you already know why. By naming God as a defendant, there isn't a newspaper in the country who won't glom onto it as one of those insipid human-interest stories." Headlines about the kid's church refusing to help save his life would cost the church big bucks in publicists to tame the firestorm of bad press. The church agrees to settle and pay for the experimental treatment.

The firm's more conventional case is also off-kilter. Harvey Kent wants to plead manslaughter for the attempted shooting of his wife's lover. The catch is, he didn't succeed in killing anyone. "I tried!" Harvey protests. But Fish tells him that the heat of passion can only mitigate murder, not attempts. "Next time, finish him off, you'll do less time. Bygones." Harvey caught his wife and her lover in bed and shot at the lover in his rage. He can't remember shooting, and he's still heartbrokenly in love with his wife.

DA Renee disdains Cage's "achy-breaky heart" defense, but the jury lets Harvey off on temporary insanity.

Eric fights for life, and Ally tells him about the time she glimpsed a blimp after the death of her kid sister and mistook it for a sign from God. "Were you a really stupid kid?" Eric inquires. Still, he suspects that Ally might be his own personal angel.

Eric dies. Ling seems less than sympathetic. The kid had terminal leukemia, what did you expect? Only as Ling leaves do we see her tears. While walking away from the hospital, Ally glances up to the sky where a blimp mysteriously appears, bearing the words, "Just Looking." Ling secretly paid for the blimp, but she takes no credit for it, because she likes to keep most tender emotions to herself. "Just Looking" is a phrase that captures the heavenly aspiration of everyone in Ally's world: They are always yearning and searching for signs of undying love in their lives.

SONG LIST:

"Rainbow Connection"

"This Old Heart of Mine"

"Vincent"

"Always Chasing Rainbows"

"Going the Distance"

PYRAMIDS
on the nile

written by David E. Kelley, **directed by** Elodie Keene

THE BRIEF: A Fortune 500 company hires a seven-attorney army to crush Cage/Fish's case against its prohibition of unauthorized office romance. Greg butters Ally up in a big way—and Billy enganges in utterly unauthorized office romance.

A young couple gets busted for violating the Cobb Company's strict, rather paranoid, anti-sexual-harassment rule, "Date and Tell." To make sure nobody sues the company for tolerating harassment, all couples must confess their dating status the instant they get together and sign a "love contract" insulating Cobb from lawsuits arising from dangerous displays of affection. The couple, Callie Horn and Steve Cloves, don't fess up, are discovered, get fired, and demand compensation for the loss of their jobs.

Cobb's counsel says it's the harassment law's fault, not theirs. "Now single incidents can give rise to lawsuits ... we have to set rules to prevent atmospheres that could foster any incidents .... As a prophylactic, we cut off all sex talk, period." Even talking about Monica Lewinsky is forbidden. "As silly as it sounds, conversations about national news can amount to sexual harassment under today's laws."

"You love her," Cage tells the fired office swain on the witness stand. "That must have just broken all *sorts* of rules. We can't go around having people *love* one another." Cobb's lead lawyer objects. "I'm sorry," says Cage. "It's just that sometimes I get overwhelmed by common sense."

Billy gets overwhelmed by some unidentified emotion after a ruling goes against them on a case he and Ally are handling. He yells at Ally for going into court unprepared. "You were unprofessional to the point of malpractice!"

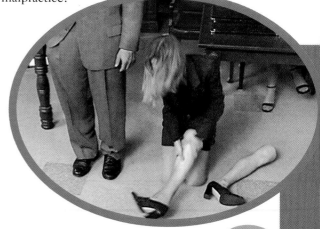

But as the episode's title reveals (it's his and Ally's old song, the one they dangerously danced to in the office one night), Billy's anger is actually a cover for his jealousy. He's just seen Greg Butters bring Valentine's Day flowers to Ally. He couldn't see the dancing baby dressed as Cupid spraying Ally's heart with arrows, but he can't miss Greg's direct hit on her heart. Like kerosene on a banked fire, the sight makes Billy's old passion for her flare up. Just like old times.

He pretends he needs to talk to Ally about the firm's big scandal—Fish is hiring Ling as their newest associate. When Ling walks into the office, the Wicked Witch of the West theme plays, sum-

ming up her image in the eyes of most of her new colleagues. "Asset. Firm. I'm human," Fish says, referring to Ling's lucrative accounts and alluding to her posterior's effect on his dumb stick.

Billy is upset about Ling's arrival but confesses that what's really bugging him is his quenchless passion for Ally, despite his love for Georgia. Now Ally's angry. At home she confesses to Renee that she loves Greg and Billy both. Since Billy has no kids with Georgia, Renee advises going for him.

"Billy told me about your little talk," Georgia tells Ally, who goes white—or rather, her face goes black-and-white while the rest of the scene stays in color. But Georgia means the Ling situation. Ally isn't busted. Not yet.

Cage defends office romance by citing the failure of his recent courtship of co-counsel, Nelle— he's better off having tried and failed then not having ever tried. The jury awards the fired couple $942,000.

Alone late in the office, Billy gives Ally a long passionate kiss. How will the jury of their peers react to this?

OPPOSITE (left to right): Ling prepares to make Fish sizzle; (fantasy) Ally is cut off at the knees in court when she has no defense. ABOVE: Billy and Ally just before the infamous kiss.

SONG LIST:

♪ *"100 Tears Away"*
"Tell Him" ♪
♪ *"Mustang Sally"*
"You Belong to Me" ♪
♪ *"Going the Distance"*
"You're the First, the Last, My Everything" ♪
♪ *"Georgia"*

SIDESHOW

written by David E. Kelley, **directed by** Alex Graves

THE BRIEF: Ally and Billy freak out about the implications of their kiss. They talk it over with Dr. Tracy, who confesses that she's an adulteress herself and belts out "Tainted Love." Poor Greg gets left in the dark about his largely theoretical cuckoldry.

"Do you realize what I've *done*?" Ally says to Renee.

"It's not like you made love," Renee says placatingly.

"There's no greater betrayal than a kiss!" Ally says. "There's more intimacy, more emotion, more connection in a kiss than any other physical act."

Just then, Greg shows up at the door. Ally has made him wait for sixty-plus minutes in the restaurant on one of his very rare nights off work. "What's the deal?" he asks.

"I just had to come back here and . . . lie. Lie *down*," Ally stammers. She's about to confess all, but Renee pinches her ear, drags her across the apartment out of Greg's earshot, and orders her not to tell him.

"What kind of a way is that to begin a relationship—dishonesty?" Ally says.

"Every relationship starts with dishonesty, you dope! It sets the stage for marriage . . . . You can't tell him you were kissing—Billy!"

Billy suddenly shows up. While Renee distracts a suspicious Greg with improvised lies, Billy criticizes Ally for spilling the big-kiss beans to Renee. Improvising various excuses, Ally and Renee whisk the men out the door.

Ally flees to Dr. Tracy. "Deep, deep down we both know what you are," Dr. Tracy tells her. "A slut....The way to your heart is through your Fallopian tubes."

Ally hotly denies it.

"Come on, Ally. When you watch the Nature Channel and you see the snake swallow the thing four times its size, you ever wonder why you reach for Bounty, the quicker picker-upper? You love sex!"

Ally stands and starts marching out in disgust. Tracy hits her stereo remote button and the couch lurches forward, knocking Ally's feet out from under her and making her sit and listen.

"You're afraid you like Greg, but you're afraid of falling in love," explains Tracy. "So you're looking for some kind of guardrail to reach out and grab onto—and it's Billy! You kook!" The only solution: Ally has to go home and have sex with Greg, to see

if they're meant to be. "If you see a blimp on the way, ignore it."

Renee and Fish tell Ally that sex is the acid test of true love. Ally insists it's all in the kiss. "I can't go another day without making love to you," Billy pleads. Ally makes a date to meet him in her apartment.

But at the office, she can't take the heat from innocent Georgia, who's so out of the loop that the only one she's eyeing jealously is Nelle.

Ally keeps having guilt hallucinations: She sees a knife in Georgia's back, and when they're in the elevator together, she hears a pounding sound, and the entire elevator begins expanding and contracting like the beating heart in Edgar Allan Poe's "The Tell-Tale Heart."

Ally and Billy both go see Dr. Tracy, who tries to goad them into analyzing their true feelings. It's real simple: They've got to find out whether they're a couple or not. They quiz Tracy on her own past: She confesses that she was involved with a married man herself, so she knows what she's talking about.

Billy says he dumped Ally because he feared she'd be too insecure to be monogamous. "Love is wasted on you, Ally, because you'll always be unhappy!" Billy thinks she will always be dissatisfied with herself, with her life, with all the love any man could ever give her.

Ally passionately denies it, though nothing Billy ever said has hit her this hard. "I'm gaining on happiness," she insists, "and I am going to get there one day."

They reiterate their love—and walk out on each other again.

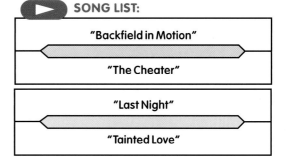

OPPOSITE (top to bottom): The kiss; Dr. Tracy sings her own sad song of "tainted love" past. ABOVE: The walls close in on Ally as she stands next to Georgia in the elevator.

▶ SONG LIST:

"Backfield in Motion"
"The Cheater"

"Last Night"
"Tainted Love"

sex, lies, and POLITICS

written by David E. Kelley, **directed by** Arlene Sanford

THE BRIEF: Georgia learns about Ally and Billy's kiss. A senator feels no guilt about falsely smearing an independent bookstore as a porno emporium in order to court right-wing voters. Cage sets up Ling's first shot at courtroom glory, and she scores.

Ally's bad conscience makes her hallucinate—she hears people passing by in the street dissing her, the Pope walks by muttering against her. Ally asks Renee if she just saw the Pope, too. Renee tells Ally to see Dr. Tracy for guilt counseling. A little dog contemptuously piddles on Ally's foot. "Did a dog just piddle on my foot?" Ally asks. This time Renee did see what Ally saw. "I'm afraid that was real," says Renee.

ran TV ads claiming her store on Beacon Hill sold smutty books. She's suing the senator for damages. Benson dangled a $500,000 settlement to lull Cage into complacency, then reneged. Desperately, Cage asks Ling to help him try the case.

Meanwhile Ally cracks under pressure and blurts the truth to Greg: She kissed somebody else. Greg storms off as Billy walks in. Billy demands, "What did you tell him?"

"That we kissed . . . but I couldn't be sure if we made love on account of you having such a microscopic penis," Ally hisses. Greg's exit hurt Ally, so she takes it out on Billy.

At the office, Ally again hears the "tell-tale heart" sound and sees Georgia's head expand and contract in sync with this aural symbol of guilt.

Benson, the slimy, high-priced lawyer of the slimy, high-profile Senator Harold Watkins, stabs Cage in the back. Cage's client, bookstore owner Shirley Peterson, went bankrupt because Watkins

In court, Benson accuses Shirley of selling "books graphically describing sex acts." Shirley notes that these were books by the likes of Herb Ritts, John Irving, Balzac, and Chaucer. Benson accuses Shirley of quashing the senator's free speech. "He saddled me up to raise funding from right-wing constituents," Shirley replies. Ling ruins Benson's rhythm by acting even weirder than Cage in court: "Objection! *Every* politician lies to get money!"

Cage ridicules Senator Harold Watkins by comparing him with Professor Harold Hill in *The Music*

**But you can see from my sad face...
I'm sympathetic.**

OPPOSITE (left to right): Busted. Ally and Billy exit the private place where they discussed Billy's confession to Georgia just as Georgia walks into the Unisex; (fantasy) Ally's eyes react to the sight of Georgia. LEFT: Ling sways the jury by emotionally quoting in Mandarin what she claims is a wise old Chinese saying (in reality, she's saying, "It doesn't matter what I say here, because none of you speak Chinese"). BELOW: Ally tries to apologize to Georgia for kissing Billy. Georgia asks her to leave.

Man and launching into Hill's rabble-rousing, moralistic "Trouble" anthem, which claims that "the idle brain is the devil's playground." The courtroom erupts in dancing and "mass-teria."

Cage and Ling win $1.2 million for the bookstore owner. Billy risks his marriage by blabbing to Georgia about his illicit kiss. Ally tries to explain to Georgia the emotional logic behind her kissing Billy: When Ally found out Billy had deliberately dumped her once he met Georgia, it made her question whether Billy had ever really loved her at all. But if Billy still loves Ally now, then he did love her in the past—and so true love is possible and Ally can still hope to find it out there somewhere.

Ally grants that she and Billy weren't meant to be. She tells Georgia that the stupidest thing about kissing Billy was the damage it did to her cherished friendship with Georgia.

"Could you leave now?" Georgia says quietly.

SONG LIST:

♪ *"Friendship Train"*
"And I Love You So" ♪
♪ *"Shake Your Tail Feather"*
"Trouble" ♪

As rivals for Billy's affection, Ally and Georgia bring their catfight into court in "Civil Wars."

civil WARS

written by David E. Kelley, **directed by** Billy Dickson

>>

THE BRIEF: It's Ally and Cage versus Georgia and Richard in court. They represent, respectively, a man and a woman who've gone from love to war, but the lawyers tend to forget whom they're representing and play out personal arguments about the firm's own internecine combat. Nelle represents a man in a sweat over the IRS.

Paula Hunt swooned for Kevin Wah the night they met. "We left the party, went out for coffee, and I'm listening to this man speak my life. We stayed up all night talking." Soul mates! Lovers at first glance, in love forever! Next came sex, dreams of marriage . . . and abrupt disillusionment. "Everything we 'connected' on, he learned from my chat room on-line," Paula bitterly testifies in court. "He evidently was *in* it pretending to be a woman." Now Paula's suing for fraudulent seduction and civil date rape. "He stole my thoughts off the Internet!"

Paula is Ally's client. But Kevin's dad, Harry Wah, is one of Fish's biggest cash cows and asks him to represent Kevin. He doesn't care if the opposing counsel is employed by Fish. In fact, he orders Fish to represent Kevin or the firm is fired.

Ally teams up with Cage on Paula's behalf, and Georgia with Fish in Kevin's corner. Georgia thinks it's probably good for one's professional performance not to think of your opposing counsel as a friend. She tells Ally, "It probably just becomes easier for me to look at you as, I dunno . . . a conniving backstabber who kissed my husband."

Georgia cross-examines Paula, probing to discover whether Paula ever faked enthusiasm for a football team to impress Kevin, a fan. "I don't pretend," retorts Paula. "I like Denver, I used to live there, I follow the Buckos."

"Broncos," Georgia corrects her. "I'm just trying to show everybody does a little pretending." Glaring at Ally, she adds, "Some women even lie and still think they're blameless in life. Some even cheat!"

Cage rises and apologizes to the judge. "Ms. Thomas has recently undergone a little strife in her marriage. I think it explains this inappropriate and cruel line of questioning."

"Objection!" Georgia yells.

Typically Fish, he asks Kevin, "Why own up to it? It's not like she was ever going to find out. Why this overriding compulsion to be honest?"

When Cage gets his shot at Kevin, he puts events in a harsher light: "You took this information from the chat room, used it to move in like a Trojan horse, then popped the Trojan condom!"

Meanwhile, Nelle is at war with her own soul. She's representing the remarkably sweaty and unattractive George Chisholm—Ling calls him a

where her ER doc is—you got it, Greg Butters. She gets her honest reward: a butterfly bandage and a kiss-off instead of a kiss.

♂♀ OPPOSITE: Ling, Ally, Georgia, and Nelle's catfight in the Unisex. **LEFT:** Nelle and Ling apply sweat-suppressing liniment to IRS audit victim Mr. Chisholm. **BELOW:** Dr. Butters treats Ally after the Unisex fight. "That's all I'm gonna get out of this relationship—a tetanus shot?"

"soggy hog"—who's being audited for extraordinarily bold interpretations of ambiguous IRS deduction rules. Marsh, the IRS rep, finds Nelle extraordinarily attractive. To make matters worse, Chisholm's drenching sweat makes him look even guiltier than he is.

Though Chisholm isn't an outright chiseler, Marsh would be well within his rights to sink him with a fat bill for back taxes and interest, if not big penalties. Nelle feels the heat.

"Marsh likes you. You know this....Let your hair down tomorrow," Ling suggests.

"I don't want to win that way, Ling," Nelle protests. "The only thing worse is—"

"Losing," Ling says.

Nelle bats a thousand by batting her lashes at Marsh. Chisholm gets off with paying what he honestly owes, and no more.

While the court is deliberating, Kevin and Paula reconcile and call off the case. He really did love her. Mr. Wah pays both sides. It's win-win for Cage/Fish and Associates.

And how do they react? By getting in a pigpile fight in the Unisex. Ally winds up in the hospital,

▶ **SONG LIST:**

"Wrong Number"

"Going the Distance"

those lips, THAT HAND

written by David E. Kelley, **directed by** Arlene Sanford

THE BRIEF: Ally and Cage defend Albert Shepley, who was arrested for holding onto his wife's hand—which unfortunately was detached from her arm. Renee has no intention of losing this slamdunk case to Cage and his bag of courtroom tricks. Georgia and Billy represent an insurance salesman who can't face the bald facts.

Facing her mirror just before her twenty-ninth birthday, Ally spots a wrinkle, freaks, and shrieks. "Women reach their prime in their thirties," Renee says soothingly. "Says who?" "Women in their forties," admits Renee.

At work, Ally gets a client who also can't bear to be without his soul mate: Mr. Shepley, whom cops stopped for speeding through a stop sign. He was upset: Mrs. Shepley had just had a fatal heart attack, he'd chain-sawed her hand off and was off to his mortician brother to preserve it. He loved her so much, he testifies, "I couldn't let go."

It looks awkward for Shepley at best, and prosecutor Renee makes him admit that he didn't call 911 and that he'd been hoping she'd die—she'd been in a vegetative state. Furthermore his wife's medical care was costly.

Cage is in no shape to help Shepley: He's distracted by his impending thirty-fifth birthday, which has him as much on edge as Ally's twenty-ninth does her. "Have you ever been in love?" Shepley asks Cage. Referring to prison, Cage retorts, "Your love life could improve," at Shepley, "but it won't be what you had in mind!"

Only Ally can save Shepley—by her defense of her own mad romantic hope to "be with someone I can't bear to live without . . . I envy a little what he had."

Meanwhile, Billy and Georgia are suing Ross Fineman's employer, an insurance company, for replacing him with a young salesman at half the salary. His boss's attorney says it's not ageism, it's Fineman's undermining his salesman's credibility by the enormous coiling comb-over he wears, unsuccessfully concealing an almost entirely hair-free scalp. "This is my real hair," Ross accurately protests. But the boss's lawyer has a point, too: "A comb-over by its very nature is a fraud."

So is romance without sex, Fish decides. He dumps Ling for stringing him along with hair massages and finger sucking. "I feel like I might explode," says Fish. "I'd like you to be part of it." Ling is reluctant, because she's "amazing" in bed. "No matter what I do, it always comes out as the best sex the man has ever had, and suddenly it's no more talking, no more movies...it's sex, sex, sex!"

Ross's comb-over and solves his problems. In the Bar, Fish shows Ling the knee-pit caress, a trick from his own erotic treasure chest. The knee-pit caress brings her to an ecstatic state. Cage is beyond orgasm when Nelle unveils her birthday surprise: a serenade by Barry White—no hallucination, the flesh-and-blood real thing. The whole firm surrenders to White's spell.

Cage has been thinking along the same lines. He steals a smooch from a startled Ally, apologizes, then takes it back. "I'm thirty-five, dammit!" he tells her later. "I've never met anybody I felt like chopping up! And nobody's ever wanted to chop me up! I haven't lived!"

Renee battles Cage's sneaky, foot-and-nose-squeaky court tactics with better ones. She gets a pathologist to say it looks like Shepley's wife's coronary may have been caused by the amputation. She revs up a chain saw. Judge "Whipper" Cone, the presiding judge, makes her turn it off, but the saw does buttress Renee's closing: "This isn't what loved ones do to each other."

Ally's emotional defense of endless love acquits Shepley (who takes it manfully when she says he still can't have the hand back). Cage kisses Renee after the ruling, in the grip of birthday seize-the-day obsession. "*John?*" Renee says, startled, but perhaps not entirely displeased. "Life is for the living," says Cage.

Ross's employer will hire him back if he ditches the comb-over. So Ling, a gifted barber, severs

SONG LIST:

"39-21-46" ♪

♪ "Hey There, Lonely Girl"

"My Pledge of Love" ♪

♪ "Let's Hang On"

"Miss Gulch's Theme" ♪

♪ "You're the First, the Last, My Everything"

👨👩 OPPOSITE: Georgia and Billy eye Ross Fineman's elaborately coiled comb-over. ABOVE and RIGHT: Barry White serenades Cage in the Bar; celebrating with Cage.

let's DANCE

written by David E. Kelley, **directed by** Ben Lewin

▶▶

THE BRIEF: Ally refuses to defend an employer who allegedly discriminates against women associates who become mothers. Nelle gladly takes the case. Billy and Georgia face a therapist as outspoken as Dr. Tracy: the gum-snapping Dr. Hooper. Elaine is devastated by losing her partner in a swing-dance competition, and Ling steps in.

Fish tries to talk Ally into doing what disgusts her: helping Nelle defend a firm accused of discriminating against women associates who become mothers. (It's not just the case that disgusts her, it's being forced to work with Nelle, whom she loathes.) Fish tells Ally any law firm would hire a man over a woman: "[T]he period once a month, that's good for three days of subperformance, PMS, tack on another day, add the 3.2 more hours per month women spend in the bathroom...and the single ones, forget it, all they want to do is meet a man, and—actually, Ally, maybe we should introduce you as an exhibit!"

"This case offends me, I don't want any part of it—and Nelle, I'm a little disappointed in you," Ally chides.

"There goes my self-esteem," Nelle icily replies. "I so live for your approval." Fish's idea of a legal defense is that "women are inferior."

Nelle fights a good but doomed court battle against the sympathetic plaintiff, Marianne Harper, who had a baby and fell off the partnership track, and against feminist expert witness Margaret Camaro. Later, we discover what lurks behind Nelle's own refusal to face Ms. Harper's fate: Nelle won't have kids, because—as Cage surmised—she was scarred by her parents' divorce. "Two houses, two rooms, two sets of clothes, I even had two favorite teddy bears, one for each bed. How many kids get that?" Nelle demands rhetorically. "Too many, I suppose," Cage muses.

Ally's spends this episode caught up in another drama: Elaine's heartbreak when her dance partner's ankle goes out on him just before a big dance contest. Ling turns out to be a superb swing dancer, but the prospect of sweating and blistering turns her off. In the Unisex, Ally begs Ling to

is intrigued. Later, she asks Fish for a quick knee-pit hit in court; her large hair pops right out of its bun, and her eyes go wide.

Elaine and Ling qualify for the swing-dance finals. The dance goes on in the Bar—for everyone but Nelle, who's home alone grieving over two teddy bears stored in an old box.

👨👩 LEFT and OPPOSITE BOTTOM: Ling and Elaine get in the swing at the dance contest. OPPOSITE TOP: Ling as Elaine's dance partner. BELOW: Renee enthusiastically embracses Cage as he demonstrates his knee-pit technique.

SONG LIST:

♪ *"Slow Hand"*

"Baby Don't You Break My Heart Slow" ♪

♪ *"You Turned My Whole World Around"*

"You're the First, the Last, My Everything" ♪

♪ *"What Am I Gonna to Do With You?"*

"Jump with My Baby" ♪

♪ *"Miss Gulch's Theme"*

"You and Me and the Bottle Makes Three Tonight" ♪

♪ *"Mr. Pinstripe Suit"* ♪

"The Boogie Bumper" ♪

reconsider: "Listen, you and I, we're lawyers, [we] do important things on occasion. Think of Elaine's life. There's a reason she's out there inventing face bras and glow-in-the-dark condoms...there's something a little pathetic there. And this dance contest, if it can help make her feel, I dunno, good about herself—"

At which point, Elaine stalks out of a Unisex stall, glaring at Ally. Later, Elaine eloquently nails the mortified Ally with two stern truths: Ally is "an elitist snob," and Elaine doesn't need nor want her pity, because Elaine likes not being a lawyer and consequently having time for a life outside the office.

Billy gets busted even harder by the therapist Dr. Hooper. "Forty percent of all married men cheat," Billy argues. "I just *kissed*."

"If you were my husband, I'd kick your ass," says Hooper. "You're an awful person . . . not just to Georgia, but this Ally person." Billy wonders whether he's in for a fair trial. But does he deserve one?

Cage, taking charge of his life upon turning thirty-five, takes Renee on a date to a familiar setting, the Bar. She's unimpressed. Until Cage demonstrates the knee-pit action he has recently coerced Fish into teaching him. One touch and there's nothing left of Renee but slow, moaning ecstasy. Across the dance floor, Nelle sees this and

only the
LONELY

written by David E. Kelley, **directed by** Vince Misiano

THE BRIEF: At long last, Elaine gets the Face Bra infomercial of her dreams. But it all turns into a nightmare of betrayal. The firm defends a boss who has a monthly "Beach Day" in the office, encouraging employees to wear bathing suits. An offended female employee sues. Cage finally gets his real date with destiny—Nelle asks him to a rap club. Ally confronts Dr. Greg Butters one last time about giving her one more chance.

Deep-pocketed Ling, realizer of dreams and infallible entrepreneur, backs Elaine's Face Bra infomercial. Elaine is in a state of bliss: She has joked before about being "1-800-ELAINE" (i.e., an easy sexual conquest), but now she's the proud possessor of a real 1-800 number and a TV spot that sparked 800 orders overnight. She knows she'll be rich. Better yet, she's sharing the moment with her dearest friends at Cage/Fish at a screening in the office. And she promises she'll never leave the firm, no matter how much cash she makes.

Then her aunt comes in with a summons, suing Elaine for stealing the Face Bra concept from her cousin Martha, recently deceased. The day before an accident killed her, Martha told Elaine's cousin and half a dozen others she feared Elaine would heist the idea. Martha left sketches and a March 2, 1996, patent application (predating Elaine's filed patent). In court, Elaine's surviving cousin testifies that nobody would bring their boyfriends around

when Elaine was there because they were scared she'd steal them and Elaine always was desperate for attention. It all has the awful ring of truth.

Ally looks doubtful. Georgia comes right out and suggests settling. "It's your word against a dead woman with seven witnesses." Elaine says, "No way." Nobody's taking her invention from her. In the Unisex, Cage dismounts and accidentally knocks her into a bowl. "Last night was the greatest night of my life," says Elaine, dripping. "Today I go headfirst into a toilet." Her dream's been flushed.

Billy and Ling tackle the case of Vicki Sharpe, who's suing her boss, Mr. Volpe, because his monthly in-office Beach Day makes her feel harassed. Nobody forced her to wear a bathing suit and women weren't singled out, but seeing others wearing them made her feel self-conscious about her slight weight problem—and seeing men's beer bellies on display made her feel even worse. "I suppose they could have a wet T-shirt contest and justify

The MIRACLE FACE BRA

"Shave years off your appearance"

that by having men compete as well," says Sharpe's attorney, who also has bathing-suit beauties walk into court to refute the boss's notion that near-nakedness in a professional setting is just good fun that doesn't punch people's sexual buttons.

Billy's sincere defense saves Mr. Volpe, but the altogether persuasive and sympathetic Ms. Sharpe buttonholes Billy in the hallway. "I'm sure you're a nice man, but you really don't get it...Just because men and women both wore bathing suits, that doesn't make his policy gender neutral. Men aren't judged by their bodies; women still are."

Meanwhile, Elaine is ranting about her late cousin's family's posthumous show of loyalty—why, when it was Martha's birthday, nobody came except Elaine. Bing! Elaine remembers and retrieves the video she made of the birthday party,

OPPOSITE BOTTOM: Elaine's Face Bra infomercial. OPPOSITE TOP and BELOW: Cage attacks Nelle's knee-pit and she freaks. ABOVE: At last, Cage makes the right move on Nelle.

hit the sexpot!" Fish exults. Ally confirms this fact. Later, Nelle confirms it in the flesh.

Ally gets depressed: "There are no good men. I read this article, on average there are about two good ones per state. I had one of them, and I let him get away." After dropping hints with eleven unanswered phone messages, Ally goes to see Greg in person at the hospital where he works. She sees him emerge with a lovely woman on his arm. He doesn't see her. It doesn't seem likely he'll be seeing her again.

While Cage and Nelle are making sweet love, Ally and Renee sit home eating Super Chunk ice cream.

during which Martha asks about the Face Bra and Elaine explains the whole thing. Elaine wins. Asked by a TV reporter how her family and coworkers feel about her success, she says they're all "cheering for me." Watching the interview, Georgia in particular sees the pain in Elaine's smiling lie. Ally believed in Elaine; Georgia was filled with doubt.

Nelle invites Cage on a date to a rap club; Cage invites Fish and Ling along, and the two men redeem themselves by doing a wacky rap dance. Nelle asks Cage home to cook him dinner. "You've

SONG LIST:

"Tears on My Pillow"

"You Turned My Whole World Around"

"I'm Qualified to Satisfy You"

"Happy Birthday, Baby"

"All-Out War"

"Big Girls Don't Cry"

"You're the First, the Last, My Everything"

the green MONSTER

written by David E. Kelley, **directed by** Michael Schultz

▶▶

THE BRIEF: Ally hires a man to serve as her date to make Greg Butters jealous. Georgia's dishy new look makes Billy jealous. Cage represents a jealous woman wronged.

"I want both of you to be everything people hate about lawyers!" Bonnie Mannix orders Cage and Fish. After eleven years of marriage, Bonnie's husband claimed he had to work late but instead went to a party with his mistress and openly nuzzled her in front of his wife's friends. So Bonnie got a crane and—in front of her husband as he came back from the party—dropped his antique $100,000-plus grand piano on his $170,000 classic Porsche.

Mr. Mannix sues for vandalism; Cage tries to sue for emotional distress caused by Mannix's adultery, but it's a no-fault state, so Cage's case is a no-win argument. "You ruined that relationship, she ruined a car and piano—who did more damage?" Cage demands. Bonnie's case boils down to the jealous rage of the betrayed. "I know you're in no mood to copulate—*capitulate*," Cage tells Bonnie.

Ally is depressed. Her relationship with Greg Butters has burned out and she can't seem to rekindle it. Ling has a male escort service— "Nothing depraved, it doesn't involve sex"—and she urges Ally to hire one of the stupefying studs in her stable as Ally's date to some event where Greg can glimpse them together and get jealous. Ally hires the breathtaking Kevin to faux-nuzzle her at Cage's thirty-fifth birthday party, an event that will be staged under false pretenses. "We need to make a green monster," Kevin tells Ally.

Renee invites Greg to the party. Convincing John to allow the party, Renee explains it's all a scam for Ally and demonstrates the existence of green monsters by thrusting Cage's head to her bust in front of Nelle. "Get his head out of your breasts," Nelle says. "That's jealousy," Renee tells Cage. "That's what we need from Greg."

Georgia craves a new look. Ling designs her a drop-dead slit-skirt dress that makes men's heads snap to attention and Billy go green. "What I am I can no longer deny!" Georgia says. "Hot!" Billy flings his coat over her. "I say I'm hot, you think I'm cold," Georgia notes.

Greg comes to the Cage party—with his new sweetie, Kimba. "Rhymes with 'Bimba,'" Ally snaps, and accuses Greg of being "rude" to have brought a date. Kevin pulls Ally onstage where they croon "All I Have to Do Is Dream" together, faux-romantically. Greg, the sexiest singer this side of Barry White, retorts with a duet of "Your Precious Love" with Kimba. Alas, Georgia is inspired to do a Dusty Springfield medley, possibly the worst ever sung.

The next day, Billy agrees to be more supportive of Georgia; she agrees to quit singing in public.

Cage gives a great closing argument, but Ms. Mannix is found guilty. Guilty verdict notwithstanding, the jury fines her a total of 35 cents.

Greg asks Ally out for coffee, proving green monsters can exert a morning-after spell. But Ally's no longer sure; she now has a crush on rent-a-date Kevin, who politely declines the honor of a real date. He's a professional!

"So you are basically still stuck in no-man's-land," Renee chides Ally. They chime in on an upbeat version of "Bye Bye Love."

SONG LIST: (*listed on page 193*)

love's
ILLUSIONS

written by David E. Kelley, **directed by** Allan Arkush

▶▶▶

THE BRIEF: Cage and Ally defend a woman whose husband discovers she's not in love with him—she has an imaginary lover. Fish finally talks Ling into bed and gets the last thing he ever expected. Ally reveals the excruciating secret behind her sky-high dreams of matrimony.

Looking in the mirror, brushing her teeth, Ally finds herself flashing back to scenes from her childhood and winds up blinking back tears. Renee tries to comfort her: "You're a lonely, pathetic, big empty sack with bad hair who stoops to using escort services. Who wouldn't cry?"

Not comforted, Ally goes to court to block Barry Philbrick's fraud case against his wife, Kelly. After two years of what he considered happy marriage, he found love letters Kelly had been writing (for eleven years!) to a perfect guy who existed solely in her mind. Kelly isn't crazy. She knows the perfect guy is pure fiction. She loves her husband but isn't passionate about him.

Kelly poured out to her phantom pen pal her loneliness on her wedding day. In court, she testifies, "As much as I told myself the passion wanes anyway, for my wedding day, which I'd spent most of my life romanticizing, it was a bitter disappointment. . . . But I did love you, Barry. And I still do."

Barry bitterly charges that Kelly's love was a lie: "Basically, she was thirty, wanting to get married, I was good husband material."

Ally wonders whether Barry doesn't have a point. "Oh, please," says Cage. "Men lie to get women into bed, women lie to get men into matrimony." Ally would never settle for less than true love, Cage grants—and then wallops her with his theory on why she has such a vivid fantasy life: "The truth is, you'll probably be happier alone . . . the only world that won't end up disappointing you is the one you make up."

Billy complains to Georgia about the cooling of their passion for each other. They impulsively have what Renee later calls "a little booty call" in a Unisex stall. Ally walks in with Cage, berating him for marital pragmatism. "There has to be passion! There has to be passion!" Ally shouts—just as Georgia and Billy tumble out of the stall. "Figures the one marriage that would have passion would be theirs," she laments.

Fish figures the one lover who would give him passion de maximus would be Ling. But when she at last consents to sex, she yells "Action!"—and Fish's dumb stick goes limp as string cheese. "He turtled! You scared him!" Fish says. Later, Viagra saves the night for Fish and Ling.

But Ally must face her demons. "My mother never loved my father," she tells Renee. "They're still together." One night when Ally was three, she caught her mom in bed with a stranger. "People want to know why I've been able to romanticize love into some big illusion. It's 'cause I got an early start. Maybe it's just sex and checkbooks and liking the same movies."

"No," says Renee. Now she's truly comforting Ally, but Ally's beyond comfort. She can't even cry.

Back in court, Ally's closing argument wins the jury over to Kelly's side: The real fraud, Ally says, is romance. "The men or women of our dreams—they live in our dreams."

Over a shot of Ally walking home alone, Vonda sings Joni Mitchell's ode to romantic disenchantment: "It's love's illusions I recall / I really don't know love at all."

SONG LIST: (*listed on page 193*)

i know him
BY HEART

written by David E. Kelley, **directed by** Jonathan Pontell

▶▶

THE BRIEF: Ally's hallucinations are starting to take over her life, and her friends are worried. Nelle is worried about the way the firm's world revolves around Ally. Single lesbian Margaret Camaro retains Cage/Fish to force her insurance company to pay for artificial insemination. Ally argues she and Margaret are sisters under the skin.

In the previous episode, Ally hallucinated a judge turning into Al Green. Now she rolls over in bed and sees him singing "How Can You Mend a Broken Heart?" She chimes right in, and Vonda's backup singers appear in bed, too, backing up her duet with Al. Why get up and face the real world when your fantasy makes your inner world go round?

Ally refuses to go to work, so the firm has to send somebody to snap her out of it. Fish argues that Cage would simply connect with Ally "on a 'cracker' level," and they'd be two attorneys down. Billy might kiss her, so Fish decides he's the rational man for the job.

Fish tells Ally to stop waiting for the right guy to just come along. "If you want a guy, you gotta go out and grab him, just grab him—that's why God gave man the handle, for women to latch onto, Fishism." Sound advice. Unfortunately, Fish adds his bizarre idea about women. "You need a guy . . . you think it makes you weak, a bad feminist,

when in truth every woman out there is exactly like you. They're all weak." When Fish says, "I am woman, hear me whimper!" Ally tries to wither him with a Ling stare. Instead of an intimidating Ling growl, all Ally can manage is a teensy chipmunk growl. Still, she kicks Fish out of her room.

After Renee realizes that Ally has flipped over last week's case of the woman who made up an imaginary lover and Cage's traumatic opinion that the guy Ally's looking for doesn't exist, that she only ever be happy in her own pretend universe. Renee determinedly takes Ally on a date-a-thon to find each of them a real man. The guys all prove to be self-centered, boring, or wing nuts. Ling offers to find Ally a desirable date and effortlessly rounds up a large order of stunningly attractive men for her, but Ally rejects them all, reasoning that any man responding to such a cattle call is suspect. Romantic hope is on the ropes.

And so is Cage's budding romance with Nelle. For the first

time, Nelle really loses her cool, jealous of the way Ally connects with Cage's extraterrestrial wavelength. "The next time she comes to your office looking for emotional support, I'd like you to ask her to leave. Through the window."

Nelle's ire is more than mere green-eyed pique. She objects to Ally's entire philosophy—"that it's OK to live in fantasy land . . . that there's a soul mate out there for everybody." Retreat into childhood whimsy is okay for Ally, but Nelle knows John tends to do it, too, and that's why Nelle disapproves of Ally's influence.

When Cage takes Ally's side and attacks Nelle's anger, Nelle says, "Pokip pokip pokip poop, *get out*! And that smile therapy thing: hate that!"

Margaret Camaro asks the firm to help her force her insurance company to pay for her artificial insemination. Because she has not been diagnosed as infertile and because she has not tried to get pregnant "the old-fashioned way," the insurance company won't pay. Margaret insists that sex "the old-fashioned way" should not be required.

Camaro defends her right to have a child and her sexual identity, too.

"Why do you even want a baby, Margaret?" Ally asks rhetorically. "I'll tell you why: Because at the end of the day, you don't feel whole alone. You need to love another person. Well, so do I."

Camaro is sympathetic but torn by her independent principles: "I don't condemn you for wanting somebody to love. I guess I just reject the notion that your life is empty without him."

"It's only half empty," Ally replies.

Nelle does not have an inner world like Cage and Ally, and Cage will have to accept it. Nelle feels that love doesn't require the Ally two-souls-in-one notion. "I want to be with somebody different from me," she says.

All Nelle has to do is learn to love—not like—Barry White. "That one's nonnegotiable, Nelle," says Cage.

Everybody gathers to dance and bond in the Bar. Vonda sings a song that strikes a giant chord with everyone and with no one more than Ally: "I know he's out there somewhere just beyond my reach . . . No we've never met, haven't found him yet / But I know him by heart." The last shot is Ally's face, lonesome but open.

We all hope love will win out.

SONG LIST *(for episode 222):*

♪ "Both Sides Now"

"Dulcinea" ♪

♪ "You're the First, the Last, My Everything"

"Addicted to Love" ♪

♪ "Keep on Pushin' Love"

"Miss Gulch's Theme" ♪

♪ "Born to Be Wild"

"Do Ya Think I'm Sexy" ♪

♪ "Play That Funky Music"

"Waltz of the Flowers" ♪

♪ "Chicago Hope Theme"

"Love Machine" ♪

SONG LIST *(for episode 221):*

♪ "This Is Crazy Now"

"Bye Bye Love" ♪

♪ "Son of a Preacher Man"

"It's Over" ♪

♪ "So Very Hard to Go"

"Bye Bye, Baby" ♪

♪ "You Turned My Whole World Around"

"All I Have to Do Is Dream" ♪

♪ "Your Precious Love"

"You Don't Have to Say You Love Me" ♪

SONG LIST *(for episode 223):*

♪ "I Know Him by Heart"

"Did You Ever Have to Make Up Your Mind" ♪

♪ "How Can You Mend a Broken Heart?"

"You're the First, the Last, My Everything" ♪

♪ "Cupid"

"Keep on Pushin' Love" ♪

love
TRIANGLES

CENTER: Fish, Cage, and Ally ponder the frailties of romance. ABOVE: Cage romancing Nelle and Renee. BELOW: Fish's amours, Whipper and Ling.

 **ABOVE: Cage practicing the Vacuum Kiss with Elaine and kissing Ally for real, and Ally faking a kiss with Elaine. BELOW: Billy romancing Ally and Georgia—who *hates* triangles.**

ally's
PASSIONOMETER

"I drink a lot of coffee," Ally confesses to a cute guy (in "The Green Monster"). And there are a <u>lot</u> of men in her life. So it's only natural, given the sensual charge of coffee in her world, that she thinks a <u>lot</u> of thoughts that are fragrant and full-bodied. But always with heart and soul. Here are some of the love interests who in one way or another interest Ally, how they rate, and what they mean to her.

there's so much history there, the merest smooch risks a huge investment in the emotional futures market. One thing is for certain: Billy may be true to Georgia, and he may sometimes yell at Ally, but his love for both is here to stay.

BILLY THOMAS

Passionometer Reading: Formerly blazing, still capable of reaching the red zone.

Ick Factor: Nonexistent.

Meant-to-Be Index: An early high-water mark.

Maybe it was because it began when they were little kids who were wowed by how much they'd grown together. Billy sure had a head start on all the other guys in her life. They say you can't reheat a soufflé, but you wouldn't know it from these two. They went out in college and in law school and trembled on the very brink of a dark deed in the late-night offices of Cage/Fish and Associates. Ally's feelings for Billy can get incendiary, and they have a half-life like plutonium. That's why it's such a scandal when they kiss: It goes no further, and God knows Ally's lipstick has not gone unsmudged by others, but

THE DANCING TWINS

Passionometer Reading: Zero.

Ick Factor: Not applicable.

Meant-to-Be Index: Zero.

Although Renee likes to refer to dancing at the Bar with these guys as "snacking on a Twin," they have no nutritional value whatsoever. They are the pleasure principle in purely vertical form. Sex doesn't enter the equation with these guys—their love is too pure for words. They are the real lords of the dance, but the goat dance is not in their job description.

DR. GREG BUTTERS

Passionometer Reading: Sky-high. Unfortunately, at its peak, Ally's passionometer reading for Billy goes sky-high, too.

Ick Factor: Zip.

Meant-to-Be Index: At first sight, it sure looks like eternal love. Afterward, it gets ambiguous.

At first Ally thinks this sweet, funny, delightful physician must be gay, because he's attentive yet elusive. Turns out he was headed for a new job in Chicago and didn't want to succumb to the tug of her love only to turn tail like a cad. He saves lives; he's a surgeon without a hypertrophic ego; his singing can bring a roomful of women to their knees—and probably to his room later. She knows it's a serious crush because she gets all pitted when she sees him. It's serious for him, too, because her smile can make him run a stop sign and wreck his car. But that stop sign is a metaphor for their stop-and-go romance.

As Ally sadly told Dr. Tracy, "There could be something here—he's got ex-husband written all over him."

KEVIN, THE MALE ESCORT

Passionometer Reading: Give Ally air, or she may faint at the sight of this hunk of rentable glutes.

Ick Factor: Zero.

Meant-to-Be Index: Dream, dream, dream, Ally. Then wake up, smell the coffee, and get your own glutes the heck outta there.

It was all Ling's idea. See, she has this escort service for women who just want a handsome man to hang with. Ally hires Kevin to pretend to be her date to make Greg jealous, and he is a pro. In one sense, Wyatt is the ultimate fantasy, a smart man who is utterly, selflessly devoted to making a woman happy. But while they're practicing their stagy Eskimo nose nuzzle for Greg's benefit (or rather, for Ally's), she gets a funny fluttery feeling and gives Kevin a big wet kiss. We should have known it was a risky sign when she hallucinated wrapping her mouth around his head at first sight.

THE INFLATABLE DOLL

Passionometer Reading: He's not a boy toy, he's just a comfortable presence in her life, like a teddy bear.

Ick Factor: Not applicable.

Meant-to-Be Index: Zero, he's made of plastic.

Sure, he was thin-skinned and empty, but he was always there for Ally, which is more than any other guy can say. She took him out dancing now and then, but he was essentially the male of last resort when she had nobody else to come up to her room. He treated her right. And when flesh-and-blood men don't treat her right, she has the doll to take it out on. On the night that Greg spurns her overture, Ally out of frustration sits on its head until it pops.

MAYO-MOUTH (D.A. JASON ROBERTS)

Passionometer Reading: A high spike, then a steep plunge to nothing.

Ick Factor: Major.

Meant-to-Be Index: Zero, but at first Ally misread the signals.

Poor Ally fell down in Jason's presence and fell for him as a smart, accomplished man, an attractive colleague of Renee's. But his appalling table manners turn her right off. He keeps dropping salad dressing on his chin and neglecting to wipe it off,  hence his nickname. Why cry over spilt mayo? Unlike mustard, mayo cannot be hot. And Ally will likely never warm up to Jason again.

THE RABBI

Passionometer Reading: About two degrees higher than David the Inflatable Doll, but at least he had plenty going on upstairs.

Ick Factor: Low.

Meant-to-Be Index: Lower still.

She saw in him a moral touchstone with a sense of humor. He saw in her a funny girl, the antidote to the piety which surrounds men of faith. Her faith in eternal love must've been alluring, too. But it was not promising that Ally so half-heartedly dated him on the lame theory that since Mr. Right never seems to work out, Mr. "Who Knows" might be a better bet. But you can say one thing for the rabbi: You never catch him with a mouth full of mayo.

GLENN, THE NUDE MODEL

Passionometer Reading: To quote Ally in the confession booth after her fiery collision with Glenn: "You have no idea!"

Ick Factor: None—until later.

Meant-to-Be Index: Less than zero.

Ally never fell madly in bed with anybody as fast as she did with this unambitious, footloose, snowboarding hardbody who modeled for Ally's art class. They made beautiful music together playing "Heart and Soul" on Ally's piano, then did an encore or three on the floor by the roaring fire. The problem was, Ally didn't really treat him like a guy with a heart and soul, just a guy with what Renee calls a "meat whistle." (In Glenn's case, it was more of a meat pipe organ.) OK, she was starting to fall for the rest of him by the time he got offended and dumped her. But it was too little, too late for a man with so much to offer.

JAMES DAWSON, THE LAW PROFESSOR

Passionometer Reading: Over the top, but low-down and guilty.

Ick Factor: Low.

Meant-to-Be Index: Never meant to be.

Ally's favorite law professor at Harvard (and Billy's teacher, too) was the first grown-up love of her life. Too bad he was so much more grown-up and married with children and she wasn't nearly grown-up enough. Just a third-year student with a mind he fell head over heels for. The great man told her the tragedy of his life was that he met the love of his life too late. But he simply could not leave his family. At the funeral, the pain inflicted on his family becomes even more pointed.

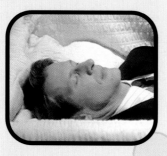

RONALD CHEANIE

Passionometer Reading: Moderate.

Ick Factor: Nothing obvious, but Ally did keep him at arm's length.

Meant-to-Be Index: Lowish.

We never saw precisely what Ally saw in this guy, but that's love for you. Perhaps it was just romantic jujitsu: He was hesitant in making a pass at her, so that's why she wanted him to.  He's a good kisser with a juicy tongue, but he scared too easily. Ally is not for wimps! Just because her favorite fictional character is Saul Bellow's Henderson the Rain King and she hurt Cheanie's feelings by turning to Billy for comfort at her late professor's funeral, Cheanie chickened out. He did say if there were ever a book about Ally's life, he'd be the first to buy it. Hey, maybe he's not such a bad fellow after all.

JASON TRESHAM

Passionometer Reading: Hot, yet somehow innocent.

Ick Factor: Nonexistent.

Meant-to-Be Index: Likewise.

Jason is a young man involved in one of Ally's cases. She may have "impure sexual thoughts" about an age-inappropriate man, but she's not just heeding the call of the meat whistle. Jason's parents are suing his ex-lover because she was thirty-nine and he a teen when their affair began, and they nosily read about it in Jason's diary and busted her for statutory rape. Jason feels it was romance, not rape at all, and his appeal to Ally is

free of sordidness. (He's a couple of years older now, too.) They both dream the same dream, of touching fingertips, and he represents the male sensitivity she needs—and which men lose when they stop being romantic boys and start getting coldly and pragmatically out of touch with their emotions. Jason takes Ally to deserted Fenway Park and they play-act a game of baseball. They both know it's not for real: He says she looks like she's "having a reunion with the fun you had before." Still, the interlude is short and sweet. (Incidentally, the couple never went to Fenway Park. What you see is a realistic computer-generated backdrop, one of the feats *Ally's* special-effects team is proudest of.)

impervious to rejection, woos her with flowers she hates, and drives her to stage a lesbian kiss with Georgia to drive him away. He's a homophobe on top of everything else. Yet he means well: He gently breaks it to her that he cannot abide her gay lifestyle—but promises to pray for her.

WALLY PIKE

Passionometer Reading: Can't read it, the instrument's frozen.

Ick Factor: Infinite.

Meant-to-Be Index: A flatliner.

Ally gets dragged by the ear by Renee to go out with Renee's date Ben and his friend Wally. If she'd known what Wally was like, she might have let Renee tear her ear off. True, Wally is, as Ally says, "the most boring man on earth," but that's only the beginning of his awfulness. He can make a bowling date go from dull to worse. He has no sensitivity to her feelings and less sense than God gave a bowling ball. He is

"FITZY" FITZPATRICK

Passionometer Reading: Deep freeze.

Ick Factor: Infinite.

Meant-to-Be Index: Not.

Another flower-toting, hint-missing fool for Ally's love. But the old lesbian ruse can't fool Fitzy—since Ally isn't the first girl to feign lesbianism (or even death) to avoid dating him. His date idea is karaoke, not bowling, and he's got some talent for this ghastly pastime. The other girls in the room act like he's Greg Butters up there at the microphone, though Ally is unmoved by his rendition of "Puppy Love." Face it, Fitzy:

To Ally you're a Dumpster-bound dog. At least he's wily and manipulative, guilt-tripping her into a second date after she insults him. Wally would never have had the smarts to try that ploy.

BOBBY DONNELL

Passionometer Reading: Through the courthouse roof.

Ick Factor: Nope.

Meant-to-Be Index: Maybe someday.

Although this clinch had the potential to pop the thermometer and break the record, Bobby Donnell and Ally are star-crossed lovers: one has to wonder whether the planets of TV production can ever align again to put them in the same place at the same enchanted time. But it was hot while it lasted, in a crossover episode made everybody look good. After they kiss ("Full alignment!" Ally gloated when she told Renee), Bobby breaks it to

her that he has emotional "baggage" (including Helen Gamble of *The Practice*, who practically hisses at the sight of Ally). But Bobby can't bring himself to rule out a rematch. Ally sarcastically calls his vague vow a kind of "layaway" plan.

JOHN CAGE

Passionometer Reading: Give it a moment, maybe it will give a reading one of these days.

Ick Factor: Alas, that's easy to see.

Meant-to-Be Index: Not meant to be lovers, perhaps, but meant to be something of mutual import.

It don't mean a thing if it ain't got that swing, and Ally's thing with Cage had less swing than the collected works of Lawrence Welk. It's not a good sign when your face cracks into a million icicle pieces at the man's mention of a first date. As far as true love and understanding go, though, Cage and Ally do click. They slow dance in "Silver Bells" most movingly, and they can read each other's hearts like nobody else. Not even Billy has this rapport with Ally. When she instantly discerns Cage's lifelong unrequited love for his opposing counsel Hayley Chisholm, she tries to fix them up at once. "I act on feelings, even if they're not mine!" says Ally. But she does have feelings for Cage, and their courtship was not in vain. She's had steamier slow dances, but never a warmer one.

RAYMOND BROWN

Passionometer Reading: Events prevent Ally from finding out, but his real thing is for Georgia.

Ick Factor: Plenty.

Meant-to-Be Index: Their future went right down the toilet.

Brown is the lawyer for a Cage/Fish opponent, but the only reason he asks Ally for a no-big-deal drink is that Georgia told him Ally had eyes for him. In fact, Georgia does, because he's the guy she dated once just before meeting Billy. Ally is late for the jive date because Cage's remote toilet-seat device flips up as she's sitting down, and her hip flexors flex so firmly in the bowl that firemen must break the john (and John's toilet-adoring heart) to free her.

GEORGE MADISON

Passionometer Reading: High, but she has no right—he's Elaine's squeeze.

Ick Factor: Not a problem.

Meant-to-Be Index: Could be, but Ally won't open her eyes and blot her conscience.

Ally's client, Elaine's boyfriend George Madison, makes her spill foamy cappuccino on him and hallucinate slurping it off, fantasize wrapping her legs around his neck (or higher yet), and generally lose her cool. He hears songs in his head, just like she does—soul mates!—and he's as bugged as she is by the prospect of hurting Elaine. Nobly, Ally sends him packing when she yearns to shack up and listen for songs only two can hear.

203

"I have a great imaginary world but sometimes I just need things to happen for real."

"This isn't pain I'm feeling, it's just nostalgia."

"Take me."

"Balance is overrated."

"It's not that I object to sadness. It's just, every time I get depressed I raise my hemline. Unless things change, I'm bound to be arrested."

"You might think there's an explanation, but you'd be wrong."

"I'm gonna have to whip out my Freud book."

"Maybe I should buy new stockings to get the support I don't get from you."

"You're supposed to be able to send your life to the dry cleaners and it all comes back pretty and neat on a hanger."

"Single and on the market."

"Sorry. A little voice told me to."

"Don't look at me like I'm a nut."

"I know that I appear insane, but it's just a legal strategy."

"Men are like gum. After you chew awhile, they lose their flavor."

"Where does it say that women can't act like men sometimes? You only live once—be a man."

—ALLY McBEAL, *McBealisms*

AWARDS

Ally McBeal arrived with a bang. Not only was it the most popular new show of the season, it was the only breakout hit of 1997. "*Ally* had buzz right from its debut in September," observed Phil Kloer of the *Atlanta Journal-Constitution*, "and now is crossing over from cult to mainstream, something that took *Seinfeld* more than two years." Critics liked the way the show hurdled high genre boundaries in a single take, mixing melodrama, pratfalls, social satire, legal critique, lightning-flash hallucinations, and pop-music interludes with daft, cleverly calculated abandon. The very thing that made it distinctive, its multiple personality, made the show tough to submit for prizes—should *Ally* compete as a comedy, a drama, or something in between? But double Golden Globe awards for comedy got the *Ally* ball rolling, and more prizes followed. Here are a few of the courts of appeal in which *Ally* has won favorable judgment.

GEORGE FOSTER PEABODY AWARD, 1999

SCREEN ACTORS GUILD AWARDS:

★Outstanding Performance by an Ensemble in a Comedy Series, 1998

Nominations, 1998
–Outstanding Performance by an Actress in a Comedy Series (Calista Flockhart)
–Outstanding Performance by an Actor in a Comedy Series (Peter MacNicol)
–Outstanding Performance by an Ensemble in a Comedy Series

Nominations, 1997
–Outstanding Performance by an Actress in a Comedy Series (Calista Flockhart) (1997)
–Outstanding Performance by an Ensemble in a Comedy Series (1997)

EMMY AWARDS

★Outstanding Sound Mixing for a Comedy Series or a Special, for the episode "Boy to the World," 1997–1998

Nominations, 1998–1999
–Outstanding Comedy Series
–Outstanding Writing in a Comedy Series, "Sideshow" (David E. Kelley)
–Outstanding Lead Actress in a Comedy Series (Calista Flockhart)
–Outstanding Supporting Actor in a Comedy Series (Peter MacNicol)

EMMY AWARDS *(cont.)*

–Outstanding Supporting Actress in a Comedy Series (Lucy Liu)

–Outstanding Guest Actor in a Comedy Series (John Ritter)

–Outstanding Guest Actress in a Comedy Series (Tracy Ullman)

–Outstanding Art Direction for a Series, "Making Spirits Bright"

–Outstanding Casting for a Series

–Outstanding Costume Design for a Series

–Outstanding Directing for a Comedy Series (Arlene Sanford)

–Outstanding Single-Camera Picture Editing for a Series

–Outstanding Sound Mixing for a Comedy Series or a Special

Nominations, 1997–1998

–Outstanding Comedy Series

–Outstanding Lead Actress in a Comedy Series (Calista Flockhart)

–Outstanding Art Direction for a Series

–Outstanding Casting in a Series

–Outstanding Costuming for a Series

–Outstanding Directing for a Comedy Series (Allan Arkush and James Frawley)

–Outstanding Single-Camera Picture Editing for a Series

–Outstanding Sound Mixing for a Comedy Series or a Special

GOLDEN LAUREL AWARD
(Producer's Guild of America)

Nomination, 1998

–The Norman Felton Producer of the Year Award for episodic television (David E. Kelley)

GOLDEN GLOBE AWARDS

★ Best Television Series—Musical or Comedy, 1998

★ Best Performance by an Actress in a TV Musical or Comedy Series (Calista Flockhart), 1997

★ Best Television Series—Musical or Comedy, 1997

Nominations, 1998

–Best Performance by an Actress in a Supporting Role in a Series, Miniseries, or Motion Picture (Jane Krakowski)

–Best Performance by an Actress in a TV Musical or Comedy Series (Calista Flockhart)

–Best Television Series—Musical or Comedy

Nominations, 1997

–Best Performance by an Actress in a TV Musical or Comedy Series (Calista Flockhart)

–Best Television Series—Musical or Comedy

NAACP IMAGE AWARDS

Nominations, 1998

–Outstanding Drama Series

–Outstanding Supporting Actress in a Drama Series (Lisa Nicole Carson and Jennifer Holiday)

TELEVISION CRITICS ASSOCIATION AWARDS

★ Best Individual Actor, Comedy (Calista Flockhart), 1998

★ Program of the Year, 1998

★ Outstanding New Series, 1997

VIEWERS FOR QUALITY TELEVISION AWARDS

★ Best Comedy Series, 1998–1999

★ Best Actress, Quality Comedy (Calista Flockhart), 1998–1999

★ Best Actress, Quality Comedy (Calista Flockhart), 1997–1998

Nominations, 1998–1999

–Best Quality Comedy

–Best Actress, Quality Comedy (Calista Flockhart)

–Best Supporting Actress, Quality Comedy (Lucy Liu)

–Best Supporting Actor, Quality Comedy (Peter MacNicol)

Nominations, 1997–1998

–Best Actress, Quality Comedy (Calista Flockhart)

–Best Supporting Actress, Quality Comedy (Lisa Nicole Carson)

–Best Supporting Actor, Quality Comedy (Peter MacNicol)

–Best Recurring Player, Comedy or Drama (Dyan Cannon)

DIRECTORS GUILD AWARDS

Nomination, 1997

–Outstanding Directorial Achievement in a Comedy Series (James Frawley, Director and Gary Strangis, UPM)

ELECTRONIC MEDIA CRITICS' POLL

★ Best Ensemble—*Entertainment Weekly* (1998)

★ The Caucus for Producers, Writers, and Directors

★ Producer Award, shared with *The Practice* (David E. Kelley), 1998

* "happiness

is going to bed with something

that makes you feel

[relax in comfy pajamas featuring memorable lines from the show.]

warm and snuggled...

now i'll just settle for pajamas"

-MCBEALISM

...isms

Ally McBeal

**Your pajamas
are available now
at fine department stores
everywhere.**